The Biography of Thomas Lang

Jonathan Buckley lives in Greenwich, London. This is
his first novel.

The Biography of
*Thomas Lang*
A NOVEL

Jonathan Buckley

FOURTH ESTATE • *London*

This paperback edition published in 1998

First published in Great Britain in 1997 by
Fourth Estate Limited
6 Salem Road
London W2 4BU

1 3 5 7 9 10 8 6 4 2

A catalogue record for this book is available from
the British Library.

ISBN 1–85702–802–3

Typeset by Palimpsest Book Production Limited,
Polmont, Stirlingshire
Printed in Great Britain by
Clays Ltd, St Ives plc, Bungay, Suffolk

## Christopher Lang to Michael Dessauer

And here come the quick in pursuit of the dead. Yes, your request did indeed arrive in the wake of a petition from Mr David Moir. Worse still, I have met Mr David Moir. A couple of months back I made the mistake of replying to a plausible letter from this young man, and within the week he had somehow cajoled me into an interview. I attribute this to a fit of lunar dementia on my part.

Our encounter took place at his central London pied-à-terre, an apartment too plush to be sustained by the proceeds of the journalism he claims to be the mainstay of his existence. With his distressed jeans and laundered Jermyn Street shirt, Mr Moir advertised himself as the dilettantish spawn of an old-money family. He drifts rudderless through the world atop the raft of his inheritance. That was my first thought and I observed nothing to make me change my mind during the rest of my confinement in the Moir residence. Not an extended period, I concede, but long enough.

He manoeuvred me into noticing the portraits tacked to the wall above his desk: Constantin Brancusi sawing a pillar of stone in a cave-like studio; James Joyce interrogating a page through a magnifying glass; Ernst Ludwig Kirchner (Oh, of course) balancing a cigarette between finger and thumb like a paintbrush; the furious life-mask of Beethoven; the doleful loony face of Georg Trakl (Really? I would never have got him). And sitting pretty in the midst of this portable gallery of the elect, there was Thomas Lang.

The picture was the advert for the second Chopin recording: Delacroix's drawing of Chopin on one side; on the other, a photograph of the performer, Signor Charisma, sitting on the edge of a table poring over what we deduce to be the score of the sonata (but, knowing Tom, was probably the weekend's football results). Uncanny the resemblance between Frédéric and Thomas, did I not think? Indeed I did not think uncanny the resemblance. Features of Frédéric repulsively vulpine in my opinion, and I said as much. This did not deter Mr Moir, who turned out to be a proponent of hairdressing as a profound spiritual expression. He lingered awhile on the leonine manes before us, as worn by so many authenticated geniuses since the coming of Salvator Rosa. Volumes of nonsense ensued: Fred. C. had a 'gypsy soul', Thomas was the very image – I am not making this up – of 'the gypsy scholar'. There was talk of 'soul' and 'resonances' and 'destiny'. Tom would have been appalled.

Mr Moir must have had his letters ghost-written for him, for it was rapidly evident that the lad knew nothing. He was merely infatuated with Thomas. He would write an article on the hypothetical agonies of the brilliant boy, and thereby come to be his posthumous courtier.

I'm sorry, Mr Dessauer, but the recollection of this episode causes a primordial gloom to descend upon me. Your letter was exceedingly touching and I am sure you are a man of much percipience and eloquence. However, it has taken me much effort to detach myself

2

from Mr Moir, and frankly I do not possess the energy to engage in another debate.

## Michael Dessauer to Christopher Lang

Thank you for replying so promptly to my letter. I was, naturally, disappointed by the substance of your reply, but I can fully understand your reaction in the light of your problems with Mr Moir. But recognising something of my younger self in his adulation of your brother, I must be more charitable about him than you could be expected to be. Years ago I too reserved my esteem exclusively for those of what might be termed an extremist temperament, motivated to a great extent, I am sure, by the hope that through my devotion I might, by a kind of symbiosis, acquire something of the incorruptible integrity of my heroes.

Yet I must beg you not to condemn me as Mr Moir's co-conspirator. I approach the task of writing this life with due humility – I do not approach it with a view to providing corroboration of a story already written. Of course I bring preconceptions to the work, but these are merely paper trails, a way of setting out. The biography of Thomas Lang is, I feel, a necessity, and I shall do everything in my power to bring it about. Please reconsider, Mr Lang.

## Christopher Lang to Michael Dessauer

I apologise for seeming to condemn your enterprise by association. Your project is, I am sure, a thoroughly different proposition from Mr Moir's deeply shallow little venture. Condemn it I do nonetheless.

It's a popular belief – indeed a truism when it comes to performers of my brother's ilk – that the lives of the extraordinary are necessarily extraordinary. They are not. We – you and I and all our humdrum coevals – live our lives down on the sea-level plains, and we look up to the Andean plateau on which Tom and his spiritual brethren conduct their lives, and are tempted to believe that life up there must be an exalted business, full of drama. But no, a flat horizon is a flat horizon, whether it be a line a mile above the sea or is the sea itself. Most lives within our experience are a landscape of little hills, little dips, more or less rocky paths, and Tom's was no exception, as anyone who set out to retrace it would soon discover. The landscape of Tom's life was as mundane as yours or mine, albeit, as it were, a landscape transposed to a different level.

Every life, I grant, has its moments of glory, its eruptions, to pursue a metaphor I feel staggering already under the weight of its own banality. But you know what these were in the case of my brother. The inventory of what lies between these moments is not worth the effort, in my opinion, and neither is the biographer's quest for explanation. If you want to explain Thomas Lang, let's just say that he had an unusually retentive mind, a perfect apparatus for the discrimination of sound, and muscles that could perform a thousand minutely graduated operations within a very short period of time. But I would insist that, with Tom dead as with Tom living, all exegesis is redundant. And, lest you raise the obvious objection, let me say that in writing this I am not proclaiming

4

my brother as a man exalted above the common rut by virtue of his greater opacity.

## Michael Dessauer to Christopher Lang

For me the biography of Thomas Lang remains a necessity. Risking the accusation of preciousness, I admit that I have the need to pay homage to Thomas Lang, in some way repay him – perhaps presumptuous of me, but not I think an ignoble motivation. More urgently, however, I need to resolve the bewilderment I feel when I think about Thomas Lang.

It was through him that I came to know the music I now love. It was thanks entirely to Thomas that I began to listen to music with the attentiveness one gives to a book. I wrote the word 'love' carelessly a moment ago, but it is the right word. This began on one particular evening in one particular place, as suddenly as falling in love.

I was a student, studying modern history. I was no more nor no less musically aware than the majority of my contemporaries. I possessed a few disconnected enthusiasms, elevated in moments of stress to the status of principles. My knowledge was chiefly a knowledge of reputations. Thus I knew that Wagner, the uncompromising comrade of pitiless Nietzsche, was a man for me – although I had yet to traverse an entire opera by him. And thus I knew that I did not care for Chopin, a salon-pleaser, a miniaturist, a delicate plant. Whenever I heard his name I hoisted my judgement like a banner, and kept it flying until the challenge had been seen off.

Then, one night in April 1971, I had an essay to finish – its subject, for what it's worth, the Suez crisis. Typically, I had overestimated my grasp of the issues, and a chance remark by a fellow student on the afternoon of the previous day had sent me back to the library in a panic. Of the intervening hours I had spent no more than three asleep and now I was exhausted, with another couple of volumes of tedious memoirs to disembowel before I could start writing. I put the radio on to keep myself alert, and within a few minutes was dozing on my arms.

In the small hours of the morning I became drowsily aware of a strange sound in the room. It was piano music, but like the relentless tolling of discordant bells. I had heard nothing like it before, and assumed the piece was modern. It was in fact Chopin's A-minor prelude, played by Thomas Lang. The next day I bought and played his recording of the preludes. The first experience of the night before had been a shock, but this was a long moment of new clarity, as if the opening of a door had let me hear a conversation I had only heard muffled from an adjoining room. Where once I had been predisposed to hear preciousness I now heard the most delicate refinement; feyness was transfigured into subtle wit; bombast became staunch resolve; slightness, economy.

Eager to validate my latest enthusiasm, I rooted through the newspapers in the college library, and quickly found a review of my record in the *Daily Telegraph*. The closing sentence I recall as clearly as if I had written it myself: 'Whenever in the future I feel the urge to bewail the lot of the music journalist, I shall simply place this record on the turntable.'

I had to wait a year and a half before I could see him play. It was at the Wigmore Hall. Anticipation tends to make an audience garrulous, but there is a higher pitch of excitement that makes people taciturn, as though every faculty were concentrated on what is about to happen, and so it was on that evening in London. I myself was so taut with anticipation that the sound of applause hit me like the din of a sheet of ripping tin. Thomas Lang's demeanour was not what I had expected. The ferocity displayed by his recordings had prepared me for a dynamic, Mephistophelian figure. Instead, Thomas Lang conveyed above all a sense of extreme constraint. He bowed to the audience four times, turning with each bow as though observing a ritual that required obeisance to certain points of the compass. His expression was one of abstracted discontent.

He played Chopin – the third sonata, two scherzi, a couple of études, the *Polonaise-fantaisie* and the *Berceuse* to finish. It was a riveting performance, which moved everyone in the hall except Thomas Lang, if appearances were anything to judge by. Straight-backed throughout, he seemed totally impassive, unless one counted the strange little nod he made from time to time, like a potentate giving permission for a flunkey to leave his presence. He seemed almost to be watching himself playing, and when each piece was over he surveyed his audience as if we were a gigantic picture hung from the ceiling. Recalled for ovation after ovation, he assumed the face of a soldier on parade, his hands behind his back with the fingers of one encircling the wrist of the other like a handcuff. He played no encore, despite the clamour; I left at least ten minutes after Lang had last emerged, and the applause was still in full spate. Walking to the train station I had to admit to myself that I was resisting disappointment at this decidedly undemonic performance, for all its excellence.

The structure of his career, so neatly partitioned, was no less disconcerting for me. Of no other musician whom I have seen would I be prompted to use the word genius – with Thomas Lang one uses it unabashed, as if it were no more a matter for disagreement than his gender. Yet it is in the nature of genius to be absolute, to intoxicate or tyrannise the one on whom it settles. The artist of genius should not allocate his time as Thomas Lang did, as if he were the master of it. Inspiration should not be a matter of decision.

But it was of course Thomas's death that set me on the path to his biography. His death, and all the other things I know or think about Thomas Lang, are points that do not begin to define a form. Rather they sketch a line that stretches off into darkness. I don't wish to embroil you in a debate of any kind. Please do not misgauge my tone when I state that I intend to proceed with this biography. Your cooperation would be less a service to me than a service to Thomas, and the book's completion may, I hope, in some way better the lives of those to whom your brother meant so much.


## *Christopher Lang to Michael Dessauer*

I have few doubts as to your sincerity and I have none at all regarding your declared intention to proceed. Go ahead. My inclination is neither to help nor hinder.

## Michael Dessauer to Christopher Lang

The biography of Thomas Lang will be written, and it may be written by someone less scrupulous than I. If one living person may be said to have truly known Thomas Lang, you are he. Your silence would leave the field to half-informed cynics or naive eulogists such as Mr Moir. This is a simple fact. By not helping you would be hindering – you would be hindering the emergence of the truth.

## Christopher Lang to Michael Dessauer

Thank you for your rather peremptory note. Your obsession with my brother is touching, and perhaps is shared by several others in addition to Mr Moir. It is possible that some of them share your desire to bring Tom back alive. You should all be deterred from your labours.

To repeat, 'the biography of Thomas Lang' is for me an absurdity, a sort of Platonic super-life, an impossible feat of pedantic devotion and clairvoyance. Thomas Lang enters the hall in Vienna in which, three hours hence, he is to play the *Hammerklavier* sonata. By what route did he get to the hall? What aspect of that journey might have left its residue with him, and for how long, and how deep does it lie? How does he see this city? Is it for him the city of Freud, of Mozart, of Schubert, or of someone whose existence is known to Thomas Lang and perhaps eight other people on the entire continent? What effect does the decor of the hall have on him? Which ghostly presences does he feel?

Do they encourage him or do they threaten him? What piece of tutelary advice does he now recall? What does he hear? What moment of no previous significance rises for the first time, unbidden, in his memory? Does he wish he were not here? Does he simply wish he had worn different shoes today?

Behold the man; behold the guesswork; behold the footnotes in ninety-nine volumes.

### *Michael Dessauer to Christopher Lang*

I think you were somewhat disingenuous in your last letter. But then so was I in mine. I will not press the point further than to enclose a photocopy of something I received from New York this morning. It's part of the concluding segment of a 'work in progress' by one Jonas Ackerman, and recently appeared in a small magazine called *ZG*, published in Santa Barbara. Mr Ackerman's 'faction', as I believe the genre is known, is entitled 'The Last Months of Thomas Lang'.

Even now, two hundred miles on, four hours on, the music will not cease. Even here the music will not stop. Just two notes, a rising third, touched softly, that spectral two-note prelude, but followed only by itself. A journey stalled perpetually at the moment of departure.

At his back the pines are packed tight to the hills, all of one height, as if razored by the wind. At the forest's edge each tier of branches is burdened with snow, a plate of snow, a fat, heavy paw of snow. A gust smacks against his shoulders, turns him a quarter-turn to see the powder spiral from the crests of the drifts and the snow fall from the nearest pines in pieces the size of sacks. They hit the ground with a gasping noise, like winded men, and then comes silence, into which seeps the reverberation of the music, as if the notes had been struck unheard beneath the silence. The note decays, fading longer than any made note could last, as the trees ripple in the wind like a cat's fur stroked against its grain, settling.

Out on the lake, the back of something breaks the surface in a spin of its body, and it seems as though nothing else moves forward, as though the wavelets were a surface of battered silver. The first note returns, as soft as before, as implacable as erosion. His ungloved hands gently contract with each recurrence, the fingers making the movements that the notes demand, while his gaze slides on the landscape, gaining a brief hold on a clump of frozen reeds splayed in the foreshore's ice, on a blue crack in the clouds imposed upon the lake's dead glare, on the distant, dim seams of rock and sky and water. He listens to the whispering of the stars, the tinkling of the crystals of his breath as they strike the crusted snow. He recalls long-gone months, trying to clamber back to his identity on a scaffold of days, cities, concert halls.

His car looks like a wound, vermilion against the whiteness. He trudges down to it. At every step the crushed snow creaks like a rusted hinge, squeaks like an electronic blip, and every second step falls at the beat of a note. The car's tracks have vanished already. The road describes the commencement of a great arc that reaches beyond the forest, beyond the next day's horizons.

As I said – 'someone less scrupulous . . .'

## *Christopher Lang to Michael Dessauer*

This exotic rubbish will evaporate as soon as it's exposed to the light of day. (I take your word for it that this piece is genuine – in the sense that it is genuinely published rubbish.) Should one day a biography of my brother appear in which he is represented in a way that requires correction, then I shall perhaps intervene. If you feel there is a danger that you may be producing just such a book, then I might agree to cast an eye over what you have written. That is as far as I am willing to go.

## *Michael Dessauer to Christopher Lang*

I am immensely grateful to you, and shall send instalments as soon as they are presentable. Every sentence, after all, is potentially a drift from the true course. In fact, I have a draft of my opening page, which I enclose.

On 5 May 1987, Thomas Lang gave a recital at the Teatro del Bibbiena in Mantova. A few weeks earlier, around the end of February or beginning of March, fly-posters advertising the event had appeared on the piazza walls and the billboards of the city. A casual visitor might easily have missed them. Small, ochre-coloured sheets of paper, they bore nothing but the name of the hall and the name of the soloist, printed black in a tall plain typeface, and underneath, in lines of diminishing height, the date and time of the performance, and the box-office phone number. Nothing more demonstrative was needed. Within days, tickets for the Lang recital were changing hands at four, five, even ten times their face value, a trade conducted chiefly at the counter of a local record shop, below a fanned-out spread of album covers and a photograph of Thomas Lang. The shop sold out of the recordings three times over.

The local press ran a full-page celebration of the pianist, whom their writer dubbed 'Cesare', partly for the 'patrician authority' of his music, partly for his looks – 'the sweep of black hair, the mesmeric contrast of the heavy black brows and pale blue eyes, a face that recalls nothing so much as the glacial beauty we see in portraits of Cesare Borgia'. When the same newspaper published a rumour that the recital had been cancelled, the box office received more than two hundred calls before lunchtime.

The concert went ahead as planned. Lang played a programme of Beethoven sonatas (numbers 13, 14 and 28) and bagatelles (opus 126), concluding with Bach's *Jesu bleibet meine Freude* – a performance of 'sublime humility', thought the critics. For twenty minutes (thirty, one reviewer insisted) the audience maintained a standing ovation, though all must have known that, as ever, Lang would play no encore. What none could have known was that the audience in the Teatro del Bibbiena on the night of 5 May 1987 would be the last ever to hear Thomas Lang play.

## Christopher Lang to Michael Dessauer

I must say that I resent this ploy to goad me into collaboration. I'll let the arty erotica go by the board

– it reflects solely on the author, whoever he may be. Doubtless I'll be encountering the 'gypsy scholar' again, some way down the road, and I'll wave him by as he trudges off to join Cesare Borgia. However, this melodramatic little overture can't be allowed to get by. If you want to tell it true, tell it straight. It's not a damned thriller, so forget the tawdry narrative gimmicks. Of course nobody could have known it would turn out to be his last concert, so why bother telling us nobody knew?

More pertinent is the fact that some people would not have been at all surprised had Thomas Lang announced his retirement the day afterwards. Whenever Thomas came off the platform there was always the possibility that he would never go on stage again. You do at least know that, don't you?

### Michael Dessauer to Christopher Lang

I am astonished by what you tell me – it contradicts a very strong impression I have formed from my early interviews, many of which have been with people who knew Thomas well. What were his anxieties about performing? Forgive my forwardness, but would it be possible for me to come down to Dorset to discuss this with you? Correspondence is an unwieldy forensic process.

### Christopher Lang to Michael Dessauer

What on earth are you talking about?

1. I am not your assistant in what you infelicitiously characterise as your 'forensic process'. I may – merely may – participate in a sporadic conversation with you, and the postal service is a more than adequate medium for such an exchange.

2. There is no possibility whatever of your entering this house. Even were it my wish, which it is not, it would be a violation of the terms of my brother's characteristically Byzantine will. My duties as executor require me to stay in my brother's house for the next month or so. You may write to me during this period, if it is strictly necessary. I don't want to read every damned word of this book. Pre-emptively may I inform you that there is no phone. There's a scoop for you – the house of Thomas Lang has no telephone. Perhaps he didn't want the sound of the piano to be interrupted by the racket of the bell? Perhaps he did not like talking on the phone? Perhaps he didn't like the colours the handsets came in? What do you think?

3. Thomas suffered no 'anxieties' about playing in public. He just didn't care for it.

### Michael Dessauer to Christopher Lang

I could suggest that a meeting within the vicinity of Thomas's house would in no way contravene the terms of his will, but I infer that there are other obstacles at least as strong as the legalistic ones, so I must let the matter drop. However, would you be able to tell me something about the terms of the will, and when it was made? The answers may shed some light on the enigma of Thomas's death. And regarding item three, my confusion is now worse than ever. The Thomas Lang I have heard about was a natural performer. Do I now have to place the testimony of my interviewees in parentheses?

### *Christopher Lang to Michael Dessauer*

No light-shedding to be derived from the will I fear. Our solicitor uncle (sole paternal, in case you're curious, which I'm sure you are) browbeat me into making one about nine or ten years ago. Peeved at allowing myself to be worn down by his sales talk (uncanny prefiguring, don't you think?), I set to work persuading Thomas to make one too – which he readily did. The names of my brother's beneficiaries are no concern of yours and would moreover be of no interpretive value to you. On this point I expect you to take my word. Of the other significant terms, I can furnish a brief synopsis, which I think is adequate for your purposes.

I am the executor of Thomas's estate, and as such I am obliged to sell this house within a specified period and donate the proceeds anonymously to a named charity. Other than myself and the five other beneficiaries, nobody shall be permitted to enter the house except those whose presence is required to facilitate its sale. All holograph material and private documents stored in this house shall be destroyed before its sale – which I am presently undertaking. From this one might conclude that Thomas was, as I believe the approved hack phraseology has it, 'an intensely private man', and also perhaps a prescient one.

Returning to the subject of your troublesome confusion, would it help to know that Thomas's problem with the concert hall wasn't psychophysiological but ethical? He detested the contract that audiences invoke at the end of a performance, the way they turn nasty when they don't get their reward for applauding so heartily. Thomas had no time for this barter. If he'd had his way, it would have been a condition of admittance that the customer undertook to be clear of the auditorium within two minutes of the last note. Whether, in the light of this revelation, you should put the evidence of your witnesses in parenthesis, in abeyance or in the bin I cannot tell you, as I do not know what you've been told nor by whom you've been told it.

## *Michael Dessauer to Christopher Lang*

Here then are the most useful excerpts from my interviews with Thomas's contemporaries from the Royal College. I've deleted my questions and their hesitations to make it easier to read. Some needed more prompting than others, and some needed a bit more smoothing over, but I have put words into the mouths of none of them. Another three to follow.

### 1. Henry Attercliff
I was amazed by him. Eighteen years old and he talked like a professor. You couldn't imagine him going through adolescent crises: he seemed to have sprung

fully-formed from the womb. He was a cantankerous little pig from the start. And he played my things as if they were Beethoven.

One teacher especially used to get on his nerves. This man was a scholar of the Edwardian type. Always saying things like – 'Chopin inherited his robust common sense from his father, but it was from his mother that he received his musical soul.' This sort of thing made Thomas apoplectic. When it came to Beethoven, the sacred book was Sullivan's *Beethoven: His Spiritual Development*. The title alone was enough to make Thomas psychotic. His idea of a good lesson was one with no proper names . . . Thomas had disagreements with virtually everyone who taught him, but he disagreed with nobody as comprehensively as he did with this man. Thomas had him marked as a sentimentalist from day one . . . Thomas's main failing was that he allowed his principles to override his judgement. The coherence of his world-view was the paramount consideration, and this often made it impossible for him to assess a piece on its own terms. So Debussy is a composer to whom Thomas never did justice – anyone who wrote for the 'hammerless piano' was by definition of the devil's party. Consequently, Thomas never got below the surface of his music. But then, if the choice is between a great Beethoven and a great Debussy, I'd choose the former.

## 2. Gwendolyn Hanna

I used to sweat blood trying to commit music to memory, but Thomas actually seemed to enjoy it . . . On Tuesdays a group of us would meet for a meal, and when the talk came round to a piece we'd just been given, you could rely on Thomas to know the thing inside out and back to front. You never questioned his recall. It was quite depressing.

A story that will give you some idea of his memory. One day it was suggested, in passing, that we might have a look at a certain sonata by Clementi. At about ten the next morning I was strolling by the Serpentine and I saw Thomas sitting on a bench, feeding the ducks – he had a morbid affection for mandarin ducks. He began grumbling that he'd been unable to find a copy of this sonata. It happened that I had a copy in my bag. Thomas had to have it, instantly. He practically dragged me off the bench. I loaned it to him, with the proviso that he return it by the weekend and that he treat it with more gentleness than was his custom – Thomas was a paper-shredder. He gave my hand a quick squeeze, the least affectionate squeeze it's ever been given, and then he was off at high speed.

I left the college buildings at about five, and I stopped in the entrance to have a word with a friend. We'd been chatting for a couple of minutes when I became aware that Thomas was hovering in the background. He could be insulting with people he knew, but he'd never intrude on a group unless he knew everyone in it. I beckoned him over and introduced him to my friend. Thomas gave him a quick nod, then whipped the Clementi from his pocket. He remarked that it seemed to be another short-winded number, or words to that effect. Anything he didn't much like was referred to as a 'number'. He definitely said 'seemed to be' which I took to mean that he'd just glanced at it.

This was a Tuesday. That evening, one member of the company, a Clementi fan, took exception – only a slight exception, mind you – to a remark made by

Thomas about his hero. He got up and played a section of the sonata which he especially liked. Thomas was not convinced. When Clementi's champion had done, Thomas roared, 'But then what happens?' Then he answered his own question by playing the passage over again, and going all the way through to the end of the movement. And then he played on to the end of the sonata. He'd learned the whole damned thing in the space of an afternoon.

What made it worse was that all the time he was playing, he had this look of complete apathy on his face. I thought he should be above that sort of childishness. And for all Thomas's distaste, his playing won me over to Clementi completely.

### 3. William Clement-Johnson

Thomas and myself were never great friends, even though we were students of the same instrument. He seemed to have this image of himself as a lone wolf, and I found it an irritating pose, like his affected passion for sherbet dips. We stayed out of each other's way as much as possible.

From the outset we were forever arguing about certain issues, but the thing with Thomas was that he could never overlook any disagreement. Perhaps we could have been friends, I don't know. But for Thomas friends and intellectual adversaries were mutually exclusive categories. Not because he took disagreement as a slight to his artist's vanity; Thomas was too arrogant to be vain. Unlike many performers – and this, I suppose, is to his credit – Thomas had no need of an entourage. Anyone unfortunate enough to be endowed with merely mundane intelligence – and differing from

Thomas on any issue was proof that one was so afflicted – was simply of very little interest to him.

Our first real set-to was over Mahler. He had an aversion to Mahler, and he never tired of airing it. Mahler's 'prolixity' was the main charge – pretty rich coming from an admirer of the windbag Wagner. I told Thomas he had a tendency to mistake the whiff of incense for the presence of the Holy Spirit. This argument ended with Thomas and myself leaving the room in stony silence and setting off in opposite directions, even though we were due in the same room in five minutes. All very silly.

You read a lot about Thomas's rigorous intellect, but this was not quite as consistent as it was supposed to be . . . all this about his scrupulousness, his adherence to markings, his avoidance of all mannerisms, fidelity to the composer and all that. But when I gave a performance of a couple of late Haydn sonatas, using a replica eighteenth-century instrument, he made a point of staying away. This was bad enough – there was quite a strong camaraderie at the college, and I'd have gone to hear him in similar circumstances. We all would. But what made it unforgivable was a comment he made to someone who asked why he hadn't been there, with the rest of them. 'I don't like fancy-dress parties.' That's what he said. It was a long time before I could bring myself to be civil to him.

### Michael Dessauer to Christopher Lang

I've just got back from a research trip, and thought I might find a reply to my transcripts. There's no hurry, but is there nothing in them you'd care to remark upon?

## Christopher Lang to Michael Dessauer

I cannot conceive why you should think the eerily lucid reminiscences of Tom's quondam colleagues might call for my observations under the terms of our protocol. However, to get myself off the hook, I thank you for sending them to me. I found the trio mildly diverting and somewhat depressing. Do these people really talk like this? Perhaps 'smoothing' entails more than you'd admit. If these are the pick of your crop, as I assume them to be, I implore you to withhold the rest. I don't want to be exposed to the monologues of characters whose only interesting dimension is that they lived within the ambit of my brother for a few years. Nobody since Homer has made nostalgia enthralling.

One final thought. These interviews make Tom sound like a prig. He might have been pig-headed, but he was not a prig. Don't make him into one just because it's easy to do so with the materials to hand.

## Michael Dessauer to Christopher Lang

You do me an injustice. I am not out to diminish Thomas Lang, nor do I believe that he will be diminished by my book. I grant you that I will be unable to present the whole man. As you suggest, such an enterprise is beyond anyone's capabilities, whether the subject be dead or alive. But it does not follow that this biography is futile. I would suggest that the Thomas Lang of my book will perhaps be closer to the whole man than the character perceived by any single person who knew him.

Here are the remaining three from the Royal College sextet. I hope you don't find them completely pointless.

## 4. Elisabeth Charniot

I used to go to the cinema and theatre a lot, and I kept trying to get Thomas to come with me. I was in love with him a little. Perhaps. I don't know. In a purely social situation he was lovely: courteous and rather shy. But with Thomas there was hardly any such thing as a purely social situation. He was so unrelenting. That could be really attractive; but, in the end, it was so exhausting.

A few times I got him to come out with me. I always regretted it. Nothing could hold his attention. If we went to a play he was bored stiff by the interval; films made him fidget. It made no difference what it was.

He wasn't a musical philistine though – the sort who would rather sit through a crashingly dull Rameau opera than set foot in the National Gallery. There were plenty of those around, but Thomas was not one of them. It was that he lacked imagination, in a sense. He found it ridiculous that adults should dedicate themselves to convincing other adults that the words they were speaking had just come into their heads, when everyone knew they had been learned by heart. Actors' skills, the devices they use to create the illusion of spontaneity, were for Thomas mere tricks. He found them demeaning. And the more moving I found a performance, the more Thomas hated it.

When it came to Wagner, of course, the rules were different. Not that he'd ever admit to being carried away by anything. We went to see *Tristan*, and there were tears in his eyes at the end. We didn't hear anything about cheap tricks that evening.

## 5. John Wycherly

It must have been a couple of weeks into our second term when Thomas moved into my flat. He came round to see the room on a Friday afternoon and said on the spot that he'd take it. He came out of the room, went over to the piano, picked out a note or two, asked if he could move in on Monday, and left. He didn't even take his coat off.

We shared the flat for more than two years, so I think I knew him as well as anyone did. He's the only bona fide ascetic I've ever met. One look at his room and you knew that here was someone who had no time for frivolities. There was not one object that could have been described as decoration. His room wasn't ostentatiously bare – it was like a monk's cell that had just been ransacked. Books and scores were everywhere. It must have taken him five minutes every night to burrow through to his bed. He had a large bookcase on each side of the door, and there were these teetering stacks all over the floor. There was a desk, a couple of chairs, an electric heater and a wardrobe. The wardrobe was for clothes that were in need of a trip to the launderette – the clean ones were draped around the room. The clean things were easily accessible while the dirty ones were hygienically locked away. It had a certain logic. And there was a record player as well, which was tucked away under the bed. That was it.

To the untrained eye it was chaotic, but everything was in its place. I could ask to borrow a book which I knew he'd not touched in the last eighteen months, and he'd tell me, without looking up from his desk – 'Second pile on the right, two from the bottom.' Sure enough, there it would be.

He possessed almost photographic recall. I'll give you an example. A trivial incident, but striking because it's trivial.

I was going down to Cornwall, and I'd agreed to take a parcel for a girl in the year above. Her folks lived near Boscastle. She'd heard from somebody that I was going in that direction and she came up to me while I was chatting with Thomas. She jotted down her address and phone number in the back of the book I was carrying.

In the rush to get going it went clean out of my mind – the key was in the ignition when it came back to me. For the life of me I couldn't remember the book in which I'd written the address. Thomas could. Then I couldn't remember where I'd put the book. Thomas told me where it was. I clambered out of the car – 'Don't bother,' said Thomas, and he told me her address and phone number. Just in case, I went into the flat to check. The address was in the book he'd said it was in, the book was exactly where he'd said it would be, and he'd got every letter and digit right. It crossed my mind that he'd been seeing the girl, but it turned out he hadn't even set eyes on her.

I've never come across anyone quicker than Thomas

at getting a piece of music into his fingers . . . It was only with people's names that he was fallible. There he was worse than average. He couldn't remember a person's name unless he'd been told it a dozen times.

## 6. Jessica Nyman

We were a stone's throw from the King's Road, and every shop was blaring out the Beatles. But most of our lot looked like we came from a different planet. Some of the girls wore miniskirts and patent-leather boots, a few went out with art-school boys, but not many. Even then it was sex in the head.

Most music students are conservative. Music has its own specialised vocabulary, which makes musicians members of a secret society. All secret societies tend to be conservative. And it's a backward-looking life. The landscape is dominated by the far distance. With us, Beethoven and Brahms were still headlines.

Thomas was the ultimate music student. If you wanted to see him move fast, you put on the Rolling Stones. His tolerance was zero. Lizzy Charniot and I dragged him down Carnaby Street once – it was like forcing him barefoot over broken glass. But I think he regarded most of us as children with unacceptably promiscuous tastes. He could not comprehend how anyone could like both Bach and *La Bohème*. To like both was to be serious about neither. He used to say that writers and painters are expected to be fighters, but musicians are expected to be enthusiasts.

I used to think it was a shame that his repertoire was so limited. He seemed to be making things difficult for himself by taking the well-trodden path. It was like he wanted his audience to think 'You can't tell us anything about this we don't already know.' But that's exactly what he did do, with everything . . . When Thomas played, he never just quoted the music.

## Michael Dessauer to Christopher Lang

In acknowledgement of your strictures, I shall try to tell it straight. The pages enclosed will appear close to the beginning of the book. Not quite in this form, perhaps, but I feel comfortable with this material as part of my opening. Simultaneously I am working on the chapter dealing with Thomas's death, which, unexceptionably I hope, shall come close to the end. Anything you might care to say about this instalment I shall of course consider with the greatest respect.

At the primary school that Thomas Lang attended, it was the habit of some of the children to go home not directly, but by a detour through the garden of a large house that stood in nearby Hayward Street, on the perimeter of the local technical college's playing field. The owner of this house was Mrs Helen Gilray, a widow in her late forties at the time Thomas enrolled at the school, in the autumn of 1950.

Her husband, an ophthalmic surgeon at Guy's Hospital, had been killed in a car accident one week after VJ day, and her life had been blighted utterly by his loss. While he was alive she had led a full social life quite independently of her husband, much of it devoted to the amateur orchestra she had founded in 1931. Under her management it performed as many as half a dozen concerts in a year, and established a strong local reputation. When the orchestra was re-formed

27

in 1947, Helen Gilray declined all invitations to resume her involvement.

Her relatives lived too far from London to visit her regularly, though her daughter Mary – then living in Galloway – persisted in her efforts to persuade her to move to Scotland. Of those that had been friends of the doctor's wife, many could find little time for the widow. A minority remained to share her evenings, during which her husband's name could never be mentioned. Perhaps seeing ever less purpose in their attendance, one by one these few allowed their visits to become irregular, and finally, with but a single exception, to cease altogether. Thereafter Mrs Gilray would step out of doors just once a week, on a Friday morning, to do her shopping alone.

The Gilrays' home, a five-bedroomed house, had always been too large for their needs. As a widow she used just part of the ground floor, sleeping and passing most of the day in what had been the dining room. Opposite the door stood her bed and a vast settee of damson-coloured velvet, which when sat upon released a puff of dust and a faint smell of rosewater. One of the arms of the settee, collapsed slightly, rested against a massive Bakelite radio, from which a thin yellow cable ran to a socket at the furthest point of the skirting. A bay of leaded panes filled much of one wall, overlooking the garden through an unkempt vine. Facing the window, a fireplace of white marble enclosed a cast-iron insert surrounding a double-bar electric heater. Each morning the marble was washed and the iron polished, and the single photograph on the mantelpiece was lifted to be dusted. Taken by her husband, it showed her under a bright canvas canopy, a hand raised to press the crown of her straw hat, a shoulder bared by the slipped strap of her dress, the background filled by a blurred wall of dark rock; on the reverse, written in ink that had faded to lilac, was written – 'Moustiers-Ste-Marie / 13–6–28 / the Little Moroccan'.

A chintz armchair occupied a corner of the bay window, a length of curtain furled over its back; it was here that Mrs Gilray sat for much of the day, sedulously reading every page of the three newspapers delivered each morning, and occasionally browsing through a music score. Slewed stacks of sheet music spread across the rugs in front of this chair, and smaller piles were ranged on the lid of the adjacent upright piano, which was kept perfectly tuned but played no more than once or twice in the course of a week.

Untended for years, the garden was overrun with convolvulus and dandelions and a weave of other weeds from which only the central area – a belt of matted grass around a dried-out fish pond – was kept free. There was a lime tree between the house and the pond, and a sumac leaned over the farthest remnant of fence, where the mowed stripes of the college playing field stopped.

A succession of schoolboy clans used the garden as their own, never seeing its owner, though she observed them. On the day Thomas Lang first appeared there, a boy on another boy's shoulders was trying to sling a rope over the lowest bough of the lime. Thomas, taller than the others, helped him secure it; the next time that group went to Mrs Gilray's, they took him along. He would play for a few minutes, but then, as the games grew rougher, would shin up the rope and on into the higher branches, often staying there after the rest had left.

One late afternoon, Thomas was at his post when a storm broke. He stayed where he was as the downpour began, until Mrs Gilray, holding out a towel at the back door, told him to come inside to shelter. She took his sopping cardigan from him, made him a mug of hot chocolate, then led him to the room in which she lived, where she sat him on cushions in front of the fire. Soon she had learned his name and the names of his mother and father and brother. She asked him if he liked school and he replied that he did. She asked which subjects were his favourites and if he liked music. If Thomas told her his favourite tune, she said, she would play it for him. Thomas chose 'Jerusalem'.

He followed Mrs Gilray to the piano, and stood directly behind her. Silently he watched her play, craning his neck to follow the movements of her hands. At the end of the piece he was asked if he wanted to hear anything else; what he wanted most, he said, was to sit where she was sitting. Mrs Gilray relinquished her seat, pulled the stool closer to the piano, and stood at his side to help him pick out the melody.

Thomas played the hymn from first bar to last, without error, unassisted. Mrs Gilray was speechless. Settling onto the stool beside the boy, she lifted from the top of the piano a wad of sheet music and shuffled through it as Thomas calmly sipped his drink. She slotted the selected score – a simple piece, perhaps by Domenico Scarlatti – into the holder and then played, slowly, the right-hand part of the first few bars. Thomas reproduced the piece with no apparent effort. Next came a passage from a Mozart sonata; it too was executed fluently by the boy. A Schubert song followed; Thomas performed it with but a few mistakes. Arms folded, he waited for Mrs Gilray to set him another test. She played scales, major and minor, letting each note fade before going on, and calling out its name as it sounded. Then, telling him to pay attention to the tones and not to her hands, she repeated the series.

That done, she told him to go and sit in the armchair by the window and close his eyes. In a different sequence, all the scales were played once more. Thomas identified each one on the mediant. Mrs Gilray gave him next a miscellany of tones; he identified each one correctly. His ear seemed infallible.

So it was that Thomas Lang's musical training began. He was nine years old.

After a few months of Helen Gilray's guidance Thomas had learned some forty pieces, most of them from the eighteenth century. Compositions that to other young musicians might have seemed arid instilled in Thomas an enthusiasm that was inexhaustible. It made no difference whether the piece were one that he could play easily or one that still caused him difficulties – he would go through studies by Clementi or J. S. Bach preludes or movements by C. P. E. Bach as many times as Helen Gilray would allow. His capacity for exercises, even the most repetitious and mechanical, was without apparent limit, and it was not uncommon for an entire two-hour session to be given over to the practice of chords, scales and arpeggios. His ability instantly to see the most economical fingering for a piece was uncanny. Thomas's understanding of the relationship between the keyboard and the body of the pianist was such that rarely did his teacher feel it necessary to correct either his posture or his movement, and his assimilation of what advice she did proffer was immediate and perfect.

By his tenth birthday he had advanced so much that Helen Gilray was often unable to improve his playing by example. Certain fugues from *The Well-Tempered Clavier* were now well within his compass, as were several sonatas by Haydn and Mozart. Works of denser texture – by

Schumann, Brahms or Mendelssohn – were being assigned with increasing frequency, and although his playing was as yet rather clipped in style, these pieces gave him few problems of execution aside from those that were unavoidable for a pianist with smaller than adult's hands.

Over the next year his tendency to excessive briskness was all but eradicated, and he would often take excerpts from a composition on which he was working and, on his own initiative, use it to experiment with the sonorities that the pedals can draw. The discrepant strength of his fingers, which formerly he had been inclined to regard as a frustrating hindrance, he had precociously come to look upon as an exploitable characteristic of the player's hand.

It was during this period that the magnitude of Thomas's potential became clear to Helen Gilray. His dexterity and his understanding of the resources of the instrument and of the performer's body were in themselves remarkable, but what impressed his teacher more than these accomplishments was the emergence, month by month, of a distinctive musical personality, a mind that could discriminate between the forceful and the crude, the understated and the undefined. He was beginning to play the music in ways he had not been taught, and his teacher was moved to feelings more complex than wonder. In recognition of this early maturity he was permitted to embark upon the piano sonatas of Beethoven, a composer by whom he had yet to play a single composition.

## *Christopher Lang to Michael Dessauer*

Well, it's all far too lush for me. On the grounds of simple good taste you should put a diminuendo on the pathos of Mrs Gilray's domestic life, touching though the story may be found by some. The image of the grandmotherly mentor makes my skin crawl, to be frank. And it's a very odd transition from the world of carpet slippers and digestive biscuits to all that Young Werther nonsense with the storm. I'd demote it to a brief shower or a stiff breeze if I were you. It may have happened exactly as Mrs Gilray remembers it, but that isn't really the point. You should give your readers the benefit of the doubt, and go easy on the symbolism. What we need is verisimilitude, not necessarily *la vérité*. If it's corroboration you're after, however, I must disappoint you – Mrs Gilray's memories will have to suffice, their fragility notwithstanding, now that the other protagonist is unable to furnish his version of events.

I would feel that I'd failed in my duty if I let your letter go without a rebuke or correction; I trust you'll take the next remark in the same complaisant spirit with which you've received its precursors. I find your faith in chronology a little worrying. A sequential story isn't necessarily a straight story. Standing at the terminus of a life, looking down over the events he has gathered, the narrator can become something like a demagogue surveying his audience from the podium, pleased with their presence, pleased with the unity of purpose he appears to have created, but unable to hear the comments passing back and forth.

Let me cavil in another way: think of biographical death as an arc lamp turned on a crowd – it illuminates some figures sharply, but many stay in shadow, and those caught in the beam are seen only as half-figures, startled, not themselves.

Tom's death – the manner of his dying, the circumstances of it – should not be presented as a riddle to which everything that preceded it was a clue. Thomas's death, like most, is simply the one episode in his life that had no consequence. Close your story with it and you might give it greater prominence than it can bear.

## Michael Dessauer to Christopher Lang

I was rather hoping that you, as Thomas's confidant, might have something to add on the subject of his relationship with Mrs Gilray. How did Thomas change over this period? How did your relationship with him change? How did he talk about Mrs Gilray? How did he talk about anything?

Sorry – this wasn't meant to read like a litany of demands. I'd just like your angle on these formative years.

## Christopher Lang to Michael Dessauer

Your last letter had a powerful effect upon me: the haiku-like concision, the sense of a passion so urgent that it forces language to the brink of illiteracy, but above all the intimation glimmering in each syllable – like a hint of fire in the depths of an uncut gemstone – of a profound and resolute ignorance. Only now is it evident how far you are from fathoming my brother. You are jammed in the starting gate, and out of simple compassion I am going to give you a good strong kick to get you going. Perhaps then you'll be able to follow the rails of your own accord.

Unless you are being very slack with your terminology, you cannot describe me as my brother's 'confidant'. Yes, Tom wrote to me regularly from the time he left home until his last month, and yes, he told me things he did not tell anyone else. But a confidant, to my understanding, is required to sympathise, to console, to advise, or in some other way engage emotionally with the confider. Tom often wrote to ask me to do things for him; he often wrote to amuse me, or amuse himself. But he never needed my support, except in the most trivial matters, and he rarely bothered to ascertain if I'd even received his letters. Had we been close in the way you imagine, he would not have written to me so frequently.

I knew next to nothing about Mrs Gilray until years after their partnership started. I knew he went to her house, but so did dozens of children, as you say. His visits weren't clandestine, but he made sure we didn't know how frequent they were. Both our parents worked, and neither of them got home before six during the week so Tom could spend a couple of hours at Mrs Gilray's without their knowing. It turned out that he would go to Mrs Gilray's house on Saturdays as well, but he covered his tracks with various plausible stories. Sundays were compulsory family days, but his behaviour never hinted that our trips to the country or afternoons of board games were any sacrifice for him. He and his friends went to Mrs Gilray's garden; Tom sometimes went indoors to look at old photos and books, or lark around with the piano, or listen to scratchy 78s – that was all we knew, in the beginning.

What changed things was the 1956 Beckenham Festival of Music and Drama. Sounds grandiose, but do not chide yourself for knowing nothing of it – it was basically a jumped-up kids' show. (An unintentional but apt ambiguity to that last phrase.) There were two ways of entering: the neophyte showperson could be entered by its school – the case with the majority – or it could pay a small fee and compete privately. There were about a dozen categories – public speaking, dramatic monologues, dramatic scenes for two actors (an especially painful display I'd imagine), solo piano, solo clarinet, violin, a few others – and each category was split into two sections, for under-thirteens and over-thirteens, a division that I suppose made sense to some functionary within the local council. Perhaps he thought it best to separate the pre-pubertals from the posts.

Tom had put in his own application, but he didn't tell our parents about it and he didn't tell me until the day itself. He sauntered into my bedroom in the morning and asked me if I'd go with him somewhere in the afternoon. So at about three o'clock I found myself walking through the park with Tom, compliantly and silently abetting whatever conspiracy he had devised. Then he produced a leaflet from an envelope secreted under his armpit, and he pointed to a list of names. His name was halfway down, piano section, small division. (It turned out he'd found the fee by charging his classmates for his assistance with their homework. The project rebounded after the competition, when he withdrew from the scheme. His paymasters promptly got lower marks and Tom's racket was blown. We had two mothers on the doorstep demanding a refund.)

To resume. Tom said nothing more despite inter-
rogation all the way to the school hall where the
Beckenham F of M & D was being held. I was
pretty sure of what he was doing, I just wanted to
know how far he was going to push it. Tom's entry
was an appalling practical joke, hatched with some
of his less reputable schoolmates. They were always
pulling stupid stunts. His best friend spent a Saturday
morning wandering around Forest Hill with a beach
ball, asking the way to the sea in a ludicrous German
accent, a prank of Tom's devising. But how far was
Tom going to go this time? Did the dare oblige him
to get on stage and then feign illness? Was I going to
reach the hall and find the back row packed by his
half-witted crew?

At the hall the first person we met was our school's
official representative, a child pompous beyond his
years. He assumed that our presence was a homage
to his prowess, and he let us into his wicked little
joke – the piece he was going to play was in reality
his own composition. The name of the obscure French
composer appended to his application form was in fact
an anagram of his own name, with a couple of acute
accents thrown in. Tom smiled serenely at him, and
said nothing.

There were three judges, sitting on a bench to the
left of the stage. The middle judge – the spitting
image of King Farouk – stood up and called the name
of the first competitor, thereby initiating a procession
of prim little girls and Brylcreemed little boys, who
squeaked across the parquet, slotted their score onto
the baby grand, and proceeded to deliver 'Für Elise'
or something similar. All perfectly competent as far

as I could hear, but only my anxiety about Tom's party-piece kept boredom at bay. At this point all I had ever heard from Tom was a tuneless version of 'Greensleeves' on the recorder.

Then came Tom's name. He shoved his chair back, slapped me on the knee and gave me a grin as if we'd planned this escapade together. My heart dropped three feet. Someone behind me commented on the way Tom was dressed – he was the only boy wearing short trousers, and they were a scruffy pair he sometimes wore to play football. I fixed my eyes on the dust between two tiles, and prayed it would finish quickly.

For the first few seconds I couldn't connect the sound I was hearing with the fact that it was my brother on the stage. What he played – though obviously I didn't know it until he told me afterwards – was Beethoven's *Bagatelle* in E flat major. It starts with a stampede of notes, then a silence. When the pause came I looked up, as if expecting to see that Tom had been replaced by someone else. But no, it was Tom, looking down at his hands as if they were bits of paper blowing about on the keyboard.

My first sensation, I think, was a feeling of loss. I suddenly couldn't comprehend the person I was looking at. It wasn't just that I couldn't understand him as my brother. I couldn't understand him as child. I could, just about, have comprehended how a child could have the proficiency necessary to play the notes of something that required a good memory and good hands. But how could a child play this particular piece, having no understanding of the feelings underlying it? My brother could not have experienced what

Beethoven had put into this music; but on the other hand, I'd never heard it before, and the only reason I knew that it expressed these emotions that Tom could never have known was that Tom was expressing them. There was something horrible about the spectacle. It was as if he was fabricating the soul of a person, and showing that it needed no effort to do it. No part of him except his hands seemed to be involved in making the music: his face was impassive and his eyes followed his fingers as if he were watching another pianist, and was not particularly interested in what he was being shown. He was insolently blank. He seemed to be saying: 'There's nothing more to this than hitting the right note at the right time with the right degree of force.'

He became a boy again right at the end of the piece. As the last notes faded Tom raised his fingers a few inches from the keys and left them suspended for a second or two, with the fingertips downturned. Then this nasty little smirk appeared. I'd never thought of Tom as being competitive in this childish way, but I was relieved to see that smile. He wasn't quite my brother, but at least he was comprehensible, momentarily.

There was a silence, as though everyone in the hall was as taken aback as I was, then came a crash of applause. Now Tom was wholly himself again. He shot off the stool as if someone had jabbed a pin into him, blushed scarlet, bowed, and stumbled down the stage steps. He scuttled past the judges, was called back to collect his other copy of the score, and resumed his seat clutching the envelope to his chest as if to hide something he'd stolen. I glanced at him every now and again, but he managed to avoid my look.

Tom had put a hex on the opposition. The girl who came after him walked up to the piano in her sleep and made a complete hash of her number. The pompous one was next and he played as if he'd never seen his own composition in his life before. It was like that all through the second half – one botch-up after another. Tom showed not the slightest interest, but stared dumbly at the back of the chair in front of him, looking so glum that I began to feel guilty. I couldn't think of anything to say to him.

When the results came, Tom was top with ninety per cent. The chief judge told us that in normal circumstances eighty-five was considered the maximum. The prize was a small silver shield and a certificate that we had to collect ten minutes later, after a secretary had written Tom's name on the dotted line in mock-Gothic script. From the way Tom slouched down the aisle when his name was read out you'd have thought he was being awarded a broom and told to sweep the building. The other two judges came round the front of the table and surrounded Tom, who accepted their compliments by mouthing 'Thank you' silently while eyeing their waistbands. He was out of the door before Mr Davenport, our music teacher, could close in on him. I got caught.

'We had no idea that Tom was so talented,' he said.

'Neither had I,' I was thinking. I got away with a shrug and the excuse that I had to catch up with Tom.

He was striding down the street with his back bent and his chin tucked into his collar, as if he were walking into a gale. We didn't speak, and then he stopped in his tracks and said 'I'm sorry I did that.' I didn't know what 'that' was exactly, but I didn't press him. 'I wanted to surprise you,' he added after a minute or two.

'You certainly did that,' I said, and then it was back to silence all the way home. It was left to me to break the news of Tom's success. Our mother was flabbergasted and rather hurt; father seemed more amused than anything else. He suggested that Tom probably hadn't wanted to show off in front of them – to which mother replied that he hadn't minded showing off in front of a bunch of total strangers. It took me a while to wheedle Tom out of his bedroom, where he was pretending to believe that a row was in progress. I prodded him downstairs, and mother grabbed him as if he'd just been snatched out from under the wheels of a juggernaut. Tom surrendered the trophy and the certificate, and smiled bashfully when father called him a dark horse – I'm not sure he knew what it meant. Back in his room later, he gave me what I think he took to be a rueful smile. 'What have I done?' he said, and he sounded like someone twice his age.

There, a story from me. I think I might now be due another period of silence.

### Michael Dessauer to Christopher Lang

Next instalment.

To delay for so long so talented a pupil's contact with

masterpieces that dominate the literature of the piano may seem perverse, especially when one bears in mind that Thomas Lang's introduction to the instrument came late by the standards of many virtuosi.

However, this delay was a perfectly rational decision as far as his tutor was concerned. Helen Gilray was convinced that it would be a mistake to expose the young musician to Beethoven's works as soon as his technique had reached the necessary level. She was determined that 'his fingers should not outstrip his heart', that she should not nurture a prodigy who would turn out glitteringly shallow performances. 'Beethoven's sonatas are the most intensely personal ever written, and they cannot be played by anyone who has not achieved independence of mind.'

It would of course be ridiculous to suggest that a ten-year-old boy might be capable of interpreting Beethoven's music from a basis of emotional empathy. But Helen Gilray adjudged that Thomas could do justice to this music through, as she put it, a comprehension that was 'purely musical'. His extraordinary awareness of the cohesion of a whole movement (indeed of a whole work), his acute sensitivity to nuances of tone, his sense of phrasing – these qualities enabled him to recreate emotions of which he was himself innocent. By way of analogy, Helen Gilray put the imaginary case of a supremely skilled young sculptor, who is able, through his dexterity and his observation of the masterpieces of the medium and of the planes and angles of the human body, to produce figures in which were expressed states of mind that were unknown to him. Similarly, we do not believe that the actor impersonating King Lear is actually experiencing, or has ever experienced, Lear's suffering and madness, so why should we demand absolute identification from the performer of music? If

Thomas's interpretations bore the weight of many years, of what relevance was it that those years were illusory?

The partnership of Helen Gilray and Thomas Lang was astonishingly harmonious. Trusting in the wisdom of his teacher and possessing both patience and a precocious capacity for self-criticism, Thomas had accepted without protest her proscription of Beethoven's music and applied himself to the elimination of his weaknesses.

Their first and only disagreement was brought about by the 1956 Beckenham Festival of Music and Drama, a minor competition that drew its participants chiefly from the local schools. At the end of a Saturday morning lesson Thomas showed Helen Gilray a flysheet announcing the festival and told her that he would like to enter. She instantly declared herself against the idea. Did she think he wouldn't win? he asked her. No, the others would be competing for second place, she assured him; but music-making was not a sport. ,

He would not be playing for the competition of it, he claimed; he would be happy if there were no others in his group – just himself and the judges. She asked him why he needed somebody else to tell him how good he was, and at this Thomas could only shrug his shoulders. 'It will be too much of a distraction,' Mrs Gilray continued. Thomas had his answer: a short piece was all that was required; there were a few months to go before the festival; it would take only a part of each session to prepare something thoroughly. If she thought his studies were being neglected, he'd drop out. She had no choice but to concede, fearing it would be more damaging if she were to refuse to accommodate a wish that was so tenaciously rooted. He had, it turned out, already chosen the piece he'd like to play. Hesitantly, as if handing in a scrappy item of homework, he teased from under his cushion a copy of Beethoven's E-flat major bagatelle, opus 126.

It had been Helen Gilray's customary procedure to preface a lesson with some remarks on the salient points in the piece to be studied, making suggestions on tempo, dynamics and so forth. The preparation of the bagatelle was quite different – Thomas was given a free hand and his teacher confined her advice to details of shading, advice which, she was at pains to establish, he was perfectly entitled to ignore. As a rule he did just that. For the central section of the bagatelle Thomas at the outset chose a tempo which Helen Gilray considered far too slow. This was not a surprise. Unusually for a young musician, Thomas had often shown a predilection for very slow speeds, taking great delight, in his teacher's words, in 'playing as slowly as the music could bear', as if he were taking it to bits to see how they worked. Thinking it best to let the boy come round to a more tenable speed unguided, Helen Gilray voiced no criticism; Thomas stayed with his tempo, and soon she was finding it hard to imagine how the piece could ever be played more quickly.

He showed his winner's certificate to Mrs Gilray at the first opportunity, on the Monday following the festival. She congratulated him, shared with him a cake she had baked for his inevitable success, listened to his account of the competition and its aftermath, and then, having lost one third of the lesson in talk, placed on the piano the score of the Mozart sonata on which they had been working the previous Friday.

As Helen Gilray had anticipated, the competition did bring about a change in her relationship with Thomas, though it was not, as she had feared it would be, a change in its quality. Thomas Lang's first taste of acclaim had not the slightest detrimental effect on his attitude to humdrum practice: he was as diligent as before and equally compliant. The more conventional piano lessons which came as a consequence of his debut of course reduced the time Thomas spent with her, but did not weaken the bond between them. The tuition provided by his new teacher – Mr Davis Narayan, a graduate of the Juilliard School – was more rigorous than that which Thomas had been receiving from Helen Gilray and had the effect of modifying (one might say liberating) the sessions he spent with her.

Everything we know about the part played in Thomas's development by Mr Narayan, who died in 1970, is derived from second-hand testimony, but although we are looking at the subject, as it were, through an array of lenses – some more opaque than others – it would seem fair to say that between Thomas and Mr Narayan there existed none of the affection that was a characteristic of the boy's association with Helen Gilray. The infrequency of Thomas's visits to Mr Narayan after the commencement of his studies at the Royal College of Music – in contrast to his loyalty to Helen Gilray – lends support to this conjecture. Although Mr Narayan's methods were congruent with Helen Gilray's insofar as he never attempted to make Thomas conform to any disciplines that were inimical to his natural style, his teaching was more tightly structured and more formally conducted. Each lesson had a number of precisely defined goals, each designated at the end of the previous one.

Technical exercises came to be the preserve of Mr Narayan, by whom Thomas was also introduced to compositional theory, work for which he immediately displayed a keen aptitude. In what was consciously a compensatory reaction to the more systematic instruction given by Mr Narayan, the lessons at Helen Gilray's became looser and less predictable. There was no loss of seriousness in their work but a playful element was now present too. Thomas would perform uninterruptedly an entire sonata movement, and then create a reading of the music that was, if not quite its antithesis, then a commentary on the original version. In successive renditions he would accelerate a *Three-Part Invention* as if to find how fast he could go before the voices became an unintelligible tangle; Chopin would be played ever more softly, to the edge of inaudibility; Debussy played so hazily that the music seemed to deliquesce. And when, after these caprices, he came to play the pieces soberly, as if in public performance, his interpretation would invariably emerge enriched. As many felicities were struck upon through parody of the composer's intentions as were produced by solemn study. Only with the Beethoven sonatas was he permitted no licence. Before these mighty creations, with which the name of Thomas Lang was later to be associated inextricably, an attitude of hierophantic dedication was the only one possible.

## *Christopher Lang to Michael Dessauer*

Not quite 'hierophantic dedication' on the home front, old boy. Straight after the Beckenham furore our parents bought a piano for the newborn star – a gift which, incidentally, some of us knew must have entailed considerable financial sacrifice, but the other received as though the thing had fortuitously materialised out of thin air. Anyway, Thomas used to plough great tracts of Beethoven on this noble if superannuated Broadwood, but nothing in his playing suggested that a lifelong affinity was in the process of being forged. For quite a while Tom tended to play everything in a manner unalleviated by anything that could be characterised as expressivity. It was like watching a ballet dancer hopping about in diver's boots.

Tom wouldn't deny that he was not playing 'properly' – the usual excuse was that it helped him 'to see the bones' of the music. As an alibi he once reeled off a list of the great pianists who had employed this irritating mode of practice. I made him write them down, then I checked them in the library. The names were genuine, if nothing else. When I requested a fuller analysis of the technique's merits, Tom said he understood the good it did him but could not put it into words – an unconvincing but unbreakable defence.

Sometimes I became so frustrated by his evasions that I really pressed him to talk. He averted the threat by showing me a little musical puzzle or code he had 'discovered'. Schumann – a composer I'm sure he never truly liked – was a particularly fecund source of diversions: the 'Abegg' variations; the birthplace of Schumann's fiancée hidden in the score of *Carnaval*; the disguised version of the 'Marseillaise' in *Faschingsschwank aus Wien*. All very clever, but nothing more, and nothing to do with the working of Tom's mind.

For a long time Tom was as reluctant to play for us as he was to talk about what he played or the way he played it. An inability to concentrate when people sat close was the professed reason for this reluctance, but that was nonsense – he suffered not from poor concentration but from embarrassment, as if he thought we'd take the music as some kind of confession. Some evenings he'd perform a batch of short pieces or a sonata, and sometimes he could be cajoled into playing for visiting relatives, but he made sure it was a dutiful business.

For certain kinds of practice he never minded an audience. If he were playing chord progressions, or scales, or trying different pedallings, he would not be distracted by company. Sometimes he would actually invite me to sit beside him while he demonstrated an effect. He was happy to show the piano's capabilities, but not the pianist's.

He was, however, more willing to oblige in the two or three years before the Royal College, when the label 'pianist' had glued itself permanently to him. He was still no extrovert, but we could stray into the room while he was playing and he wouldn't slam the lid down as if he'd been caught pilfering the silver. He wasn't voluble, but he wasn't shifty either. Tom carried on like the sole occupant of a fortress. We weren't invited in, but at least he'd peer over the parapet at regular intervals and give us a report on life inside.

Hope this helps. It's been a strain.

### Michael Dessauer to Christopher Lang

Episode three.

That Davis Narayan was immediately impressed by the calibre of his new pupil may safely be assumed; that within a few months he was envisaging a solo career for the boy and endeavouring to persuade him to channel all his efforts to that end, we know for a fact.

Advice regarding his future was given persistently but, we may deduce from the lengthy delay before Thomas's decision, was of limited influence. Helen Gilray, on the other hand, abjured all such guidance, deeming it wiser to wait until her opinion on the matter was requested. When the request came – and it came only once – it was scarcely imperative. Thomas was a few days past his thirteenth birthday when, with the air of someone who was being pestered for a loan by an unreliable friend, he told Helen Gilray that his other teacher had asked him why he couldn't see that his 'destiny was staring him in the face'. If he didn't see it soon, Mr Narayan had said, it might be too late. 'If you want to go far, you've got to go light,' he had admonished him. 'You've got to throw away everything that isn't essential.'

Thomas's tone suggested that he was seeking not advice but commiseration for the harassment he had endured, but Helen Gilray saw that it was advice he wanted. She told him that she agreed with Mr Narayan, but that he must not force himself. Single-mindedness was not something that could be implanted. If he really had to think about his decision, then he had already made it.

At his next session with Helen Gilray, Thomas told her what he had decided. He explained his decision with an uncharacteristic ponderousness, as though called upon to articulate his assessment of the potential of a third person.

He accepted that a choice had to be made, and that it should not be postponed. Thus he had compared his accomplishments. His marks at school were good in all subjects except history and religious knowledge, and his teachers all predicted that he would make a first-class scientist. However, something troubled him about these subjects in which he especially excelled, and that was the impossibility of imagining the work he might do in whatever scientific discipline he might take up. To opt for the sciences would be, in a sense, to choose the unknown. By contrast, although his talent was by no means fully developed (and he used the word 'talent' quite easily, as if it were merely an aspect of the growth of his body), and although his knowledge of the literature was very restricted, he could nonetheless see more clearly what would lie ahead were he to go the way Mr Narayan was pushing him. Therefore, without agonising, he had chosen.

Helen Gilray was uneasy with Thomas's decision – or rather, with the manner of it. It was, she said, a little like discovering that a cherished painting is not by the artist to whom it had been attributed, but by an artist she had previously disliked. She had emphasised to Thomas the necessity of a sense of vocation in order to push him into a period of self-examination through which he would arrive at a realisation of what he really was – an artist. This idea, that Thomas might one day be surprised by his true nature, like a traveller awakened to his deep identity by an encounter with a fellow countryman in a foreign land, was one that Helen Gilray was obliged to relinquish, albeit slowly and with great regret. Thomas was patently not burdened by any sense of destiny.

## Michael Dessauer to Christopher Lang

No reply. May I assume I'm on the right track? Anyway, here's more.

The four years preceding his admission to the Royal College of Music constitute a third phase in Thomas Lang's musical education. His lessons with Helen Gilray were now transmuted into private recitals, and it is notable that the pieces he played for her were drawn from the repertoire that was to form the backbone of his solo career. Whereas with Davis Narayan he ranged over virtuosic pieces by Liszt, Scriabin, Rachmaninov and a variety of musicians whose work he was later to shun, at Helen Gilray's home he chose to play little that was not written by Beethoven, Schubert, Chopin or Bach.

Helen Gilray could no longer properly be called Thomas Lang's teacher, as it had become all but impossible for a situation to arise in which she could make a suggestion that had not occurred to Thomas already, and his dexterity had long since surpassed her own. She now saw herself as his first audience and critic, though she rarely heard anything to question in his playing, except for a tendency to 'underplay the lyrical in favour of the discursive'. When Thomas was accepted by the Royal College, there was no celebration. Both Thomas and Helen Gilray accepted his success as the simple corollary of his decision to be a pianist.

In later years Thomas Lang played for his old teacher whenever his schedule permitted, but she never heard him play in public. In late January 1965 she suffered a stroke that left her with impaired hearing and partial paralysis. Christopher Lang, Thomas's older brother (and, as Thomas's brother, instantly secure in her trust), has been a frequent visitor ever since.

### Christopher Lang to Michael Dessauer

Despite the insinuation of your latest instalment, I have nothing to add on the subject of Thomas and Helen Gilray. We do indeed meet from time to time, and we talk about Thomas more often than not. She talks about him as if he were still alive – not, I think, because she finds the past too turbulent a country, but because it's the highest compliment she can pay him. Message ends.

### Michael Dessauer to Christopher Lang

No insinuation intended. Helen Gilray has provided me with ample material for my chapter on her part in his life. I simply thought that you should receive some tribute for your devotion to an admirable woman whose strengths would seem to be of little interest to anyone else. If you'd prefer, I shall delete this reference to you, though I think your complete deletion from the dramatis personae would be a flaw in the biography of Thomas Lang.

Since last writing to you I have spoken at length to a certain Ian Matthiesson, a schoolfriend of Thomas as a teenager. Perhaps you remember him? He has provided a few neat touches of portraiture. He talked about Thomas's combination of 'dreaminess and determination', for instance, and of the impression he gave 'of being preoccupied with things that hadn't yet happened' – a nice turn of phrase I thought. He confirmed Mrs Gilray's image of Thomas as a boy who stood outside the ever-shifting alliances of the classroom, but augmented it with the observation that although Thomas belonged to no one's clique, he was the one boy whose approval everyone sought or required. Evidently Thomas was seen as an individual to respect right from the beginning.

I'll be following up these points later this week, as I've succeeded in tracking down a couple of other friends from this period. I hope you're keeping well.


## Christopher Lang to Michael Dessauer

Ian Matthiesson was not a 'schoolmate'; he just happened to be in the same class as Tom for a couple of years. As I recall – and in this instance I recall with extreme precision, believe me – he was an athletic, good-looking and formidably dense child, open-minded with the emphasis on 'open', as in 'wide open': that is, with an amazing capacity for believing two entirely contradictory ideas in the interval of half an hour. His face habitually registered slowly emerging wry amusement, a non-committal expression that could be readily adjusted in the direction of hilarity or thoughtfulness or whichever way it became apparent that it was expedient to go. Like looking at a painted face on an inflating balloon. Remarkably dogged kind of brain he had: if you told him a joke he'd really stick at it. You'd see him on his own on the top deck of the bus, suddenly breaking into a grin as the penny dropped. Not an unpopular boy, chiefly on account of his all-round sportiness, with special proficiency in football, rugby and any other game that entailed a high risk of percussive cranial injury. To give him his due, he was a very good cross-country runner as well, though it was like watching some sort of high-velocity ruminant. I believe that for a while he was the feebly twinkling star of the geography class: nice simple principles (rivers flow downhill, trees like rain, ice wears things away, cows can't graze on sand), and lots of lovely facts and figures to remember. I'd imagine he's now something big in fertilisers.

In short, you are to be congratulated on your achievement in selecting, out of a field of dozens, the most obtuse extant observer of my brother's schooldays. I find it inconceivable that Ian Matthiesson and my brother would ever have been party to anything that could be described as a conversation, and equally hard to imagine that your witness would have seen any reason to focus his stringently circumscribed mental faculties on anything he was not ordered to engage himself with. The lad was pathologically incurious.

He's just telling you what he thinks you want to hear, and it's alarmingly possible that he has read you correctly. I mean to say – 'dreaminess', for God's sake. Thomas was as dreamy as a wolverine. And if Mr Matthiesson really came up with that little aperçu you find so cute, he must have been going to phrase-mongering classes at the neighbourhood adult institute for the last twenty years. During which time he evidently lost sight of his subject over the horizon of the past.

I'll tell you what. Give me a week and I'll submit an essay in the biographical mode: 'Selected Scenes from the Childhood of Thomas Lang'. A glimpse of life at home, with literary enhancement at no extra charge. Nothing special, nothing revelatory, but I think you'll be attracted by my thematic consistency, the specious sine qua non of the memorialist's art. And at least my memory is on nodding terms with reality.

## *Christopher Lang to Michael Dessauer*

Thomas Lang, aged 7, was enthralled by dinosaurs, a common enough fascination. A small library of books circulated through his classroom, each page illustrated with watercolours of pin-headed reptiles, freakish predators with numberless teeth, weak-flippered whale-like things, herds of elephantine cud-chewers eyed from the glossy undergrowth by tigers the size of horses. Unlike his friends, however, Thomas was little interested in the monstrousness of these creatures.

Using his father's ticket, he would borrow each week a book from the prehistory section of the local library. For every half-hour absorbed by pictures of reconstructed jawbones and cross-sectioned clay beds he would spend an hour on the index of the book. Asked, when reading, which were his favourite dinosaurs, he would not – as many children would do – turn to an artist's impression of a rampant *Tyrannosaurus rex* or its hapless victims, but instead recite a list of names, a list of variable components but constant length, recited as his friends might reel off the forward line of the Manchester United team: diplodocus, triceratops, stegosaurus, mastodon, archaeopteryx. If asked to explain his preferences, he would reply that their names sounded right.

The focus of his enthusiasm shifted to the hominids, and he was to be heard on occasion declaiming their names in a sort of marching song as he tramped the landing between his bedroom and the head of the stairs: 'Cro-Magnon, Neanderthal, Java, Piltdown, *Homo habilis.*'

For his eighth birthday he received from his parents a book titled *The Young Person's Guide to Life on Earth.* Within the day he was loudly chanting the name of the animal for which, he insisted, he had the greatest affection:

Aitch eye
Double pee
Owe pee
Owe tee
Ay em you ess.

On his next birthday he was given a collection of Arthurian tales, a volume as fat as a ledger, illustrated with misty pastel scenes. That August, on his mother's birthday, he performed for her a 'poem' he had learned by heart, and presented her with a copy of it, written in indigo ink on a scroll of plain wallpaper adorned with little drawings of knights on horseback. Though the writing has long ago faded to the faintest bloom on the yellowed paper, his brother still keeps the scroll framed above his desk. The poem runs:

A shrewdness of apes
A sloth of bears
A clowder of cats
A dule of doves
A herd of elephants
A charm of finches
A trip of goats
A siege of herons
A smack of jellyfish
A kindle of kittens
A deceit of lapwings
A labour of moles
A watch of nightingales
A parliament of owls
An ostentation of peacocks
A covey of quail
An unkindness of ravens
A sounder of swine
A knot of toads
A gam of whales

(What element of this list, we may ask, is the more significant: the music of the ensemble, or the esoteric nature of these collective nouns? Should we resist the temptation to find additional meaning in his rejection of the obvious 'plague of locusts' in favour of the more recondite 'deceit of lapwings'? And what revelation might there be in the coexistence of 'unkindness' and 'charm', 'ostentation' and 'shrewdness'?)

Thomas Lang was an obsessive child. As a ten-year-old he was fascinated by cars, worshipped Malcolm Campbell, knew the story of every racing marque, the location of every major factory, the insignia of every make. In his last months at primary school he then conceived an interest in racehorses, though he had never seen a race (and was never to see one). He studied bloodlines, learned the curves and gradients of courses not just in Britain but in the USA and Australia too, and could recount the victories of animals from Sceptre to Phar Lap. Once the eleven-plus exam was out of the way, he wrote a project on the evolution of the horse, complete with multicoloured evolutionary tree and a bibliography.

From the time he transferred to grammar school his obsessions changed with accelerating frequency. In the first term it was geology. Photographs of scintillating stones and cross-sections of faulted strata went up on his walls, displacing the horses and the hominids. Thomas wrote an essay on the classification of rock that prompted the form master to enquire of his parents whether they had given him some assistance; they looked at the essay, and confessed they didn't even understand the first page.

Before Christmas he had embarked on a digression through the obscurantisms of heraldry, decorating his bedroom with invented coats of arms, each with its blazon appended. Next he was on to astronomy, a passion that endured for several months after his twelfth birthday, when he persuaded his parents to give him a telescope he'd seen in a local junk shop. Within a few weeks he could reel off lists of stars, nebulas and satellites, and the names of the world's main observatories, as well as the details of the telescopes installed there. His family could point to any part of the night sky and he'd duly recite a catalogue of light-year distances. On cloudless nights he could be found lying on a blanket in the garden, underneath the kitchen chair on which he had propped the telescope. He might lie there for hours, and come indoors in a shirt dripping with dew.

Shortly after the start of Thomas's second year at the grammar school the telescope was discarded. Gone were the slabs of agate, the lions couchant, the descent of man and the star charts. Chemistry had now taken hold, and every weekend he would take a train up to central London and spend part of the day in the Science Museum. For as long as this phase lasted he was friendly with the local doctor's son, who supplied Thomas with tubs of unlabelled powders and liquids, which would be brewed in test tubes over the gas ring. His mother became used to finding flasks of virulent-looking concoctions in the kitchen cabinets, and the basin in the bathroom was regularly stained with things that bleach could not shift – though Thomas would arrive with a home-made potion that would erase the mark in seconds. Two vast posters hung over his bed: one of the periodic table, the other a chart of the metallic elements. His skills were in constant demand. He turned out capsules of foul-smelling mixtures and a powder which, mixed with water, produced an unstoppable eruption of pink foam.

Chemistry held his attention into the new year, but in the spring term Thomas was spending much of his free time in the biology laboratory, a prefabricated hut behind the cricket nets. His brother recalls seeing him often at the window of the lab, holding a flask against the sun or preparing a specimen for the miscroscope. Whenever Christopher Lang called by during a lunchbreak, Thomas would explain the aims of the experiment he was conducting, show him its results, elucidate what they meant. He was far more expansive about this extra-curricular work than he ever was about his music. His manner, however, was sometimes slightly distant, even condescending, as though he were showing his work not to his brother but to a young newcomer to the school.

On his thirteenth birthday he was given a copy of *Dixon's Encyclopaedia of Mammals*, a weighty volume with a photo of a duck-billed platypus on the front cover and a rhinoceros on the back. Soon after, on a cousin's birthday, the Langs went to Regent's Park zoo, where Thomas proceeded to demonstrate that he had memorised most of the book. Should the caption on an animal's enclosure be lacking certain details, Thomas could usually supply them, whether it be the gestation period of the mouflon, the habitat of the jackal, the diet of the caracal, the sun bear's life expectancy, or the average weight of the tamarin. Every few minutes the group would stop, consult the boy, and he would recite the information with an air of compromised modesty, as though embarrassed by the volume of material he could remember.

Until then, if anyone had asked him what he wanted to be, he'd say a zoologist, or a research chemist, or an immunologist; never a musician. Then suddenly he changed. The spare-time researches were dropped, the labs abandoned. He told his teachers that the amount of work was becoming too much for him. None of them believed him, but none of them could fathom what was going on in his mind. It wasn't as if his interest in these subjects had palled. It was more that he had decided to deny himself that interest.

Only his brother was not surprised by this volte-face, for the very intensity of Thomas's dedication to the sciences had made him increasingly suspicious of its depth. As Christopher Lang wrote to Michael Dessauer in 1990: 'When he rattled through his lists of facts it was as if someone had switched on a tape. His passionate interests often seemed to be factitious fanaticisms.'

## Michael Dessauer to Christopher Lang

It's not difficult to reconcile Helen Gilray's account of your brother's 'conversion' with your reading of it. (I'm assuming that you mean what you quote yourself as saying.) Thomas may have thought he was exercising his free will, but he was in fact acting out a course that was preordained by his talent. Inevitably he was going to make the decision he did make, and his formulation of reasons for that decision is ultimately an irrelevance; he would have done what he did even had such rationalisations not been to hand. After all, how many lives appear in retrospect to have been the fulfilment of the laws of social class, whereas to their subjects every significant development could be ascribed to chance or choice?

Or perhaps Thomas was aware of the working of this 'destiny', but needed to provide a rational camouflage for something he found it difficult to accommodate, an objective sanction for something that was supremely subjective? Of course, the fact remains that Thomas not once expressed any sentiment that Helen Gilray could hear as a declaration of vocation, so this second version, while getting me out of what initially seemed something of an impasse, adds weight to another problematic aspect of Thomas's genius – his secretiveness.

P.S. Ian Matthiesson is now an acupuncturist, you may be surprised to hear.

### Christopher Lang to Michael Dessauer

I liked your last missive. I like anything that smacks of theological legerdemain. However, I must say I don't have any problem with the fledgling virtuoso's lack of openness, though I sympathise with your difficulties. I was certainly shocked by Tom's coming out, as I've already told you. It was a brutal way to be robbed of one's tacit belief in the ingenuousness of children, but such sentimentalism had to be abandoned sooner or later. The ability to lie is a great step forward for a child. A lie demonstrates the ability to conceive of the world as it might be perceived by someone other than oneself. Please feel free to exploit this off-the-cuff and possibly untenable idea if you wish – lying as a self-interested liberation from egocentricity.

While we're at it, please don't use the word 'genius' again, unless you wish to upset Tom's ghost. I remember Tom reporting that he'd been categorised as a genius by the school's music teacher. What impressed Tom about this incident wasn't that he'd been elevated to another sphere of existence. It was that a professional teacher had used such sloppy language. If you care to compare the sleeve notes on the individual Chopin records with the booklet enclosed in the boxed set of those records released in 1984, you'll notice that 'genius' has been expunged from the text, the consequence of an attritional correspondence campaign by my brother. I can recall Tom uttering the dread word just once, and that was in relation to a melody from *Death and the Maiden*. He must have been thirteen at the time. The comment – 'That's genius you know,' or something like that – seemed odd at the time and even more odd later, as Schubert was a composer in whom he had evinced not the slightest interest, and whose music he wasn't to play in public until well into his career. So was this a prescient observation on the music, a sudden flash of light amid the murk of incomprehension, or was it an ironic comment on the word? At the time I took it as the latter, but I was never sure. One did not ask Tom for clarification. It would have been like asking the Delphic oracle for a paraphrase.

Anyway, don't lose sleep over the enigma of young Tom. As musical prodigies go, he wasn't the weirdest. Friedman at the age of nine knew by heart all forty-eight preludes and fugues of *The Well-Tempered Clavier*. Wee Carl Fitsch copied out the whole orchestral score of Liszt's F-minor concerto from memory. Liszt said of him: 'When this little one goes on the road I shall shut up shop', but the wunderkind was dead by fifteen. Tausig was said to have memorised the entire classical repertoire before he'd reached the age of seventeen. Their brothers died insane, I should imagine.

## Michael Dessauer to Christopher Lang

I'm working in a few more reminiscences of Thomas as a child. This page stands a good chance of surviving the rewrites unchanged.

A few friends of the Lang family were very occasionally permitted to hear young Thomas play. Of course they recall the bewildering sureness of his playing, but they also remark upon the unusual manner in which the boy seemed to regard his own virtuosity. He was not bashful, as a less extraordinarily talented child might be, nor was he in any way conceited, which would have been forgivable. His attitude was rather one of intense interest in the phenomenon of himself.

He appeared fascinated by himself and by the piano, and fascinated in exactly the same way. He could be heard playing the same chord over and over again, entranced by the various hues he could create with just the slightest alterations of pressure. And as he played, he would often look not at the keyboard but at his hands, as if they were merely part of the intricate transmission that ended with the hammers, strings and dampers.

His memory was startling, not just with regard to music. In geography classes he would play a game in which a friend would open his atlas at the map of the world and stick his pencil blindly onto the page. He'd tell Thomas the name of the country he'd selected and then nominate a compass bearing. Thomas would then recite the names of all the countries that lay along that line, in the right order, without hesitation. He could do the same trick right round the globe, starting from the named point and heading north, south, east or west. He could do it with the states of the

USA, with the islands of Polynesia, with the peaks of the Himalayas.

In the debates that were a feature of each term, he would deliver his speech from memory, and could recall verbatim the speeches of his opponents. As if such abilities were not intimidating enough, his manner seemed calculated to crush his rivals, though these were often his nearest friends. His words were generally facetious yet were delivered with a solemnity that had the effect of keeping his audience one step behind him, unsure that they had gauged correctly the tone of what he was saying. He also had a habit of pausing for a moment, to scrutinise a spot midway between the floor and ceiling, as if the exact word that would settle the argument were imprinted on the air there, at the same time placing a hush upon his voice, conveying the sense that it was for his own sake, not his audience's, that he sought precision.

I'd really like more on how he was perceived by his friends, but I think I've milked the current sources for all they're worth. Could you help me out at all?

## Christopher Lang to Michael Dessauer

Who are these 'few friends of the Lang family'? The only non-relatives who were even semi-frequent guests in the Lang household were Joe Armitage (father's boss), his wife (Margaret) and his two creepily pallid daughters (Judith & Clare). The girls developed simultaneously a sad crush on Tom during the ghastly phase of his adolescence (circa 1959) in which he chose to cultivate a mien of Savonarolan ferocity. The younger (Judith) became convinced that her passion was reciprocated, notwithstanding the absence of any evidence detectable to others, and awaited humbly the moment when Tom would cast off the secret burden that prevented the disclosure of his soul. For a year she nurtured her half-stifled torment, but Tom's heart remained unmortgaged and so it was suddenly revealed to her that he was a big-headed cold-hearted boor. Clare was more tardy in apprehending the truth, and maintained her self-denying vigil to the day her progenitor took his family off to cultivate some blasted heath in the depths of Wales.

Joe Armitage is dead now isn't he? The girls can't be judged reliable, as they spent most of their time in a swoon or a sulk. So that leaves Margaret, an unimpeachable witness I'm sure, but a singular unimpeachable witness. So one must perforce ask if these 'friends' are a trick done by mirrors? I'm not carping, however. The observations attributed to these dubiously plural people are valid, and I commend your tenacity in winkling them out.

I assume the source for the classroom pranks is Matthiesson again? Still, the story rings true, and I can't be of much use to you here anyway. I couldn't say with any certainty what Tom's crew made of him. As far as I was concerned, Tom's friends were apprentice boys, and I didn't waste my time with them. Most were in awe of him, I think, but that was to do more with the ease with which he could tackle their schoolwork than with his musical prowess. I think his piano-playing was just a given, like being double-jointed or seven feet tall.

I'd say his friends liked him because he made them

laugh. Or perhaps it's more accurate to say that they thought him a wit, on the basis of his penchant for overworked wordplays and puns. I remember the one he chalked on a classmate's blazer – 'I do not care for your haircut, but I shall defend to the death your right to wear it. Jacques Asson-Gou.' And the note he pinned to the gym door just before a football match in sub-zero temperatures – 'God does not temper the wind. Sean Lamb.' Or the time Tom and I were sitting in the local fish and chip shop when the lights went out: 'The dark night of the sole'.

An especially tortuous creation now comes to mind. Tom must have been twelve or thirteen. We were filing into church for some festive ritual, a combined operation with the girls' school. Tom and I had positioned ourselves behind a girl of whose precociously curvaceous form I was a fervent admirer. At the church entrance the girls were shepherded off to one side, the boys to the other, and as the object of my lust disappeared from view, Tom muttered to me: 'We enjoy heavenly pleasures, and leave the earthly behind.' (The quotation, he later explained to his obtuse sibling, was from Mahler's Fourth.) It has taken me ten minutes to remember the real name of the earthly behind: Katharine Wilton. The sort of gratuitous detail that might create an aura of authenticity.

Why not go back to your Royal College specimens and ask them if Tom was ever funny? You might learn as much as you did by asking for recollections of the budding star. Ask them about postcards.

## Michael Dessauer to Christopher Lang

Not a terrifically productive line of enquiry, sorry to say. Only one item has come to light. John Wycherly recalls a party at which your brother gave a spoof recital in the guise of various keyboard greats. For the first part of the show he was de Pachmann, striding into the room wearing garish odd socks revealed by trousers at half mast. Having doused his hands in cold tea from a brandy bottle, he dashed through one of the *Davidsbündlertänze* while swapping insults with John Wycherly: 'Stop fidgeting, you fat moron!' – 'Shut up and play it properly!' et cetera, et cetera. His Friedman routine required a change of costume: reappearing in a jacket stuffed with foam cushions, Thomas waddled over to the piano, dumped himself down onto the stool, regarded the keyboard 'like a man looking down on his one thousandth consecutive breakfast of bacon and eggs', and played a note-perfect Chopin mazurka. Thomas as Liszt was the highlight of the evening, it would seem. I confess to finding this episode a wearisome example of student humour. I might use it. I don't know yet.

The enquiry about postcards drew a blank: nobody knew to what the question was meant to refer, and as I didn't either, we were stuck. No mirrors, by the way; the explanation is far simpler – Joe Armitage is not dead. And neither was Matthiesson my source – it was a different former schoolmate, Colin Mitchelham, now something big in insurance. With reference to a comment you made on one of our early days, the earliest I believe – I take it Thomas liked football?

## Christopher Lang to Michael Dessauer

Tom hated nearly all sport. That would have been part of the joke, I assume, but I can't recall what it was now. I'm surprised that nobody took you up on the postcards. Whenever Tom's travels took him to a part of the world where it's chic to flaunt one's familiarity with Anglo-American tastes, he would look in shop windows for examples of finely warped English. Every time he played in France, Spain or Italy, I'd get a postcard with no message other than a garbled slogan and its source. He always did this, so I assumed I was not the unique recipient, but perhaps I was. Here's a batch of ten Roman cards for you.

1. 'The set of knapsacks thought for metropolitan use will last unaltered also after exasperated use'. (Label of a leather bag.)

2. 'Free life hand tools by the spirit of West Canada Furs Company great era'. (Windcheater.)

3. 'Paul Jomes (american creative). Culturally borned in one of the best american's university, Paul Jomes succeeded by his personality to become a leading artist in the difficult and contrasted world of fashions. In every thing, his clothes shows his purity, style and semplicity of line.' (Jacket label.)

4. 'Bear & Pool – Dive Your Own'. (Slogan in four-inch-high low-relief lime green plastic lettering on purple sweatshirt.)

5. 'The adaptability of this garment is deducted from an accurate study of urbane behaviour of all modes'. (Label on reversible cardigan.)

6. '20 Years of My Life – The End of the Journey – Exhausteds and Immovables'. (Text on two scrolls woven above and below a printed scene of unleashed huskies and snowbound sled; on front of sweatshirt.)

7. 'Tutti frutti all the way here – pickle on blue, lemon on rye'. (Jeans label.)

8. 'One two three Detroit set. Prairies College, wide outdoor. Team strive'. (Anorak.)

9. 'Hawaii
Stimulation personal adornment
5–0 College League
Fashion is a Human Expression Permanently
Do You Know?'. (Sweatshirt.)

10. 'The perfect outfit of good times.
Education is the key to self-knowlegde'. [sic] (Satin bomber jacket.)

Every life needs a bit of leavening. Surely you should do something with the Liszt gag? How about this for a bit of colourful ersatz reportage?

'From behind twin swags of scarlet plush Franz Liszt appears, his powdered face framed by black, lank locks, with a central parting like a trail of chalk dust.

From neck to shin he is cased in a black surplice, a heavy silver crucifix at rest on his chest, a rosary of coral-pink beads tucked negligently into a wide black belt. He prowls to the keyboard and there pauses, turns, bows, his face cracked into a sanctimonious smirk. Claw-like, the hands are raised till they brush his ears; a moment's cruel pause, and then they fall, tearing a *Transcendental Study* from the instrument, like a lion ripping the guts from its prey.

The music runs out from under his fingers; he leans back and turns his head to survey his audience, primed to glare at any untransported celebrants. Satisfied that due reverence is his, he returns his gaze to the piano. His eyes blaze as though outstaring a demon squatting on the strings; the arms flail, the hair leaps, the crucifix bounces on the passion-racked torso. As the fury subsides, a beatific smile dawns on his face. As gently as the petals of a flower at dusk, his eyelids close, and he is lost in the wonder of being Franz Liszt. The ecstasy endures some seconds beyond the final bar. Wiping an eye discreetly, he rises, one hand pressed to his breast, his features aglow with humility. He bows once, and gravely departs.'

## *Michael Dessauer to Christopher Lang*

Please don't think me ungrateful, but I'm not sure if I can use the material you've just sent me. I find the end-of-term play-acting something of an embarrassment, and the 'funny foreigners' stuff tedious. But more importantly, I remain to be convinced that this material is central to any life of Thomas Lang. A mention of

Thomas Lang's sense of humour might be warranted if he were a notably humourless character or the reverse, but in this respect he would seem to have been entirely average. It would be as pointless to make reference to so unremarkable an aspect of my subject as it would be to give space to his favourite types of food. Perhaps I'll give the postcards a mention; we'll see.

### *Christopher Lang to Michael Dessauer*

If you find play-acting an 'embarrassment', it seems damned strange that you've decided to write the life of a performer. But still, you are of course at liberty to select from the countless millions of pieces of information floating around the world those that help you clarify the picture you are drawing. As long as you remind yourself from time to time that what you're doing is tracing faces in the clouds.

Anyway, here's a salutary tale for you. It will be my last word on the subject of Tom's humour.

Martin McLellan, at the time of my tale a junior journalist with *The Times*, first encountered the name of Thomas Lang when a colleague (my source for much of this tale, by a route too circuitous to relate) brought into the office an Italian news magazine containing a story about the pianist. According to this report, a press photographer had come across Lang and a young Italian actress in a Modena restaurant. Placing himself at a nearby table, the paparazzo bided his time until Lang and his companion seemed absorbed in each other, then released the shutter on the camera he had hidden in a plant pot beside his chair. Instantly the 'stupendous blonde' turned round, and in a moment she had seized the offending instrument, detached its lens, and emptied the contents of a large wine glass into the open body of the camera. The ensuing altercation was carried into the street outside, whither the protagonists were ushered by the embarrassed head waiter. Next day, the reporter declared his intention to sue for damages both to his equipment and to his reputation. Lang had, it was alleged, called him a 'truffle pig' before an audience of several onlookers.

Shortly after hearing this story, Martin McLellan determined that he would be the first person ever to obtain an interview with the publicity-shy and cantankerous 'English legend'.

His first assault was launched within the week. A lunchtime's research in the Westminster reference library, rifling through back-copies of *Gramophone*, gave him all the background he needed. In the afternoon he composed his letter to Tom's agent, assuring him of his integrity, embellishing his curriculum vitae with a few fictitious heavyweight articles and his praise of Tom with a few phrases taken from the record reviews he had read in the library.

Had Joshua Thorpe retained all the similar propositions he had received since the start of his professional relationship with Tom, he would have had enough paper to redecorate his office three times over, as he had been fond of telling any supplicants bold enough to telephone him with their request. To Martin McLellan he dispatched his standard response.

'Thank you for your letter regarding the possibility of an interview with Mr Lang. Your comments on Mr

Lang's work are greatly appreciated but as you may be aware, it has never been Mr Lang's custom to discuss his work. Therefore regretfully I have to inform you that we must deny your request. Please do not think that this refusal is a reflection either on yourself or on your publication.'

McLellan then dispatched his letter to the publicity department at DRG Grammophon, who informed him that his communication had been conveyed to Mr Lang but that no interview could be arranged. He telephoned the publicity department at DRGG to ask if they might tell him Tom's address. The person to whom he spoke, an easily irritated young man by the name of Miles Craxton, suggested that he try the office of Mr Joshua Thorpe. Again he tackled Thorpe, whose secretary told him that in no circumstances would his employer release the address of any of his clients. Under pressure, she relented slightly. If Mr McLellan cared to post his letter to Mr Thorpe's office she would be prepared to forward it to Mr Lang.

Before embarking on this approach, Martin McLellan did a few hours' more research. From the catalogue in a West End shop he copied the list of all Tom's recordings, which he then tracked down in the Westminster music library. He photocopied their sleeve notes, then all the reviews he could trace in the library's music magazines. The character and career of Thomas Lang thus given flesh, he devoted an evening to his petition. He noticed that although half a dozen different writers had reviewed Tom's recordings, certain key notions had been common to their commentaries. The pianist's technique was 'aristocratic', 'refined', 'highly articulated', even, perhaps 'a little cold'; his interpretations were 'fiercely intelligent', 'closely argued', and often made 'demands' on the listener. What Martin McLellan wanted to reveal, he declared, was the man behind the music, the man, as he resoundingly put it, 'behind the mask of music'.

On 1 June 1978, McLellan posted the letter, and every subsequent day he read it through before leaving for work. A week later, he discovered he had made a mistake. He had paraphrased convincingly one reviewer's particularly arresting remark on Chopin's E-minor étude, but then misattached the remark to the étude in C minor. Desperate with anxiety, he phoned Thorpe's office. Had his letter been forwarded? he asked. Yes, it had.

What Thomas Lang thought of this gaffe he still had not learned when September came around. Working himself into a state of some indignation, he again spoke to Mr Craxton. Could he tell him when Mr Lang might next be recording in London? Mr Lang hardly ever recorded in London. What was the explanation for this particular idiosyncrasy? It was not an idiosyncrasy, it was simply a fact of Mr Lang's career. Where would Mr Lang's next recording be made? Mr Lang's next recording was scheduled for Salzburg. It might take place in Salzburg. Then again, it might not.

A fellow *Times* journalist restored McLellan's hope of success by informing him that Thomas Lang would be performing at the Royal Festival Hall in November. Within an hour he had his strategy devised, complete with contingency plans to circumvent any obstacles. On the day before the recital, he phoned the management of the Festival Hall, introducing himself as a journalist writing a piece on the legacy of the

Festival of Britain. The article really needed a couple of photos of the Festival Hall – would it be possible for him to come round on the following day to take a few shots?

Mid-morning was suggested as the best time. Martin McLellan replied that the afternoon would be preferable from his point of view. That wouldn't be possible, he was told, as the hall would be in use during the afternoon. From what time? he asked.

'From two o'clock, all afternoon,' came the answer, thus betraying the time at which the quarry would be rehearsing. Martin McLellan eventually arranged to arrive at one o'clock and to be finished within twenty minutes. He turned up at one-fifteen, clicked the shutter a dozen times on his unloaded camera, went for lunch at the ground-floor café, and at two-thirty made his way to the uppermost storey. A member of staff was loitering within a few feet of the door by which McLellan had planned to enter the auditorium. He could hear scales being played, methodically, at perfectly even volume. This neutral, passionless sound, produced by Thomas Lang, was unbearably exciting. Thwarted by the presence of attendants at all entrances, McLellan dawdled up and down the staircases for fully half an hour, as tantalising wisps of music seeped out of the hall. At last one of the attendants folded his magazine, placed it on the floor, and crossed the landing to the toilets. Martin McLellan prowled over to the unprotected door, eased it open, sidled through the gap, eased it shut again. On stage, crouched over the body of the instrument, like a car mechanic changing the spark plugs, was Ronald Cruickshank, the piano-tuner.

That evening Martin McLellan endured all of Book One of *The Well-Tempered Clavier*. When it was over he dashed towards the dressing room, and arrived with no more than half a dozen fans in front of him. All were turned away. He commenced a vigil at the artists' entrance to the building, where he remained until the last light went out in the backstage offices. He saw no sign of Thomas Lang.

It was then that McLellan launched his campaign of saturation correspondence. The evening after the abortive concert he composed a letter to Thomas Lang, care of Thorpe Associates, in which he pleaded for 'an audience with the most electrifying performer at work on the concertstage today'. He adumbrated the course of his career, emphasising those commissions on which he had been required to exercise the 'highest degree of discretion and tact', and quoting salient paragraphs from those articles which he thought, 'in all modesty', displayed best those qualities which guaranteed the value of their 'projected collaboration'.

At seven o'clock the next morning he posted the letter, and last thing the following night he turned out another copy of it, which he posted first thing the following morning, a routine he maintained until he received, three weeks later, a note from Thorpe Associates, asking him to desist. Still McLellan did not give up, even when a second letter informed him that none of his letters would be forwarded in future. Instead, he disguised his duplicates in envelopes of different sizes and colours, addressed with pens of different inks by various colleagues and friends.

Finally, after a total of some thirty-five camouflages had been employed, Martin McLellan's ingenuity and perserverance were rewarded. On 19 March 1979, he received a postcard from Gstaad.

'As you are so intent upon getting your man, you shall have him. Ring the Hotel Suisse at 7 p.m. London time on 30 March, and ask for room 107.' The number of the hotel was appended, in place of a signature.

By the designated day, Martin McLellan had scripted twenty pages of questions. Calling from his office desk, he phoned the Hotel Suisse on the stroke of 7 p.m. and within seconds heard the voice of his prey. Though the interview lasted no more than ten minutes, McLellan was delighted with the remarks he had succeeded in extracting. His editor found the transcript on his desk in the morning, and at eleven he summoned McLellan to his room. The verdict was not favourable. Comments such as 'Horowitz is a performing seal' were, McLellan was told, no more interesting than 'some bilious old dowager wittering away about her in-laws'. Most of the rest – 'it's a monastic life . . .' – was just confessional cliché.

The story was spiked. This, though he was never to realise it, was a piece of extremely good fortune for Martin McLellan, for at 7 p.m. London time on 30 March 1979, Thomas Lang was being shown to a table at Intermezzo, Herenstraat 28, Amsterdam.


## *Michael Dessauer to Christopher Lang*

Is your story true? If so, I'll find some way of using it, but perhaps in relation to his subterfuges as a child (Beckenham etc.), rather than as an example of 'humour'. Here, in the meantime, is my most recent episode, as yet unrevised, so make allowances please.

The piano is not a passive object, a mere box of steel strings and hammers with which to strike them. To play the piano is to dance, and the instrument is a partner in the dance, resisting and answering the player's touch. The keys yield like another's fingers, and no two instruments yield in an identical way. The resonating strings, set in motion by a movement that may have its source deep in the player's body, make the piano tremble like a body in response. The body of the pianist, it is often said, requires the touch of the instrument as much as the instrument requires that of the pianist. The arms, wrists and fingers need the keyboard, just as a dancer's body comes fully into existence only when tested by another's weight. Practice is not solely the means by which a performance is refined – it is a physical imperative. In the words of Gwendolyn Hanna, Thomas Lang's contemporary at the Royal College of Music, 'to go a day without touching the piano would be like spending the day with one's eyes shut'.

Yet here we have Thomas Lang's view on the matter. 'To go a day without touching the piano,' he rejoined, 'is essential if you want to stay sane.' Variations on this theme were favourite Lang provocations. 'How could anyone bear to hear the sound of the piano every day?' he once asked. 'That's why I like the piano so much. Its sound is so unseductive it forces you to hear the music, not the instrument.' Such proclamations may have been partly tactical; they were not wholly so.

To achieve a state of concentrated repose the pianist may resort to strategies or rituals that demand a degree of concentration barely less than that demanded by the recital itself. One famous soloist, for instance, would play through his entire concert programme immediately before his appearance on the platform, but would play the notes without expression. Others detach the right-hand part of the piece from the left-hand, and play the two in sequence; or play the piece as quickly as possible, or as slowly; or memorise a poem or list of trivialities, to be summoned at the piano stool as a way of cleansing the mind, as a blockade against the audience. Before the keyboard can be touched, some performers have to extinguish all sounds and sights except the imagined sound of the first notes and the imagined pressure of the keys, creating a fated event, as it were, which the body can then only fulfil.

As students, many of Lang's contemporaries developed techniques to ease that initial moment of contact with the piano. One would 'rehearse' on a phantom keyboard; another could be heard in the hour before an examination repeatedly playing the opening bars of her designated piece with relentless brutality. Thomas Lang, however, was rarely to be found anywhere in the building until a minute before he was due to play, and his manner of beginning a performance could not have been more intimidating had he contrived it to be. To quote Gwendolyn Hanna again, Lang's way of entering a room suggested that he was simply 'in a hurry to get away from the place he'd come from'. He would begin to play immediately, with as much apparent forethought as a 'bus driver starting his day's work'.

Only once in all his time at the Royal College did this 'aggressive nonchalance' fail him. He was to play the *Waldstein* for Professor Brian Heathley and an external examiner. For all its complexities, the sonata was not a piece that had caused him any noticeable difficulties before, and the experience of critical scrutiny was one to which he had previously seemed indifferent. On this occasion, though, Lang strode to the piano with his customary speed, and then froze, his hands resting on his thighs, his eyes fixed on an indefinite space above the keyboard, his brows slightly tensed, as if suddenly perplexed by something that had occurred some time before.

A few months later, in the chapel of King's College on the Aldwych, a percussion octet and two keyboard players gave the premiere of Henry Attercliff's *Aleatorius IV*, the score of which (circulated to the meagre audience in mimeograph form) bore a dedication to Thomas Lang. Stapled to the five pages of graphic notation was a 500-word text headed 'Notes for *Aleatorius I–IV*'. Towards the end of this long unbroken paragraph of more or less connected phrases occurred the following passage:

'Mallarmé and the horror of the blank page / the horror of the first note / the act of performance as a destructive act / the plenitude of silence / in silence all potentialities are open / with one tone the possibilities are reduced / every note is an erosion, an imposition of limit, a death . . .'


## *Christopher Lang to Michael Dessauer*

Musings on musicianship like watching an elephant waltzing over daisies. There is no reason to be ashamed of dedication to the quotidian, as Tom might once have told me, *aetatis* VIII.


## *Michael Dessauer to Christopher Lang*

Chastised, I forsake speculation for the interim. You'll find nothing but raw facts in this letter, even though these facts, more than any others in the life of Thomas Lang – and I am not forgetting your earlier strictures – warrant, indeed demand, speculation.

1. On 25 October 1987, three weeks after his return from a two-week trip to Norway, Thomas Lang posted to Joshua Thorpe a proposed schedule of recordings for the next five years. The major project he put forward was a chronological cycle of those Beethoven sonatas he had not previously recorded, with a view to completion at the end of 1992. Within that period he also planned to release a disc of the complete Schoenberg piano music as well as recordings of works by Orlando Gibbons, some of Beethoven's bagatelles, and some Brahms – most probably the opus 10 *Ballades*.

2. On 26 October, Thomas Lang took an Air France flight from London to Nice. There he collected a hire car in which he drove to Cotignac, in the Haut-Var region of Provence, where he booked a room for two nights at Lou Calen, a hotel on the village square. That night he ate alone in the restaurant of Lou Calen; the following night he ate at a restaurant called Le Mas de Cotignac, a short distance south of Cotignac. On this occasion he was joined by Konrad Seibert, described in the British newspapers as a 'long-standing friend'. The two men parted at approximately 10.30 p.m. Seibert, who had that day driven from Turin, continued west to the house of his sister-in-law, Cornelia Bernal, on the outskirts of Aix; Lang returned to his hotel.

3. Shortly before 10 a.m. on 28 October, Thomas Lang checked out of Lou Calen. Some time around

82

midday he stopped at a café in Salernes, and in the afternoon he was seen at Le Thoronet, a Cistercian monastery a few kilometres from the hamlet of Entrecasteaux. That evening he was in Aups, where he ate, unaccompanied, at the Framboise restaurant on Place Maréchal Foch. He left no later than 9 p.m.

4. At 7.35 a.m. on 29 October 1987, the body of Thomas Lang was found underneath the Pont du Galetas, where the waters of the Verdon river flow into the reservoir known as the Lac de Sainte-Croix. Lang's car was found soon afterwards, about one kilometre upstream of the Pont du Galetas and several hundred feet below the road.

The car had breached the roadside wall on the northern side of the Verdon gorge at a point some fifty yards beyond the nearest bend; there were no marks on the road surface to indicate that Thomas Lang's vehicle had gone out of control at speed, neither did anything suggest the involvement of another vehicle. Police retrieved the car from the gorge on the day of Lang's death. The boot was found to hold a single suitcase, containing various items of clothing, an unloaded camera, eight reels of film, Thomas Lang's passport, a ticket for a flight from Nice to London on 1 November, a wallet holding nearly 10,000 francs plus travellers' cheques to the value of £500, a paperback copy of *The Book of the Courtier* by Baldassare Castiglione, and a chequebook containing six blank cheques plus a seventh for the sum of £2,000, made out to one Marcus Taylor.

Since constructing this rudimentary narrative I have

tracked down Konrad Seibert. He is based in Lyons, where he runs a film and video production company. He seems eager to assist my researches, and we have arranged to meet next week in Munich: he will be there to record a period-instruments performance of *Così* in the Cuvilliés Theatre; I shall take the opportunity to conduct interviews with a few key figures from Thomas's record company. Is there anything you know about Seibert that you feel I should know? And who was Marcus Taylor?

### *Christopher Lang to Michael Dessauer*

Herr Seibert may indeed have been a 'long-standing friend' of my brother (alarming, your use of quotation marks – I thought for a moment you were fingering him as a murder suspect). Such might be the inference from the fact that they knew each other as lads and would appear to have been on friendly terms a quarter of a century later. For all I know, however, their final day at college and their encounter in Provence could have been the parentheses of years of silence. Rifling through my concordance to the correspondence of Thomas Lang, I can find no mention of the man, and if we turn to my collection of printed memorabilia, the cupboard is again bare, but for the enclosed item of ephemera.

This brittle, frayed and dusty document (for me, its wavery typeface and watery ink instantly evoke the dread-filled classroom: endless tests on unmemorable Saxon kings, religious wars and Dutch trade treaties) was offered to the public by way of a programme note for a shoestring production of *Don Giovanni*, mounted in September 1965 by a makeshift outfit styling itself 'The New London Opera' (i.e. half a dozen ambitious students, a complement of willing drudges from the lower years, a couple of stagehands moonlighting from repertory companies and a woman with a sewing machine). This happy crew was whipped into tolerable order by the instigator, director and all-round *Kunstführer*, Konrad Seibert – a trumpeter by calling. A good job he made of it too, even if the end product lacked the euphonious qualities that professionalism usually imparts. Strident violins and mistimed percussion, I recall, and a strangulated pop-eyed Donna Anna – but incontestable brio. Grotesque rotund frog-like chap singing Don Ottavio as well. No matter.

To resume, the text stencilled onto this A4 page purports to be a conversation between Seibert and a certain Harold Glenn. This Glenn character was a figure for whom the adjective 'shadowy' seemed excessively corporeal. Nobody knew who he was. His interlocutor was substantial enough, but in his day-to-day persona he spoke in sentences that consisted of short, breathy little outbursts in strangely mashed English, rather like a string of soft sausages, and very unlike the speech patterns transcribed below. Tom helped out at the rehearsals, for certain. Only Tom was an adequate audience for Tom. Put two and two together.

H.G.: Would you agree that this is an unusually static presentation?
K.S.: No point in denying it.

H.G.: And how would you justify this approach?

K.S.: On the grounds that *Don Giovanni* is a static opera.

H.G.: I think most people would, on the contrary, describe it as the most dramatic of operas.
K.S.: It has dramatic episodes but is not a dramatic unity. Unlike *Così*, for example, it does not have the dynamics of a well-crafted play.

H.G.: Surely it is characterised above all by its momentum?
K.S.: The momentum lies in the music, not in the play. *Don Giovanni* is a supreme confidence trick, in which the music loans a structure to the drama that the action doesn't possess. We have tried to be faithful to the energy of the music, while bringing the construction of the play to the fore.

H.G.: A production with its bones showing, then?
K.S.: Precisely. The plot of *Don Giovanni* proceeds not by development but by juxtaposition. Simply ask 'What happens to the Don, and why?' At the start he kills a man; at the close the ghost of his victim drags him to hell. What happens in between establishes the grounds for his damnation but does not bring it about. The vendetta of Don Ottavio and Donna Anna creates a lot of noise but is impotent.

Don Giovanni's character is revealed chiefly not through solo declamation, but through a rapid succession of exchanges, each of which adds a new facet to the man. In the first meeting with Donna Elvira we see his rapacity, his courtesy, his brutality. With Zerlina we observe the dispassionate technique of seduction, and then, with the assault, we have evidence of the near-suicidal strength of his appetite. The deception of Elvira is a display of the improvisatory wit that is the hallmark of the true libertine. And so on. Entwined with this serial revelation is a dialectic carried by characters who are themselves constructed of opposites: think of Leporello's vacillation, the ambivalent passions of Donna Elvira, the over-asserted virtue of Donna Anna.

H.G.: So what we see is a trial of sorts, a trial in which the witnesses incriminate themselves or switch from the prosecution to the defence.
K.S.: Quite. The Don is a monstrous delinquent; the opera is his spell on probation.

H.G.: But isn't it a fact that *Don Giovanni* can never be rescued from the Devil's party?
K.S.: I hope not. You have only to pick up *Paris Match* to see the Don as he should be seen – a man with a December suntan and more weight round his wrist than between his ears. We've had enough of Don Giovanni as the primal Douglas Fairbanks Jr. There's just one heroic figure in this opera, and he's dead.

Marcus Taylor was a general odd-job man who made a few improvements to Tom's house.

## *Michael Dessauer to Christopher Lang*

It turns out that when Thomas and Konrad Seibert met in Provence, they were seeing each other for the first time in three years. Following lives that were similarly peripatetic, they found that their paths would rarely cross. Over the years they had stayed in contact through phone calls made on the spur of the moment; their conversations, says Konrad, always had the tone of a talk that had been interrupted only days before, though often they would not have spoken for months. Throughout 1978 and 1980 they didn't speak at all. Konrad would write a brief letter perhaps once a year – the reply might be a call at 7.30 in the morning, out of the blue, six months later. At least, this was the pattern until Thomas's final year.

Konrad Seibert is a strange character. His assertively bohemian appearance – he affects a chequered waist-coat, Gramsci-style glasses and a waxed moustache – is completely at odds with his almost timorous sincerity. I can see some elements of the figure you described in him. His sentences commence in an urgent whisper then trail off into silence, as though the words he had meant to speak had been eclipsed by the ones he would have to arrange for his next utterance. Congenial and self-distracted is how I'd characterise him. An unlikely media mogul and aspiring polar explorer (more on this in a minute), and, I'd have thought, an unlikely candidate for your brother's friendship – I would have attributed Thomas with rather sterner tastes. Still, I'm learning something daily.

I quickly discovered that during the year preceding their final meeting, Konrad Seibert and your brother had been in closer contact than at any time since their student days. Thomas telephoned Konrad in July 1986 to tell him that he intended to cancel all the concert engagements planned beyond the end of the year, and to retire from the stage. This was not the first occasion he had spoken of his disenchantment with live performances ('the inspiration business' he called it), but this time he had other plans for his life. He said he had it in mind to work with Konrad, as a writer of sorts. He foresaw a partnership in which he would sketch the scheme of several short films, which Konrad would then take up and develop, free of Thomas's interference. He imagined a sequence of a dozen or so pieces, perhaps wordless, interconnected by a theme that would remain unstated – a sequence whose visual language would be entirely of Konrad's invention, so that 'nothing but the idea' could be said to belong to Thomas.

This idea, little more than a format for a relationship, never developed much beyond a half-formed outline of a documentary to be entitled *The History of Ice*, in which images of ice types were to be accompanied by a soundtrack of texts – episodes of Arctic adventure and shipwreck, biologists' notebooks, Inuit tales, reports from meteorological stations. Konrad still intends to make their film, and is planning to spend several months in Canada, up on Banks Island.

When Konrad and Thomas shared their meal outside Cotignac, however, they discussed a quite different collaboration, and one that bore little semblance to the scheme that your brother had originally sketched. Thomas brought a manuscript to that meeting, a manuscript which Konrad still keeps in the manila folder in which Thomas carried it, and which I have now read. He handed it to me with no word of explanation, and left the room for a moment so that I could examine this momentous item undisturbed. Inside the folder were three documents, bound with string ties. Loose, on top of the uppermost document, was a sheet torn from a spiral-bound notebook, bearing a few pencilled words that were, in all probability, the last your brother wrote. Since embarking on this book not a day has gone by when I haven't listened to a Thomas Lang recording, but I confess that no recording has ever stirred me in the way that this page did. My first glimpse of Thomas's personal mark, the last he ever made, suddenly made his absence an immediate experience, as though I had entered a room and seen the door closing behind him as he left for ever. Please do not think me impertinent when I say that I felt something akin to a pang of grief.

Resembling nothing so much as the trace of a seismograph (so unlike the neat, compressed script I would have expected), the words were all but illegible. I thought I could make out 'unimportant music' as the first phrase, followed by '. . . abused' and '. . . love so . . .', fragments that prompted me to speculate about the autobiographical revelations I was about to read. Konrad soon put me right. The words were to be deciphered as: 'v. important, music not to be used, only speech, leaves, water, footfalls, hooves, so on', an instruction to be transmitted to whoever might become the recipient of the three items contained in the file. For what I was holding was a trilogy of scripts which Thomas and Konrad referred to as their 'triptych', sketches from which they were to create a scenario for a full-length film.

Konrad tells me that this manuscript passed backwards and forwards between them several times, but that – although the name appended is that of Konrad Seibert – the credit for its creation and revision must go mainly to Thomas. He gave me copies of the first two parts (enclosed); he's promised to forward a photocopy of the third component as soon as possible.

## AMORFLIEZ AND TARRAULT

The story commences with the death of a king. His two sons quarrel, and when the lawful heir assumes the throne his brother will not declare his allegiance. Storming from the hall of the coronation with a train of malcontents, he proclaims that the crown will be his.

A year passes, and then comes word that the rebellious brother has established his own court in the territory south of the river that bisects the land, and has made it known that he will not rest until he has annexed his sibling's kingdom. The elder brother dispatches a rider with an edict imposing on the braggart the penalty of death. Thus are born the twinned and warring kingdoms of Amorfliez and Tarrault.

The opposing forces clash upon the bridge that links the two kingdoms, and when the knights draw back from their first charge the dead are more numerous than the living. Three times more the well-matched armies fight, until at last the brothers acknowledge the futility of the battle, and an armistice is agreed. But the peace does not hold. There are further skirmishes, further fragile treaties, before the strife between Amorfliez and Tarrault assumes a pitch of ferocity without precedent. The land around the border becomes a perpetual battlefield.

At length, the king of Tarrault proposes that each should nominate a champion to fight on the bridge where the war had commenced. Two champions are selected, fight, and receive wounds that sap the life from them within one month of their inconclusive duel. The pair that follow fight for three hours until each champion falls into the arms of

91

his opponent like a man meeting his beloved brother after years of absence, and dies. In all, thirty knights ride to that place, there to lose their lives.

The king of Amorfliez prevents the contests continuing to Doomsday by proposing that they stake their kingdoms on a bloodless battle.

As boys, the kings of Amorfliez and Tarrault had been taught a game played on a particoloured board, with pieces that stood for lords and fighting men. Its object was the capture of the opponent's king, and such was its complexity that it was said a man could play it all his days and never plumb all its mysteries. Both boys had achieved some proficiency, and thus the suggestion of the king of Amorfliez is that their struggle be transferred to the chequered board, and that the brothers themselves compete for their kingdoms.

It is agreed that the contest be concluded when one of the contestants has achieved a margin of victories equal to his age in years. In a tall satin tent, erected at the midpoint of the bridge, the players come together and begin their first game. It is drawn, as are the second, third and fourth. The fifth is won by the king of Tarrault, the sixth drawn, and the seventh as well, but the next goes the way of the king of Amorfliez. By the time the leaves begin to lose their colour, the brothers have fought fifty games: ten have been won by each. They adjourn to their citadels for the winter, and in their absence a hall of oak panels is constructed, the contest now being judged to merit a more imposing arena.

On the summer solstice of the following year the one hundredth game is played, and the tally still is equal. Then, in August, the king of Tarrault falls ill with a fever. His brother demands that play continue without interruption, as the rules state that no interval should be called without

92

mutual consent. The king of Tarrault remains in his seat and loses the next five games, but delight makes his enemy careless, and within a month the deficit has been reduced to one. It takes the king of Tarrault until November, however, to obliterate that solitary point.

Two years later the bridge has become the foundation of a long hall made of brick and adorned with courses of stone. The next adjournment is prolonged to allow for the construction of a marble room in which play can be conducted. The next decade sees a proliferation of chambers on both the Amorfliez and the Tarrault sides of the marble room.

In time, the courts of both kings move to the bridge, the knights and ladies of the warring kingdoms sharing the same palace, as they share the same preoccupation. Once in a while the kings of Amorfliez and Tarrault dine in the one hall, though they never converse directly.

Every few weeks messengers are sent out to spread word of the duel's progress throughout the two kingdoms. The messengers are welcomed wherever they ride, for the game has become the guarantor of the people's contentment. Theorists of the game write treatises on gambits and strategies: there is not one member of either court who does not play for recreation. The forms of the pieces appear in heraldic designs, and the chequered pattern of the board is woven into sheets and tunics and carved into chair backs. A dance is composed in which the figures emulate the game's hither-and-thither of attack and defence. Travellers make long journeys to see the two players, as others might embark on a pilgrimage to the relic of the True Cross. And these travellers report that the kings of Amorfliez and Tarrault daily instruct their sons in the arcane science of the game, in preparation for the day when they might play to keep their kingdoms.

# KORLUS

The subject of this tale – known as Korlus the Pure, the Just, the Panther, the Basilisk – lives in the greatest austerity. No banquets ever cheer his hall, and the daily dress of his retinue is as drab as sacking. Seven times each day he summons his knights to the chapel, and at night he lies down in a bare granite cell. In one respect only does Korlus lapse from his severity. Three generations ago, his forefathers discovered the way of making a steel of exceptional brilliance. Being softer than was common, this metal was useless for weaponry, and was used solely for trinkets such as Korlus abominated – salt cellars, ornamented clasps, combs. Yet notwithstanding its fragility, Korlus ordered his smiths to forge breastplates from this steel, embossed with the words: I COME NOT TO SEND PEACE BUT A SWORD.

For one thing above all is Korlus celebrated, and that is his ferocity. Inexorable as fire, he falls upon the enemy in a whirlwind of wrath from which few escape. Such is the contrast between his wit in the fray and his taciturn manner in peace, that it is said he thinks not in words but in plans of battle.

The story begins in the fortieth year of his life, with the arrival of a message from Gragoris, whose citadel stands some ten leagues distant. The message states that Gragoris and his court have recently attended a tournament as the guests of a prince of a neighbouring land. The invitation has turned out to be a ruse, for their hosts have abducted a lady of the court, Olmita by name. Gragoris intends to rescue Olmita and punish the villains for their treachery. He is confident of success if Korlus will ride with him, and promises his help in any campaign Korlus might undertake.

The ensuing battle commences with the charge of the knights of Gragoris. Suddenly, on the peak of the hill from which Gragoris has galloped, a second sun seems to rise. All eyes turn to its glare as yet another sun flashes from a clearing in the trees. From all quarters, their armour blazing, the knights of Korlus overrun the field. The enemies of Gragoris cower as if below the flaming sword of Saint Michael.

That night Korlus is honoured with a banquet which would have impressed the most profligate of princes. He takes but a platter of meat and a goblet of water. The court of Gragoris looks to the high table at the man with whom their master has made alliance. When the lady Olmita is presented to Korlus, her ladies deplore his demeanour, which softens by not the slightest degree. Here, however, they misconstrue, for Olmita has in a moment disarmed the warrior whom no knight could ever vanquish.

Next morning Korlus receives a message from Gragoris, requesting his presence. The message intimates that Gragoris is waiting for him alone, but when Korlus enters the chamber he finds Olmita there as well. Gragoris hands to Korlus a letter from the defeated lord, in which he vilifies Gragoris and his 'hired dog', and warns that he will gain revenge. 'When we are ready,' the letter ends, 'we shall send our dog to invite you.'

A few days later, the sentries open the gates to find a dog skewered to the wood through its eyes. Within the hour the battle is joined, the lances meeting like the jaws of a vast animal. The company of Korlus sweeps down onto the field, as bright as a rill of mercury, culling by the dozen.

Next day, Korlus asks Olmita if she would show him the things in the city which give her most pride. She takes him to the house of a cousin of Gragoris, in whose chapel hangs a depiction of the Risen Christ. The sleeping sentries are drenched in a light that emanates from Christ's body, a light which makes manifest the hope of the Resurrection and falls upon the guards like a finger of accusation. In another house she shows him a portrait so like the living man that people have greeted it on entering the room. She takes him to the Court of the Lilies, a cloister roofed with a tarpaulin of green silk. Under the arcades of the cloister each wall is painted in such a way that the real grass seems to grow through the transparent skin of the wall and merge with a painted meadow, which dips to the border of a vast lily pond. Flowers appear to grow where the walls touch the earth of the cloister, and beads of water glint like gemstones on the petals. As if impelled to touch the fleshy blooms Korlus moves closer, and at a distance of a single pace is deceived into stooping to brush away a butterfly that has emerged from no chrysalis.

That night, in the great hall, the concert takes place. A platform is erected at one end, supporting tables laden with diverse instruments: large and small bells, strips of metal and hammers with which to strike them, flutes, drums, stringed instruments of every kind, horns of metal straight as swords and horns of wood as twisted as ancient roots. The music they produce is like none Korlus has ever heard. The strings play a continuous languid melody, augmented by the other instruments in various combinations. Twittering like birdsong, the flutes sport for a while, fall silent, then return in the guise of the moaning wind; the thunder of drums is answered by a braying of horns; the bells toll now in celebration, now in mourning, while from the chimes fall the ringing of weapon on weapon and the drip of spring water.

'Were you pleased by our music?' asks Olmita when the concert has ended, and Korlus replies that he has been pleased immensely. Thus for the first time does Korlus dissemble, for the music has been no more to his liking than the image of the Risen Christ or the Court of the Lilies. When he looked at the sleeping guards, he had seen that only a man besotted by the flesh would have taken such pains to forge the supple shadows in the crook of an arm. The painting of the soldiers' hair, of the folds of their cloaks, the little stones like knuckle-bones that lay by their feet, the thin-petalled flowers at the base of the tomb – all spoke of an infatuation with the world, and of the artist's pride in his ability to conjure its images into being. The Court of the Lilies had appeared blasphemous, for what were these landscapes if not an emulation of the Creator? And what were the voluptuous sounds of the concert if not a proclamation that God had given the world no sound that man could not counterfeit?

Yet Korlus says nothing, for nothing can provoke him to offend Olmita. Excusing by her youth and her fidelity Olmita's liking for the things she showed him, Korlus tells himself that he could imagine no woman more magnificent.

But then it comes about that the brother of the enemy of Gragoris is captured. Korlus and Olmita are standing at the gate as the prisoner and his escort pass by. With surprise Korlus notes that although the man looks directly at Olmita as he walks past, he shows no sign of recognition. At noon Korlus goes to the dungeon and interrogates the prisoner. Telling Korlus that he has ruined himself in fighting for Gragoris, the man insists that he has never seen Olmita before this day.

Korlus confronts Gragoris, who does not deny that he

has used a ploy to secure his service. 'But did my city not prove to be worth defending?' he demands. 'Did you not relish the fight? And have you not enjoyed the fruits of victory?'

'Tonight I shall abandon you to your enemies,' replies Korlus, to which Gragoris retorts that all might not go well with Olmita should Korlus desert him. A bargain is struck. Korlus will fight a third time, and in return will be permitted to leave the city with Olmita and her family.

On the morning of the first day of September a pouch is found nailed to the gates. It contains a handful of lead coins, each minted with the image of a dog. At noon the armies of Gragoris and Korlus, the enemies in alliance, ride out to meet the challenger side by side. The knights of Korlus close round the enemy, breastplates flashing like foam on the sea: there is little for Gragoris to do but cut down those who flee, and tally the number of the dead.

That evening Korlus informs Olmita that he will depart on the third morning thence, and will ride by her dwelling three hours before noon on that day, at which time she should appear if she still intends to go with him.

Just after dawn on the morning of her departure, a knock at her door brings Olmita from her bed. On the step stands a monk, and behind him a number of his brethren. The first greets her by name and states that he wishes to pray with her for a safe journey, and to give her a relic for her protection. With that the monk produces a dagger from his sleeve and orders her indoors.

An hour earlier, suspecting that Olmita might deceive him, Korlus had dispatched a man to keep watch on her house. Now this sentinel reports what he saw. A procession of monks came to Olmita's door; she answered and briefly conversed with the senior, smiling as she spoke; together they entered the house; the other monks crossed to a building over the way, laughing as they withdrew. The tip of a scabbard protruded beneath the habit of two of them.

At midday, separately and in disguise, Korlus and every one of his knights leave the citadel. Korlus becomes the most implacable enemy of Gragoris. Any man whom Gragoris has offended finds a friend in Korlus. In battle he is seized by an indiscriminate frenzy, kinsman and foe alike putting themselves in danger of their lives if they approach him. Some come close enough in the tumult to glimpse his eyes through their visor, and declare that they are like rubies.

After one year of carnage comes the day when Gragoris, at the head of his troop, meets Korlus.

'I ask for peace,' says Gragoris.

'And I refuse to grant it,' Korlus replies, and brings his sword down on the shoulder of Gragoris, opening his body from neck to seat.

Seeing their master murdered, the knights of Gragoris gallop forward into the last battle of the war. From its chaos Korlus emerges the victor, and the city capitulates. Korlus rides to the house of Olmita, to find that only her servants live there, and they will not speak to him. Eventually he finds a citizen who tells him of Olmita's death. 'And you shall learn nothing more,' she says, 'for there is not a man or woman in this city who would not sooner die than bring you consolation.'

For days Korlus wanders the streets of the city, accosting people with the same question, but none will answer him. At last he leaves; none of his knights sees his departure; no one ever sees him again.

## Michael Dessauer to Christopher Lang

I take myself to task for my naivety. Now I realise that I have tacitly maintained the belief that anyone in a position of familiarity with a fascinating person must necessarily be a source of fascinating observations. So much for the theory of contagious quality. Today I have spent hours listening to people in whom I assumed I would see mirrored something of Thomas's character. Instead, I found myself stranded amid a bog of banality, while cliché echoed cliché all about. Here's a roll-call of the null, as I could imagine you saying.

1. Klaus-Friedrich Ehrmann, Vice-Chairman of Classical Division, DRGG. Looking like something from the last days of Weimar (big cigar, triple chin, straining jacket), Herr Ehrmann behaved as though he thought that by being effusive he could guarantee a prominent role for himself in my book. Like listening to a recitation of Thomas's obituaries; dispiriting in the extreme.

2. Niven R. Chamberlain, Missouri-born Assistant Head of Marketing and Promotions. Relaxed, watchful, complacent, much given to narrowing his eyes as he listens. I think he'd like to hear himself described as a 'coiled snake'. He has a voice confused by his transplantation to the continent via Britain, and by his determination to project himself as an occupant of the same social ledge as the person he is talking to. His pitch slithered all over the place as we moved from the receptionist to his boss's office and then briefly to the post room before a quick word with the MD.

An even more enervating experience talking to this man than to Herr Ehrmann, for in the world of Mr Chamberlain to be alive is to sell, and nothing more. Death is the state a person lapses into when he ceases to move a certain number of units per annum. Thomas Lang thus joins Bing Crosby in the ranks of the immortal. Niven is very excited about a project to which he modestly lays claim: the Lang Edition, a boxed reissue on CD of all Thomas's recordings, with a bonus photo-album included. Yet he laments the fact that your brother 'never understood the potential of video', because Thomas would have been a natural on videotape, having great hands and no bad angles. He could have been talking about some bit-part actor who had made a bad career move.

I terminated our interview – more an attended monologue – shortly after Niven made a wry aside about Thomas's lifetime contract with DRGG, signed eight months before his death. He contrived to be doubly offensive here. Not only did he give the impression that the tragedy of Thomas's death consisted chiefly in that it had thwarted another marketing triumph on the part of Niven Chamberlain, he also implied that your brother could have been more grateful for the vote of confidence that this contract represented. I am sure that Mr Chamberlain is excellent at his job, but I would sooner spend a month in a tent on Luneberg Heath than spend another hour with this stereotype made flesh.

3. Erich Bielmann, Mr Chamberlain's boss, gave me three minutes of his time so that he could assure me that his admiration for Thomas Lang was immense,

immeasurable, incomparable. Imagine a talking thesaurus and you have something of the effect. Already I have difficulty remembering his face.

All was not gloom, however. At the end of the day I shared a beer with chief engineer Matthäus Kaltenberg, who unfortunately would seem to be the only person in the city who speaks English as badly as I speak German. Despite our misunderstandings, the talk was very enjoyable. Matthäus's tributes to your brother have weight by virtue of his very inability to find the right word. Although your brother was notorious for demanding long hours in the studio (he says the Schubert *Impromptus* involved two ten-hour sessions with just six hours' break), and for becoming very 'nervous' if things didn't proceed exactly as he wished (this is what Germans tend to say when they mean 'agitated'), the technicians still regarded him with greater affection than any of the other artists with whom they had to work. Indeed, one of the crew once reorganised his annual holidays when he found it would clash with a date for Thomas's sessions. Matthäus regarded Thomas as a very 'demokratisch' man, a word he pronounces with severe gravity. It's plain there's no higher honour. Thomas understood the word 'engineer' as a German would understand it, not as the English do. And as for Thomas's musicianship, he had the 'best ear and the best hand' – an observation reinforced with rampaging fingers along the tabletop and a look of rapt consternation. I'll be seeing Matthäus again tomorrow: I don't expect many more insights, but it does the soul good to find someone who is incapable of fulsomeness.

A conundrum, in parting. Matthäus keeps in his desk a memento of your brother – the score of Schubert's C-minor *Allegretto*, annotated by Thomas with innumerable little glyphs and arrows and underlinings, all in green ink. On the back of the score Thomas had jotted a few notes to himself: 'Take #6 – 1' 43' – rattle' is one; 'Dürer self-p – card?' is another; and 'Andechs – S-Bahn Wed' a third. I have no difficulties with these. The first clearly relates to a recording session; the second to the Dürer self-portrait in the nearby gallery; the third to a trip Thomas intended to make to the monastery at Andechs, which can be reached by the S-Bahn. However, sideways to these, on the outer edge of the page, is a line that reads: 'C – latest [or test, or best] stuff to Taylor.' I've scrutinised this line many times, and with the exception of that one word, there's no real scope for alternative interpretation. Neither can I make it mesh smoothly with the image of Marcus Taylor as an 'odd-job man' – I assume that the two Taylors are the same man. Any recollection of what Thomas was moving, or why? And are you 'C'?

## Michael Dessauer to Christopher Lang

Another evening with Matthäus. Learned a lot about Munich, a fair amount about electronics, but little about Thomas – except one scrap of information that has had remarkable consequences. I am staying here a while longer. Story follows as soon as I get home.

## Michael Dessauer to Christopher Lang

I decided to do a bit of sleuthing, to follow up a remark made by Matthäus. He was talking about Thomas's observance of certain routines, some of which I would have to classify as superstitions. For instance, wherever he was recording he would approach the building in such a way as to cross the road immediately opposite the entrance. Whatever the weather, on recording days he always carried an old, sand-coloured raincoat, which nobody ever saw him wearing, even when it rained. He couldn't bear to have a clock within view when recording was in progress, and apparently he had a thing about unoccupied chairs – if there were more seats than people in the studio, the surplus chairs had to be taken out.

Perhaps you already know about these foibles, and that whenever Thomas came to Munich for a concert he always asked Joshua Thorpe to book a particular room in a particular hotel – room 17 at the Wittelsbach, on the southern edge of Schwabing. I checked it out.

It's a pleasant, quite small, self-consciously anti-quated place, with lots of mirrors and Biedermeier furniture, and studiedly deferential staff in heavy maroon uniforms. The manager, Richard Voller, could not have been more responsive to my enquiries, but there was a suggestion of over-rehearsal to his reminiscences of his 'illustrious client'. Herr Voller had found Mr Lang a remarkably modest man, an 'ideal guest', and a 'very quiet person'. Indeed Mr Thorpe, when reserving the room, had reiterated his request that the chambermaids should not enter the room during the period of Mr Lang's residence. Mr Lang had never made use of any of the special amenities offered by the management, even though Herr Voller had volunteered the attentions of his kitchen staff at any hour of the day or night, and had offered personally to chauffeur Mr Lang to any place he might like to visit within the Munich area. He could have obtained tickets for the theatre at a moment's notice, but Mr Lang declined, politely and gratefully. He insisted on carrying his bags to his room, but tipped the boy all the same.

Herr Voller showed me room 17. It looked, he said, much the same as it did when Thomas Lang stayed here. The furnishings here, as in the rest of the hotel, were too oppressive for my tastes, as was the muddy colour-scheme, but I was assured that Thomas always found everything perfectly to his satisfaction. He did, after all, choose to stay in this hotel, in room 17, on several different occasions.

After my talk with Herr Voller, I went to the hotel bar for a drink, and there struck up a conversation with Hildegard Schuster, the assistant manager. This is where things became interesting. Hildegard's closest friend, one Paula Mikolajska, had been employed by the Wittelsbach as a receptionist from June to October 1976. At the end of this period Thomas stayed here, before and after a recital in the Herkules-Saal.

On the evening in question, Paula answered an urgent phone call for Thomas from a woman in England. The key to room 17 was not on its hook, so Paula put the call through. Thomas did not answer. The woman left her number, asking Paula to ensure that Thomas was informed of her call. Paula went upstairs, knocked on the door of room 17, heard no reply. Four or fives times she knocked, but not a sound came from inside. Worried, she unlocked the door.

Splayed on the bed, looking like a figure traced on the ground at the scene of a murder, were the clothes Thomas was to wear the next evening. Placed with its collar flush to the edge of the pillow, the white shirt was laid within the jacket, the bow tie folded at its throat. The arms of the jacket were neatly outstretched, the legs of the trousers pointed straight to the patent-leather shoes at their base, parallel and a few inches apart. No suitcase was visible, nothing had been moved. Other than this slough of his concert clothes, there was nothing to indicate that the room had an occupant.

Thomas reappeared the next morning at eight o'clock, carrying a small leather holdall and a camera. Paula, still at the reception desk, handed him two sealed envelopes, containing messages from the woman in Oxford (who had called back twice) and from Joshua Thorpe. He slipped the envelopes unopened into his inside pocket. Two hours later he left for his rehearsal. That night he returned to his room at the Wittelsbach. Paula told only Hildegard what she'd found, and she in turn, she says, has told nobody except me.

Obviously, the next step was to find out where Thomas had gone that night. I went back to the DRGG offices, but that proved to be a cul-de-sac. I asked Klaus-Friedrich Ehrmann if he knew of any friends Thomas might have stayed with in Munich. He came up with a couple of names, but thought it very unlikely that they would lead anywhere. Herr Ehrmann himself had offered his hospitality to Thomas, who had explained that he couldn't sleep in a room that wasn't his own. A hotel room was acceptable, we surmised, because the financial transaction made it temporarily his.

The trail seemed to have gone cold, so I set off along a new one, in the dim hope that I might attract good luck through persistence. Thomas had stayed at the Wittelsbach many times, but he had not stayed there on every visit to Munich. Three times he had come to the city solely to make a recording, and on these occasions, everyone at DRGG agreed, he had not taken his customary room. Messrs Ehrmann, Chamberlain and Bielmann were less than outstanding when it came to dredging from their memories the name of the hotel that had been Thomas's base for these sessions. They concurred that it was on the east side of the Isar, but the first thought it might have been called the Alleheiligen, the second vaguely recalled a name including the word Isar, the third gave up the attempt. Matthäus was certain that he'd never known the answer – it seems Thomas had approached these sessions with 'a special concentration' that precluded small talk between takes.

There is no Hotel Alleheiligen and there is no hotel incorporating the name of the river, so I dragooned Matthäus into the ranks of my research assistants. For a small remuneration he set to work telephoning every hotel on the east side of the water, beginning at the top end of the range. We hit the target with our last shot. We now know where Thomas stayed during the Munich recording sessions, where he had gone on the night Paula Mikolajska looked into his empty room – where he slept on the night before each of his Munich recitals.

Half an hour or so after leaving his room at the Wittelsbach – assuming he took the U-Bahn – Thomas would have turned into a side street fifty yards south of Rosenheimerplatz and walked into the lobby of the Lorelei, a one-star hotel run since 1950 by Anna-Marie Stich. Though now eighty years old, she remembers vividly the last time Thomas checked in at her hotel. She had just bought a kitten, which Thomas baptised 'Fafner', a prophetic name in view of the ursine bulk it has attained (though she decided on 'Didi'). Anna-Marie had cooked *Weisswurst* that evening, for the Auer Dult festival; Otto, her husband's brother, was coming over, bringing his wife, a 'terrible woman . . . a connoisseur of everything, especially musicians'. She invited Thomas to join them, as she always did, but as always he preferred to eat alone. Thomas gave her, as on every visit, a ticket for the following night's concert, and went up to room 5. Thomas chose it, Anna-Marie explained, because it is the only one that overlooks the street and has no adjoining bedrooms.

She showed me the room. It has double velvet curtains that could make midday as dark as midnight, and a bedside lamp with a celluloid shade that's turned the colour of caramel where the bulb has baked it. Thomas, she said, liked the photograph above the head of the bed: it shows a military parade down Leopoldstrasse, but was modified in the 1960s by a guest who, by adroit collage, turned the faces of the front-row drummers into those of Mao, Mahler and Freud. This was, Anna-Marie told me, Thomas's 'most favourite joke'.

No sign of the third wing of the 'triptych'. I'll pass it on the day it arrives.

## Christopher Lang to Michael Dessauer

Oh my oh my, aren't folk strange? Especially creative-type folk. You know the one about Nerval and his lobster on a ribbon? Piero di Cosimo and his diet of hard-boiled eggs? Schiller and his perfume of rotten apples? Pontormo's corpse-filled bathtub and his diary of bowel movements?

For the cod-Arthurian fantasia I can generate not the slightest interest, though I can see how it might appeal to your taste for melodrama. I suppose it's genuine – there's no readily discernible reason why Seibert would wish to diminish his own role in this rigmarole. (Which is not to say there isn't one.) However, I receive these arch little tales of derring-do and human folly as I receive your tales of Tom's foibles; I acknowledge their existence, tepidly regret their existence, and commence the long process of forgetting their existence. Should the third wing fail to materialise I would not grieve.

To steer you back to your true subject, please read the enclosed document. It catches something of what I believe to have been the authentic voice of my brother – as indeed it should, as it's the only piece of writing in the public domain that can incontestably be attributed to him.

You'll need supplementary documentation. The essay relates to a series of concerts given in Florence and Empoli in November and December of 1967, to mark the centenary of the birth of Ferruccio Busoni, Italo-Germanic keyboard wizard and chronically unfashionable composer. The centenary properly should have been celebrated the previous year, but the jamboree was postponed due to climatic adversities – viz., the inundation of 4 November 1966, which, as you may recall, sluiced half a million tons of mud and riverine filth through the streets of the Tuscan capital. In the period between this calamity and the rescheduled festival came Tom's triumph in Antwerp. Suddenly he was hot property, and when the Friends of Ferruccio discovered Tom's interest in their boy they lost not a moment in firing off an invitation.

They got their money's worth. Tom didn't just give a recital (sonatinas and Chopin variations I think, but you may have to do your own research on this), he wrote them this programme note for the central event of the festival, a production of *Doktor Faustus*. I find both the essay and the opera rather ponderous, and I detect more than a touch of self-satisfaction in the former as well – perhaps a characteristic of the genre as much as of the author. Tom immediately repented of it, and forthwith took a vow of silence.

## BUSONI CONTRA WAGNER

Ferruccio Busoni, the books tell us, was an implacable opponent of Wagnerianism. And yet, on first turning to Busoni's writings, we will perhaps be inclined to reflect that a man resembles nobody as closely as he resembles his enemy. Busoni deprecates Wagner's operas for subjugating music to text – but was there ever a libretto more literary than that of *Doktor Faustus*? Busoni, the proponent of New Classicism, decries Wagner's *Gesamtkunstwerk* as a vulgar agglomeration of the theatrical, the pictorial and the musical. Yet he is no less insistent than Wagner on the supremacy of the opera over all other aesthetic genres, and his proof of that supremacy is equally dubious. The greatness of opera consists, according to Busoni, in what we might term its omniverousness: 'opera conceals, united in itself, all the devices and forms which otherwise only come into practice singly in music'. The proposition is as peremptory and naive as any promulgated by Wagner, and the constraints that proceed from it are equally severe. Seeking a subject for his final contribution to this most exalted of art forms, Busoni draws up a shortlist of four candidates: Leonardo, Don Juan, Merlin and Faust. Compare Wagner's valedictory list: Christ, Buddha, Parsifal. Each man was an evangelist for his own cult, and when Busoni declares that 'in future opera will be . . . the universal and single form of musical expression and content', he might be proselytising on behalf of Bayreuth. Both display a weakness for the vatic proclamation, for ordinances both prescriptive and proscriptive.

Nonetheless, for all these congruities, Busoni and Wagner are true adversaries. Against the irrationality and splendour of Wagnerian opera, its flux and luxury, Busoni posits the values of Young Classicism, an aesthetic that demands 'the definite departure from what is thematic and the return to melody as the ruler of all voices and emotions'. Venerating the operas of Cimarosa, Mozart and Rossini, he tells us that opera 'always consisted in a series of short, concise pieces and will never be able to exist in any other form'. Wagner is arraigned for rejecting these laws of operatic composition, this being the first of his three cardinal sins. The second is his sensualism – 'sexual music is obviously out of place owing to the very nature of the art, which is purely abstract'. The third is the denial of the artificiality of the genre: 'A love-duet on the public stage is not only shameful but absolutely untrue.' To the notion of artifice we shall return later. For the present let us stay with this concept of the abstractness of music, as it brings us into an area of Busoni's thought where he seems most clearly regressive – that is, what might be termed Busoni's Platonism.

Busoni's last substantial piece of prose, an essay entitled 'Vom Wesen der Musik' (On the Essence of Music), is the most detailed explication of his Platonic creed. When Busoni writes about 'music' what he has in mind is instead a supra-mundane, quasi-mathematical universe of sound, which certain masters have been privileged to penetrate and translate for the edification of the earthbound world. No composition can show us more than a portion of this universe. 'Even to the greatest giant, the circle in which his activity unfolds must remain a limited one . . . Mankind will never know the essence of music in its reality and entirety.' This repertoire of timeless forms is sufficient for the representation of all experience that is not transient, and it is only with such experience that the composer should concern himself. Should love be the subject of his work, it should appear before us as Love itself, not travestied in the complaints and jubilations of individual lovers. It is for his fidelity to the eternal, to the abstract, that Mozart gains precedence in Busoni's pantheon.

'The Oneness of Music', Busoni's most celebrated theoretical formulation, proceeds from these ideas. Since all great music is a derivative of the abstract and essential forms of Music (the argument goes), all music is in essence the same. The eternal forms do not yield to the taxonomies of the 'tragic' and the 'comic', or the 'secular' and the 'sacred', because they are indivisibly One. Therefore their progeny – the works of our supreme musicians – are also, fundamentally, One.

To convince us of the hidden unity of all music, Busoni

adduces the fact that compositions Bach wrote for the organ can be performed as choral pieces, and that the first movement of Mozart's D-minor quartet can be transformed readily into an aria for an opera seria. The sceptic might rejoin that the Oneness of Music depends on the exclusion from the canon of masterpieces any work that displays too pronounced a degree of expressive particularity. Yet at the same time Busoni deplores anything that lacks the mark of the individual – atonal music, for example, is condemned for propagating techniques that require no emotional investment. What is needed is a classicism bearing the imprint of the world.

Writing in 1921, Busoni foresaw the defeat of the avant-garde by the forces of Young Classicism. 'The epoch of experiments, and the overestimation of the means of expression to the disadvantage of content and artistic durability is drawing rapidly towards its close.' Instead, the period which he portrayed as an aberration is now pivotal to the music of our century, while Busoni himself has become peripheral.

It could be argued, however, that Busoni has achieved a posthumous radicalism. He is perhaps more our contemporary than he was Schoenberg's. Artists of the present age are expected to acknowledge their relationships with the past, to flaunt their sources, to extol pastiche, parody and provisionality. Composing as though he stood outside of history, Wagner is now more distant than Busoni, for whom the past was always present. Equally crucial to Busoni's new modernity is his conception of the theatrical experience. Busoni's definition of the operatic work as a 'rare half-religious and elevating ceremony' might seem to place him firmly in the Wagnerian ranks. But read the line again, and in the qualificatory 'half' we glimpse the crevasse that lies between the two men. The ecstatic element in Wagner's music is anathema to Busoni, for whom music is exemplary and uplifting but not transformative. Of all operas, it is *The Magic Flute* that he takes as his paragon, and there can be no confusion between the august moralism of Mozart's entertainment and the voluptuous ritualism of *Parsifal*. In tracing the genealogy of the opera back to the mystery play, Busoni's line of argument is precise. The mystery cycles were sacred dramas, but their audiences could never forget that the figure of Christ and the craftsman allotted the task of impersonating Him were two quite separate entities.

Detachment is the defining principle of Busoni's dramaturgy: detachment of the performer from his role ('the performer acts, he does not experience') and detachment of the audience from the theatrical creation ('artistic enjoyment is not to be debased to human participation'). Busoni would have his audiences constantly aware of the artifice of what they saw and heard. To the 'progressive' artists of his day, Busoni was cursed with a nostalgia for Enlightenment certainties. To us it seems something more courageous. In Busoni's antagonism to Wagner, we perceive a foreshadowing of the battle between the bourgeois play and the political theatre of Bertolt Brecht.

## *Michael Dessauer to Christopher Lang*

As you say, there's no reason for Konrad Seibert not to tell the truth, and having passed several hours with him I would testify that the style of the three tales is not his. My 'taste for melodrama' (granting the existence of this predilection purely for the sake of argument) is surely beside the point, as I did not summon this manuscript into being, no more than I created the unusual (to use an unexceptionable adjective) circumstances of Thomas's death. The point is that we have plentiful evidence of Thomas's own taste for melodrama, in the form of the 'triptych' and his well-attested passion for Wagner. The Bayreuth festival occupied the place in Thomas's mental calendar that others reserve for Christmas – in the words of Ehrmann, the year was young or old depending on the time that had elapsed since the last performance of the *Ring*.

I might argue that Thomas at times was not averse to introducing an element of high theatre into his behaviour. What about the backstage ructions at the notorious Amsterdam concert of November 1973 – was it strictly necessary to insult the conductor in front of a dozen members of the orchestra? Or his walkout at Grenoble in the following year. Or that spell in the mid-80s when he insisted on playing with all the house lights off, in darkness relieved only by a standard lamp over the keyboard (a trait that emerged at a recital a TV company had contracted to film) – this seems to me to be quite literally melodramatic. And isn't there at least an element of melodrama in Thomas's habit of cancelling concerts at the last minute: four in 1974, three in '75, eight in '76, three again in '77, '78 was his sabbatical, then back into the routine in '79 with four, five in '80 and so on. I'm being as faithful to the truth as I can, and admit to being more than a little put out by the suggestion that I am recasting history in lurid dress.

I cease my complaint. Thank you very much for the

Busoni piece. I'll get to know the music as soon as my local shop can order the records for me. Still awaiting clarification of the Taylor issue, by the way.

## *Christopher Lang to Michael Dessauer*

When, pray tell, did the Amsterdam concert achieve notoriety in your chronicle of the twentieth century? My bet would be that this minor fracas remained entirely unknown to you until a few months ago. And your source for this episode is in error. What happened was this.

The baton-twirler quite unprofessionally decided to continue in public a disagreement on a point of interpretation that had arisen during rehearsal. Thomas, having already decided that the careers of himself and this buffoon were never to intersect again, was of the opinion that such a discussion was redundant, and hastened to conclude it by withdrawing. His egress was impeded by the twirler's instrument of his craft, which prompted Tom to remark that he would be well advised to remove the said stick if he did not wish it to become the instrument of his martyrdom. I believe he may have been anatomically explicit in this regard. A heated exchange ensued, which I believe modulated into volleys of insults when my brother was derided as a 'madman', an appellation to which he did not take kindly. Over the consequent slanging match we had best draw a veil; but Tom didn't start it.

Regarding the cancellations, which I do not deny might appear numerous to the layman, there is no case to answer when one looks at the facts of each case. Tom always had a good reason, and rarely was there any alternative but to pull out at the last minute, as often it is only at the last minute that the globe-trotting soloist is able to discover exactly what arrangements have been made at the concert hall. Let's take the four in 1979 as a typical sample, shall we?

1. January. Vienna. Cancellation number one came about when Thomas found out that the ticket prices had been inflated to cash in on his name. He always stipulated that a percentage of the house should be priced below a certain threshold, and in this instance the condition had been flouted.

2. July. Milan. The second cancellation was a similar story: a huge block of seats had been given to a local chemical company. Tom would not have his concert turned into a fringe benefit for corporate bigwigs – ergo, game over.

3. October. Orange. It turned out that the management had obtained a Bechstein rather than the specified Steinway. Exit Tom.

4. December. Boston. Here, just as the piano was rolling off the lorry, the shifters unaccountably let it drop. No substitute piano with a comparable action could be found. Finis.

I'll let Tom explain your 'Grenoble walkout' himself. *Ecco*.

Dear Chris,

Herewith the Grenoble debacle, an episode I devoutly hope will come to be seen as the nadir of my life as a fee-charging attraction.

The countdown began with a call from a very confused Joshua. He rings me at nine o'clock or thereabouts – as near as damn it immediately post-dawn. He just has to talk to me about an idea that cropped up last night over dinner with a couple of the lads from DRGG. Just an idea, not yet really thought out, but intriguing, he thinks. How about I tackle Tchaikovsky now? A one-off with the Berlin, with Karajan. He is serious. The Germans think it would be 'a challenge' [sic]. I inform Joshua that I would rather push a cement-filled Steinway across the Sahara than play a note of Pyotr's flummery, and that I am astonished he has forgotten the party line on this issue. Ah well, replies he, the subject hasn't really been discussed for a couple of years, so he was thinking that I might be reappraising the matter on the quiet. What nonsense eh? An undignified attempt to dignify a witless proposition that had bubbled to the surface of an adman's brain after his third cognac. Would you say to the Pope – 'How do you fancy joining us at Stonehenge for the summer solstice? I was just wondering, seeing as how you've kept quiet on the subject of Druidism this year.' An extreme analogy, thinks Josh. Goodbye Josh say I.

I offer this preamble not by way of extenuation, but for the sake of accuracy, you understand. I want you to relive the troughs and deeper troughs of this wonderful day, dear brother. Someone else must know that Joshua Thorpe made me talk about Tchaikovsky before breakfast.

Let us proceed apace to the commencement. A minor irritation at the hall: the manager – a five-foot minor irritation in his own right – has omitted to black out the dressing-room skylight as promised. There's a bright yellow streetlamp right outside the window and I feel as if I'm sitting in a filling station. He finds a few rags in a backstage hamper and tapes them over the glass; not a blackout, so I end up in some windowless service cupboard, where I can get a bit of peace before the evening's entertainment.

Onto the stage. In the front row, a couple of places in from the aisle, are seated three women attired in that distinctively French haute couture that's so haute it's gone into orbit above the atmosphere of good taste. One has a satin dress in turquoise and vermilion diagonals; her neighbour is wearing a black and white outfit, also in a diagonal pattern, but with the slope going the other way; and the third *tricoteuse* is clad in a trouser suit that would seem to be made out of tangerine-coloured rope. All three – Zig, Zag and Zing – are sporting hairdos for which they must have needed planning permission. I'm on the point of tearing my appalled gaze from this trio when I notice something cradled under Zag's hands, almost hidden by her gloves. A chihuahua is my initial guess, but then I see a thin black wire traversing one of her diagonals: she's got a tape recorder. I withdraw to the wings and report the woman to the boss; a minion is dispatched to escort her from the hall with the minimum of fuss – I think they made it look as if a telegram had arrived for her.

Back we go again, bestowing a minatory glance upon Zig and Zing in passing. We begin, into Beethoven op. 27 no. 1. Thirty seconds in, The Cougher starts. I know the sound instantly. This is not a man suffering a fleeting spasm of the bronchial tract; this is a man whose cough is tendered as a contribution to the evening's event. This is the vocational Cougher. Sure enough, a few bars on, he interjects once more, but the cough has undergone a subtle transformation from a simple explosive blast into a noise with a desperate inflection, as if I were an auctioneer who might overlook his bid. On the second bid the angle of my spine is sending messages of extreme annoyance, but now The Cougher puts added power into his throat, so that what emerges is like some incomprehensible declamation, a Mongolian horseman bellowing to his steed across the steppe. I stop, and turn the basilisk stare into the haze. A door clatters and the cough recedes.

Conversations have broken out, but I play over them, starting again at the beginning. A few whispers endure as far as the fourth or fifth bar, then all fade quickly, except one – a sibilant gossipy little noise that keeps going like a gas leak. I stop again. Silence. Back to the beginning once again, though there's little hope of retrieving the show. Still, the hands set off, play a couple of bars, and then it's the whisper again, but coming in short urgent bursts this time. At this final provocation I play an unmarked rallentando, turn slowly, regard the offending sector of my public with what I trust is a contempt too deep to be articulated, and leave.

A flashbulb goes off in the vicinity of Zig and Zing, and when my vision recovers I see the manager in front of me, his arms held wide in a cringing, shepherding gesture. A wheedling, mournful moan emerges from his mouth: 'But the concert.' I say to him 'That's not a concert, it's a crowd scene' – in English, though I think nothing was lost in the translation. Whereupon this oaf actually grabs my arm, making a citizen's arrest.

I swept his wrist upwards with some force. The pudgy hand may have struck the ill-formed face; I didn't look back to see. Punch him I did not, though I freely confess that in the car park I did briefly entertain the notion of returning backstage and planting on his greasy head a blow of such magnitude that by the time he woke up his house would have been sold. I have in my possession a fine piece of casuistry from the festival director, in which he would seem to be proposing that the chemistry of the bond between audience and performer varies from place to place, and that I arrived with the wrong alkalis to balance Grenoble's acids. I think he's telling me I'll never work in his town again, but ebullient hope may be misleading me.

Yours in limbo, Tom.

Hope you enjoyed it. To mop up the detritus from your last letter – Mr Taylor has already been adequately explained, I believe. And I may well have been 'C', but to the best of my knowledge the transaction to which Tom's note alluded never took place, at least not in the way he planned.

A word of advice in conclusion: before employing the word 'literally' again, do consult your dictionary.

## Michael Dessauer to Christopher Lang

Would you concede that there was something in Thomas's character, call it an inflexible integrity, that maximised the potential for confrontation within any situation? This is by no means offered as a criticism. I am just suggesting that a refusal to compromise (a refusal essential to the creative mind) might have been carried by Thomas into all aspects of his life. As is shown by the letter you so kindly released, he was not slow to reach a state of exasperation, and was the possessor of a mordant tongue.

I was talking to William Clement-Johnson on the phone last night, and he was telling me – entirely without animosity, I might add – about an abortive recording of some Schubert pieces in Paris. Received opinion is that, for whatever reason, Thomas came to this session in an uncooperative frame of mind and made the most of a few trivial misunderstandings that arose early in the proceedings – over the type of mineral water provided for him, the level of light over the consoles, a couple of other points. When they were resolved, he insisted that the piano was not in tune, even though two tuners had worked on it in the previous twenty-four hours. Problems over the acoustics then supplied what was seen by the others as the required pretext for Thomas's abandonment of the studio. William was in Paris the following week to make a recording with the same technicians, and the talk was of Thomas's 'Teutonic' outlook – his nickname had become 'The English Kaiser'.

I cannot in all conscience refuse to acknowledge that there might be a grain of truth in this caricature, but let's not fall out over this. We are, I think, looking at the same character; it's just that my view isn't tempered by the same depth of affection as yours. Thomas's letter, though, goes some way to kindling a similar affection in me, for at last I can hear the cadence of his voice. Do you have many letters from him?

## Christopher Lang to Michael Dessauer

God, you won't let this one go, will you? Sod the bloody tuners. I would refer you to page 137 of Herbert M. Goldstein's *Masters of the Keyboard* (an unimpeachably unimaginative tome), where you will find a certain Italian maestro – a man not renowned for his generosity towards his coevals – expressing the opinion that Thomas's sense of pitch was 'without equal', and that my brother could 'identify a tone to the exact cycle'. If Tom said it was out of tune it was out of tune. I grant you that the discrepancies might have been detectable to none but Thomas and whichever members of the indigenous echolocating species may have strayed into the soundscape of the Salle Pleyel, but this, I'm certain you'll concur, is an irrelevance.

In answer to your concluding question: yes I do. Many. And here's a sample, which I happen to have to hand. (William C-J is not an omniscient narrator – just thought I'd remind you.)

Dear Chris,
The snows of yesteryear have returned en masse: drifts up to the sills, car vanished, electricity intermittent, heating gone berserk and local plumber turns out to

be a larcenous incompetent equipped for no task more complex than breaking the ice on the bird bath. Wrote this so that I could walk to the post office and warm up. Received a meagre brace of letters all week: the compulsory chivvying note from our man Thorpe, and a startling piece from some snotty-nosed Albi schoolkid, all about self-overcoming and the slave mentality of the masses. I think he intends to establish a new Athens in Andorra, with Thomas Lang, the hyperborean Apollo, as cocktail pianist to the master race.

## Michael Dessauer to Christopher Lang

Thank you for your letter and the amusing – if not greatly helpful – enclosure. Are there any others you could let me have?

## Christopher Lang to Michael Dessauer

I do apologise for the failure to make my brother more compliant to your requirements. Are these useful enough for you?

1. Ich weiß nicht, was es soll bedeuten
   Daß ich so traurig bin . . .

Staring for blank minute after blank minute at my face in the mirror, thinking 'What the hell is he thinking?'

And all he's thinking is 'What the hell is he thinking?' Lassitude has come on like food poisoning. Perhaps it's the residue of yesterday's rehearsal with the preening ponce of the podium, a man so conceited that his ego has its own separate dressing room. (Lang smiles wanly, weakly reclines, nibbles a stale cracker.)

2. One of the stagehands here is a fascinating character: a Moroccan lad called Ska (sic), who works part-time here and part-time in one of the big hotels. He wants to go into hotel management back home, and is gathering experience on an extended European tour, hopping from one town to another every three months. He intends to be away for five years, and he'll go anywhere, on one condition – the town must have a branch of the Magic Circle. Tabletop magic is his speciality – card tricks, making banknotes change from one denomination into another, pushing coins through glasses, that sort of thing. His hands never leave the table, and he does his stunts in short sleeves, but you still can't work out what is happening. He had four of us sitting round a drum case, watching his hands while he made coins disappear and shuffled packs turn into sequences of all the suits. And when he'd finished, he turned to me and said – 'You might want this back.' He'd taken my watch off without my feeling a thing; another of the group had been deprived of his tie, another of a ring. And he has an astonishingly refined vocabulary. He particularly loves the words 'interject' and 'extrude'. That brings to mind 'Thomas Lang is an extrudate of music.' Was that your sneer originally, or was it mine?

### Michael Dessauer to Christopher Lang

I'm working all hours on a thematic restructuring of the biography (I'll explain soon), hence this very quick note. The two letters were perfect – I particularly liked the second, which will dovetail nicely with the recurrent theme of 'sleight of hand' (and even with Thomas's liking for, shall we say, unsophisticated humour). Very happy.

### Christopher Lang to Michael Dessauer

Yes, I thought you'd find the ideas in those letters more malleable. It was in the hope that you would enjoy them that I composed them. Sorry, but the temptation was too great.

In penance for this unsophisticated prank, I am sending three examples of His Master's Voice, all a hundred per cent pure – and pertinent to your tale from the Parisian studio, and to the dull-witted observations on Tom's character.

Paray-le-Monial
2 August 1976
Chris, be a saint would you? Pop over to Joshua Thorpe and talk him off his ledge. The man's on the brink of another synthetic nervous breakdown. I spoke to him a couple of days back from Paris, and he was in a terrible state even then. He's probably already fretted himself into a dose of alopecia and seventeen varieties of eczema unknown to medical science. You can save

him from total collapse if you take a firm line. Seize him by the shoulders and talk to him in short phrases. The facts are perfectly straightforward and Joshua will be fully apprised of them as soon as he's in the mood to listen. I spoke to him two nights ago, but he seemed less concerned with the preservation of my self-respect than with the preservation of the *entente cordiale*. Thus I put the phone down on him. That is the limit of my guilt vis-à-vis the present impasse.

The session began as a disaster and continued the way it started. In the first place, the piano was, contrary to the protestations of the etiolated little twerp who was nominally responsible for the condition of the brute, unfit for use. There could be no problem, he reiterated in a crescendo of petulance, because Paris's finest ears had attended to the piano's innards not two hours earlier. This may or may not have been the case. The fact was that since the last surgery performed by the Ears the air-conditioning had done its worst. We lost an hour on this pointless altercation, then half a day getting the thing right.

When I am finally summoned back to the hall, racked by indigestion after doing battle with a bacterial baguette, I find the engineers have gone berserk in my absence. They've taped strips of tin foil all over the place and hung what appears to be a job lot of aluminium saucepans from the ceiling. The result was deadly. I might as well have been playing inside a gigantic mattress for all that I could hear off the walls.

Then, to cap it all, the playbacks sounded even duller than I'd have thought possible, thanks to the efforts of the microphone ace they'd brought in. I'm quite prepared to believe that this boy has already forgotten more about white noise and crossovers than the combined brains of the Max Planck Institute will ever know, but he really should be venting his expertise on subjects more suited to his temperament. I shall join the world in acclamation when he brings to our astonished ears the first recording ever made of the sound of a trout digesting its lunch, but he should not be allowed within three leagues of a concert hall. He wasn't recording the music, he was recording the machinery of the piano, every creak and crunch of it, and Christ knows there were enough creaks and crunches. But of course he could not be persuaded that his microphones were producing anything other than the veritable tones of heaven. Worse, he had a manner that would have had Mahatma Gandhi reaching for his axe. Once he'd embarked on one of his interminable explications of an otiose aspect of electromagnetic theory, nothing short of decapitation was going to make him shut up. When I finally got a chance to propose a contrary point of view – an opportunity that arose only when his metabolism finally seemed to run into oxygen debt – he received the proposition with a prim grimace on his far from pleasing features, as though the effort of reducing his brain capacity to dimensions puny enough to accommodate my contribution to the debate were an experience akin to sipping pure lime juice. After just twenty seconds he decided he had sufffered enough. 'Yes . . . yes . . . yes . . . yes . . . yes' he repeated, until he'd bludgeoned me into silence. His second monologue concluded with a ringing declaration of his devotion to progress, garnished with a deeply illogical remark about the Industrial Revolution and the backwardness of England. His name was not going to appear on any recording made in the nineteenth century, he averred. I departed. His name is Simon. He has a wife, it is alleged. Must be a deaf mute with impaired vision.

Joshua will probably inform you that I am refusing to play the New York date in December. This is true. The reason is simple – at no point did I agree to play with the maestro who is now being foisted on me. His name might be divulged by Joshua, he who fears no lawyer. I agreed to play with Abbado, not with this effluvium of the music industry. Of his virtues I am fully cognisant: as who could not be, in the face of the drivel his record company pumps out. The man has the profile of the Belvedere Apollo. He also has the rhythmic sense of the Belvedere Apollo. The American public could be spared a lot of expense and discomfort if they simply stuck a metronome on the stage and wrapped a tuxedo round it. New York is off, and there's the end of it. It does not follow, however, that the Munich date is in jeopardy, whatever Joshua may shriek in his panic at the prospect of another ten per cent floating off into the wide blue yonder.

I can imagine the scene back in London. Jen answering the phone – 'I'm sorry, Mr Thorpe can't come to the phone at the moment. He's organising a house-to-house search of the continent.' Please tell Joshua that, much as he'd like to lead an Interpol team from Highgate to the gates of Vienna, there's no need. New York is a straightforward breach of contract, and there is no causative link between the Paris furore and my appointment with Munich –. not unless Sine-Wave

Simon has a Bavarian mission of which I have been kept uninformed.

Love as ever – Tom.


Paray-le-Monial
7 August 1976

Chris, why in God's name did you tell Thorpe where I was? I thought you'd have had more wit. What did he do to you to make you squeal? What horror could it have been? Did he threaten to show you his collection of celebrity writs? His Perry Como impersonation? His Rod Steiger? Not, surely to God, his Yvonne de Carlo? Anyway, the damage is done. Joshua's on my tail and suddenly France feels as roomy as a shower cubicle.

What a loss. I tell you Chris, you should see this place one day. I think of you every hour I'm here. This village could have been made with you in mind. It's as though the deity had personally asked you what things you like to see in your surroundings, what pace you like to live at, how you like your neighbours to behave – and then created the exact opposite. Dead after dark, and nothing to do during the day except look at flowers and walls, and mill around slowly with miscellaneous mothers and babies. Everyone on first-name terms with everyone else, except with those they haven't been speaking to for thirty years, since their grandfathers had a row over the price of a chicken. No one will ever hurry and no one will ever leave. The cars seem stunned by the heat and creep along at invalid speed, paced by a few arthritic hounds. You would detest it.

I've spent a lot of time in the big church in Paray,

an hour's walk away. The stone inside is grey and crude as a cliff face, and looks as if it should have moss growing in its joints, with water seeping through perpetually. You sit inside it and you feel the silence around you like viscous air. I imagine them building it, the whole village working here on the meadow, slamming stone on stone year after year. I've sat in it for a whole morning: not a sound but for the rasp of the sacristan's broom and the scrape of a chair as a pilgrim leaves.

Yesterday the door crashed open and in filed twenty schoolchildren, each in sweltering gabardine and clutching a book. They were led by an instantly objectionable character, a mustachioed martinet who appeared to regard his charges' thrill at being here as a deviation from the day's business. One broke step to gaze up at the roof for a second or two, an act of indiscipline for which he received a vicious flick to the earlobe and was marched to the steps below the altar, where he was planted to the spot with a shove on his shoulders, like a 'Trespassers will be prosecuted' sign. Around this hapless kid the brilliantined fool arrayed the rest, expediting the manoeuvre with a clip here and an 'Idiot!' there. When all were in place and each had set his face into an expression of due dedication – i.e., an expression of clenched, inextinguishable loathing – the rehearsal began.

Every town in Europe has a version of this man, a thwarted Kapellmeister bent on moulding his gaggle of recalcitrant, crack-voiced children into a choir that will provide testimony – alas, fleeting – to a talent denied its full fruition. Every gesture dripped with conceit: the hands held hovering in mid-air for the admiration of an imaginary ideal audience; the moustache stroked in specious rumination; the exasperated twitch of the head as little Jean-Claude loses his place again. Typically, he had them singing a ludicrously ambitious piece. Machaut, for Christ's sake. People make careers out of singing this stuff and nothing else. Anyone with an ounce of sense realises that it takes two years' hard work to acquire the technique for it. It takes two years just to work out what the technique might be. But here's M'sieur Tache subjecting a random sample of pubescent and pre-pubescent French youth to the rigours of Guillaume de Machaut, as though the mere fact of tenuous consanguinity were sufficient to ensure success.

The start was farcical. Tache narrowed his eyes, a cheetah taking the range of its prey. Suddenly a forefinger shot upwards at an angle of thirty degrees to the vertical, a comical gesture that suggested a forest ranger's demonstration of survival hints. 'Number two – how to stop the bear by sticking the finger up the nose.' Most of the boys were as taken aback by this gesticulation as I was, for only half a dozen of them reacted to the cue, and no more than two came in within hailing distance of the note. Incandescent glare from Tache, who extracted his digit from the phantom nostril and enjoined his choir to an effort worthy of him and Machaut. For the next ten minutes the voices slithered round the music, fell onto it like avalanches of jelly, skidded down the stave, screeched up it. A terrible sound, but a strangely touching tribute to the complexity of Machaut. A sort of allegory about the attainment of grace. And their expressions were affecting too. There seemed such an affinity between them all – perhaps with no base more profound than a shared hatred for their teacher, but a bond for all that.

I tired of Tache's antics when he expelled a rather maudlin chap for no greater misdemeanour than a failure to possess a fine voice, as if the child had wilfully lost a set of angelic tonsils with which he'd been equipped at the start of the day. I let the miscreant make his exit in dignified loneliness, then withdrew. Outside, I found him sitting cross-legged on the gravel at the back of the church, his face lifted to the sun, his blissful smile only slightly warped by the unlit Gitane clamped between his lips. He asked me for a light, but I was lighterless. No matter, he replied, turning his head towards the church door, whence with immaculate timing marched another lad, with a box of matches held aloft. Thierry and Alain introduced themselves before sharing the cigarette, and intimated that they had a plan for M. Philibert Grosjean, as Tache's name turned out to be. What this plan was they would not say, but mighty shall be their retribution.

I left the boys contentedly kippering their larynxes and went to join the redoubtable Pauline, with whom I am in love. Pauline is the *patronne* of the only bar in my exquisitely moribund hamlet. She has been on earth for thirty-five years, and not once since the day of her birth has she strayed more than fifty kilometres from her parish. I describe Paris to her and she listens as if I'm telling her of the Taj Mahal. She is not excited by the report. She simply accepts it as though it refers to a land which is marvellous but of no significance to her life, and which she knows she will never see. Pauline is genial but is impressed by little. Having accumulated half a stone for every year of her existence, she is a vast and constant being, whose pulse rarely quickens. I saunter into the village square, and through the beaded curtain over the door of Pauline's bar I spy her on her habitual stool, like a female Buddha perched atop a tulip stem. She comes out to greet me and installs me under the narrow awning. Then she fetches a carafe of chilled young red wine and a couple of stout glass beakers that are so battered the glass glitters as if it has flecks of mica in it. She is a brilliant conversationalist: relaxed, curious, modest and unpredictable.

This afternoon I discovered the true source of her great placidity. On my way to the bar I saw for the first time a name painted in whitewash on the road, on the far side of the square. Although the tarmac has become pitted and crumbly, the lettering has evidently been retouched several times, as the letters stand a couple of centimetres proud of the road surface, gleamingly white. The name – Dufray – is her own. I supposed it to be an advertisement for her excellent establishment. Not at all. It is an advertisement for her husband, painted on the road before a big cycle race came through the village in 1964. Her husband – a man from a place across the valley – was, she informed me, a 'domestique' for Jacques Anquetil that year. She thought he was the most glamorous man she had ever seen and she resolved on the spot that she would marry him, which she did eight years later. I was still in some uncertainty as to the task M. Dufray had been so glamorously performing in 1964. Being a 'domestique' sounded like some sort of apprenticeship for M. Dufray's present line of work –

chief bottle-washer and aide-de-camp to M. Anquetil, that sort of thing. Indulgently Pauline set me right.

Her husband had been a magnificent athlete. He was not, however, blessed with the gifts of the 'eternal ones' such as Anquetil. Thus it had been his role to support the great Anquetil through each day's vicissitudes, to nurse him up the slopes on days when such aid was required, to distract his opponents on other days by launching accelerations that would sap the legs of any who followed and wreck the morale of those without the strength to follow. He was to give everything in order that his leader may win the grand prize. All in return for a minuscule share of the glory of victory and, to judge by the simian gait of the infrequently glimpsed M. Dufray, permanent damage to his locomotive apparatus. Understanding nothing of the glory that accrues to the courtiers of men such as the eternal Anquetil, I commented that it seemed a rough life. By way of answer, Pauline disappeared into her rooms and appeared a few moments later holding a photograph album as fat as a phone directory.

A rough life all right. The frontispiece was dignified enough – a nice portrait of a beaming M. Dufray being embraced by a remarkably aerodynamic and disturbingly vulpine gentleman, none other than the immortal one. But what followed was a chamber of horrors: hunchbacked men under blazing skies, their eyes swollen out of their sockets, knees cross-hatched with scars and bloodstained sticking plasters, mouths barely visible under a mess of frothy saliva. I could hardly bear to look at the snap that showed, so Pauline told me, M. Dufray's finest day – the day he led the pack over the Col de Tourmalet. The wretched boy looked like a rabies case. It did explain everything though. If you've seen your beloved commit suicide and rise from the dead on a daily basis, you probably are not going to be impressed by much else. So far, the nearest I've come to unsettling my hostess was when I informed her that we do indeed produce cheeses in England. I couldn't have shocked her more if I'd told her that all Parisians have purple skin.

Shortly after my survey of M. Dufray's sporting heroics, my Eden was violated by the arrival of the serpent, in the form of an aged postman. He hurtled into the square at Mach One, borne by a seven-ton cast-iron bicycle, and slewed to a halt at our table. He ascertained my identity, then handed a telegram to me, a transaction performed with the chivalrous gravity of a commander presenting his foe's terms of surrender. He must have known the contents of the missive, or at least glimpsed its opening words – URGENT URGENT URGENT – and so was probably assuming that he'd brought news of a family disaster. Having gauged the tone of the message and verified its authorship, I stuck the note under my wine glass, where it quickly acquired a large watery pink stain. Much taken by this display of English sang-froid, the postman regarded me with humbling admiration; I invited him to join us, which he did with alacrity.

I soon discovered that he was an intriguing and versatile man. As a teenager he wrote a small book on garlic (published locally – Pauline has a signed copy), and in the 1950s he earned his living as a restorer of vintage Citroëns, until a freak gale collapsed his workshop onto his uninsured fleet. I should have liked to learn more, but tomorrow I must flee, for nothing – not even the love of Pauline – can induce me to remain here now that Joshua has obtained my coordinates. He had Jen ring every damned hotel in the Paray region until she traced me; from then on it was plain sailing, as my daily movements seem to be common knowledge hereabouts.

I will be in Munich. I will not speak to M. Turp (as he's known to the French office of telecommunications) until I arrive in Germany. Despite all, love as ever.

Tom.


9 August 1976

Safe again. A couple of hours' drive through *la France profonde* and I found a new refuge, a dandy little *auberge* on the edge of a forest of limitless oak. The building can't be more than twenty years old but the oaks give it the aura of something medieval. The forest made me think of that story you once told me about the duke of Loches, ordering every oak within his sight to be cut down when he was brought the news of his son's death.

God only knows what keeps this place in business. I can't imagine there can be that many arboreal botanists on the loose round here. Only two rooms are occupied tonight – myself and the mysterious guest in number 4. She must have been the driver of the car I heard arrive at about seven, the only vehicle to pass along this road since I bowled in at five. Twenty minutes or so after the arrival I went downstairs to eat, and I could hear the shower in room 4, at the foot of the stairs. (We've got those typically Franco-Italian showers, a bare nozzle suspended over an uncurtained expanse of ceramic tiling, an arrangement that turns the toilet paper to deliquescent mush and the mirror to streaming murk, so your face looms into view like a turtle in a slimed-up aquarium.)

Anyway, I jammed myself into a chair alongside the chimney breast, balanced the book on the oil and vinegar bottles, ordered my meal, dismissed Joshua from my thoughts, settled. I was barely into my terrine when the clicking of heels made me look up, and I saw a woman who might have strayed in from a post-premiere party. She was perhaps thirty, pale skin, pale eyes, hair the colour of the husk of a corn cob, page-boy jacket (scarlet), miniskirt, and an air of self-absorption that was barely modified for the few seconds in which she registered my presence and acknowledged it with a movement of the mouth that was less a smile than a conditioned spasm. As far as I am aware she did not so much as glance up from her meal until it was finished, whereupon she lit a cigarette and turned momentarily to face her own face in the window. Nothing in the way the waitress spoke to her gave me a clue – she may dine here every night, she may never have been here before. A perfect mystery. She turned her eyes in my direction as I passed her table, as if a noise from behind me had distracted her; then back to the cigarette.

I took the torch from the car and turned its beam down the track at the back of the house. Orphically I descended the line of light, down the soft green ruts and drifts of crisp old leaves. At a hassock of moss I sat down, turned off the light, rested my hands on my knees, and waited for my fingers to reappear out of the darkness. I waited and waited, but I could see not a thing. I raised my hands slowly and struck my forehead before I could see them. The silence was so heavy I could not think against it. When a bird took off from a tree way down the track the noise was like a car crash, and then the silence flowed back over it. I couldn't tell where my skin stopped and the moss began. Very happy.

Ho hum; *München, München, Liebchen*.

## Michael Dessauer to Christopher Lang

The final part of the 'triptych' has arrived. Here it is. Letter to follow.

### THE LADY OF DOROLAN

The story commences with a wedding in the town of Dorolan. The groom is the youngest of five brothers, and the fourth of these to marry. The one who remains single is Ruyalt, a young man who prefers to while away his time reading romances and discussing them with the scholar to whom his education has been entrusted. His father's tournaments are never as splendid as the jousts that charge across the pages of his library, and prior to this day he has found all women flawed in form or wit when compared to the paragons of the poets. But then, on the steps of the church in which the wedding takes place, Ruyalt sees a woman who in the instant wins his adoration.

Her hair is the colour of sun-struck bronze and is twisted in whorls to the nape of her neck. She places a hand upon the head of the boy at her side, and her fingers are as white as the plumage of a swan. Her smile is but a tiny motion of her lips, but to Ruyalt it is the fullest show of simplicity and thoughtfulness. Clad in satin slippers, her feet move on the flagstones with greater grace than he has ever seen in a dance. Lifting her hem by an inch, she steps from the shadow of the portico, and is gone.

In his quest for the Lady of Dorolan, Ruyalt composes a description of her, which is sent to the foremost families of Dorolan. For three months nothing is heard, then an unsigned letter arrives.

*The lady of whom you speak is known to me. There can be no doubt that she it was who was seen at the entrance of the church. She knows of Ruyalt's search and has permitted me to send this. She will not consent to meet the young man unless he can answer this question: How can a suitor be racked by love for a woman he does not know?*

Without delay, Ruyalt sets about his letter of reply. He dismisses as trivial the understandings that we gain from speech. More eloquent by far are the gestures of the hands or the movements of the eyes, for in these unconsidered forms the soul speaks without embellishment. Yet there is an art to the interpretation of this language of the soul, just as there is an art to reading the heavens. He proceeds to enumerate the felicities he has observed in the Lady of Dorolan, and to demonstrate their profundity of meaning.

A week later comes the reply. The lady consents to hear his suit in person, on condition that Ruyalt agrees to certain provisions: firstly, that she shall be accompanied by a chaperon; secondly, that she shall speak solely through her chaperon; and finally, that these constraints shall never be questioned.

When Ruyalt arrives at the door of the designated house,

he is ushered into a passageway as dark as a mine. A flaming torch presently appears and moves towards him, throwing a wavering light over the hooded head of its bearer, who conducts Ruyalt in silence through suites of shuttered rooms, through chilly hallways and musty closets and high-ceilinged chambers. Finally, resting his hand on the brass boss of an oaken door, Ruyalt's guide tells him to enter.

The halo of a candle hangs in the air. A minute goes by before he can distinguish the table on which the candle stands, and then, dimly, two figures behind it, seated and with folded arms. Ruyalt is dumbstruck, for in addition to those to which he had agreed, one more condition has been imposed on the meeting. The Lady of Dorolan is dressed entirely in black silk and veiled with scarves of black muslin. Even her fingers are hidden, encased in gloves of black satin.

The Lady of Dorolan bends to her chaperon's ear and whispers. The woman repeats what has been said. 'My lady does not believe you are Ruyalt,' she tells him.

'I am he,' replies Ruyalt.

'If what you declare is true, then Ruyalt has a poet in his pay. It is not possible that one so parsimonious in speech could be so profligate in script.'

Told that he is to leave when the guttering of the flame commences, Ruyalt begins to talk of his boyhood, and as he talks the Lady's right hand rises to a clasp at her temple, and extracts it from her hair. Taking between finger and thumb the edge of the strip of muslin thus freed, she pulls a narrow veil from her face, disclosing two eyebrows curved like the arch of a dolphin's back, and eyes of lucent indigo. Unable to speak, Ruyalt frowns at the floor, as though he might find there all the words he has lost. The hushed sibilance of the

Lady's voice, tantalising as distant music to a prisoner in his cell, lures him out of his fretfulness.

'Your time is passing,' he is told, and thus goaded he expatiates on the tiresomeness of life at court, on the meagreness of conversation and the crudity of its pleasures, the vapidity of its women and the lubricity of the men.

The flame begins to waver. Had the consequence of its expiry been the end of his life, he could not have looked at it with greater horror. The Lady of Dorolan replaces the loosened veil; her companion permits him to return the following day.

When Ruyalt next arrives he is again escorted to the room by a perverse and darkened route. As before, the chaperon and her charge are seated at a small table, a single candle before them. The Lady of Dorolan, again disguised in black, addresses him indirectly as before. Again the duration of the audience is governed by the longevity of the light.

Ruyalt resumes his monologue with the story of the wedding day. Sparing but a few words for the ride to Dorolan, the preparation for the wedding feast and the ceremony itself – as if these things had been accidental to the great scheme of the day – he hurries to the climactic scene. And as he speaks of the children who thronged about the Lady 'like a nimbus of infant faces', the Lady's hands, as if possessed of independent will, rise from the table to tease the gloves from their outstretched fingers. The naked hands are of an opalescent whiteness, touched beneath the fingernails with a pink like that which dusts the clouds at the approach of summer sunset. Her fingers seem not jointed but sinuous as flower stems, and at the base of each is a dimple, where the skin looks as soft as the petal of a rose.

Prompted, Ruyalt returns to his story, but has proceeded

only as far as the arrival of the joyous letter when the flame begins to stutter.

The next afternoon, having been conducted to the candle-lit room by the usual way, Ruyalt is describing the tumultuous emotions with which he read that letter when the Lady reaches for the veils about her head. All at once her hair falls, breaking on her shoulders in bright curlicues and waves. Doughtily the young man hastens to his tale's conclusion. Reaching it, he allows his eyes to revel. The strands of her hair are like new copper pulled to the thinnest threads, and within each lock are a hundred glitters of yellow and silver and blue.

Chided for his dullness, Ruyalt attempts to portray his brothers and their wives, but has accounted only for the former when his audience is concluded.

The preliminaries to Ruyalt's fourth audience follow the pattern of the preceding three, and on entering the chamber he sees that the Lady of Dorolan is attired in her customary fashion. Immediately he embarks upon a description of his sisters, refusing no opportunity for damaging comparison with the princess of his heart. A movement by the Lady staunches the flow of his words. Her hands rise to the veils and extract two pins: her neck is uncovered, pale and long, and the whorls of her ears, like the imprints of shells in snow. She turns, and the movement of her flesh seems miraculous, as though it were breathing alabaster.

Ruyalt's name is uttered. 'Do your brothers love these ladies?'

'Devotedly,' says Ruyalt.

'Are we to understand that your brothers are imbeciles? Show us the attributes by which these ladies earned their love.'

Ruyalt attempts to do so, and the manner of his dismissal

suggests that he has given satisfaction, for now he is allowed to put questions to the Lady of Dorolan. He requests some knowledge of her kinsfolk. The Lady of Dorolan draws close to her chaperon and detaches the veil that hides her mouth. Her lips are red as apple rind, and each as perfect as the crescent of the new moon. She whispers at her companion's ear, her mouth shaping a sigh and smiles; then she is silent, and her lips where they meet form a line turned downwards slightly, as if her thoughts are regretful but not unsweet.

The hero of the tale now told would have humbled any poet's warrior: loyal to God and his allies, unflinching in combat and gentle to his wife, he was a nonpareil, and Ruyalt's pride in him is immense. Filial emotion just as strong is stirred by the image of the mother of his Lady, the great man's spouse. Parentage of higher degree is unimaginable to Ruyalt. And when he takes his leave, he infers from a pursing of her lips, as of a smile not fully suppressed, that on the next day his advance will proceed more rapidly.

At the next assignation the Lady of Dorolan, still veiled, is alone. As soon as Ruyalt is seated she speaks. 'It cannot be that you love me,' she says. Her voice is like leaves ruffled by rain-bringing breezes.

'It can be and it is,' he replies.

'No, you do not love me, Ruyalt,' she insists. 'I am more unknown to you than are your brothers and their wives to me. These ladies are loved for the qualities I had you number. Of my own you are in ignorance. You cannot love me.'

Thus she vainly persists. Ruyalt knows her as profoundly from the tones of her voice as any other lover would know from months of his mistress's company. Each phrase she breathes is confirmation of that first glimpse at his brother's wedding, as the glimpses of these last days have been. He repeats that he loves her.

'Is it not my form that has beguiled you?'

'The form is the sign of the soul,' he responds.

'Forms may mislead you, Ruyalt, as may words. You listened to the stories of my family as if I were disclosing every wish and every fear of my heart. But they might have been mere words. The soul discovers itself in deeds, not in words.'

Words may lie, Ruyalt replies, but her voice cannot, no more than the nightingale can sing notes other than its true song.

'I shall argue no longer,' she says. 'Tomorrow you shall see me without disguise.'

To Ruyalt's surprise, the Lady's door is opened the next morning by the chaperon, and the entrance hall is as sunny as the open air. She leads him to a bright panelled chamber, with a round table at its centre, set with seven chairs. Ruyalt sits at one; six women, each wearing a veil that covers her from crown to waist, enter the room and take their places beside him.

'Young man,' says one, 'the Lady of Dorolan is here. Where is she?'

From a choir of voices he could have singled her out. 'You yourself are the Lady of Dorolan.'

The woman thus named rises. The veil slips from her hair, which is as dark as sable, as dark as her eyes.

Ruyalt is like a king robbed of his lands by a grand imposture. He stares at the young woman's broad hands as if they might be gloves fashioned to resemble flesh, which she might discard to reveal the hands that had so entranced him.

'I may justly claim to be your Lady of Dorolan,' says the dark-haired woman. 'With equal justice I could claim that you are alone with her in this chamber.'

At this the others cast away their veils, and Ruyalt scans the circle. Next to the one who has spoken sits a woman whose lips are the lips of the Lady of Dorolan; the hair of bronze flares beside her; to the fourth belongs the hands of the Lady of Dorolan; the neck of her neighbour is the one at which he had marvelled. As a leader of an army might turn to a courier whose message, he knows, will be one of defeat, Ruyalt looks to the last of the women: under brows that arch like the backs of dolphins, the eyes of indigo regard him.

'I strove to deter you,' says the first. 'From the very beginning you declared yourself inspired by the soul of your Lady of Dorolan. Stand these words on their head and you have the truth: her soul was inspired by you, for you concocted that soul from the rhetoric of love. And yet we must pay your creativity its due. Your fabricated soul proved potent indeed. Features which formerly you had not deigned to notice were, when taken over by the Lady of Dorolan, transformed into charms. You have met each of my companions, and myself, before. There are the lips at which you gazed in wonder as though they were rosebuds sprung from stone: but these very lips once smiled at you across your father's table and they did not bewitch you then. Look here, at these hands. You touched them once in a dance, but did not think this lady deserving of your deference. Regard these eyes, which now seem so to fascinate you. When they first cast their light upon you, on an Easter evening, a moment's glance was all you could spare in return. When I myself pronounced your name last midsummer, you turned from me as if my voice were less than the whinny of a mare.'

The lesson in love fails, however, for henceforth Ruyalt is attentive to a lady only if he discerns in her some resemblance to the Lady of Dorolan, whose form he had pieced together in the course of his audiences, and of whom none could ever be more than a shadow. If Ruyalt's gaze rests on a woman's face, it lingers as might a widower's on the faded portrait of his wife.

In his twentieth year Ruyalt dies of a fever. Between the pages of his books are found countless scraps of paper, each covered in Ruyalt's writing. Every night since his humiliation he has retired to his room to labour at these verses. The lyrics are as numerous as the days of the year, and their sentiments as various as the temperament of the days. Yet in one respect they are a unity: every one is addressed to a woman who is never named.

Reading them, Ruyalt's mother weeps, both for her loss, and for the man she thinks is revealed. She misunderstands, but is closer to the truth than many readers are to be. In later years, even among those who have never seen or heard a single phrase from his *Almanac of Love*, it passes for a fact that Ruyalt, the virgin prince, was the most amorous of men, and that his mistresses were beyond number.

## Michael Dessauer to Christopher Lang

The Paray letters persuade me that I'm on the right tack on a couple of issues, and they've given me ideas regarding a couple of avenues of enquiry. More on these anon. I'm beginning to get the tone of Thomas's voice now as well. I'm sure I'll quote a few sentences from Paray, come the day of judgement. I particularly liked the episode with the children's choir. Perhaps I can tie his remarks in with a quote I've found from Busoni, which I'm sure Thomas would have known and approved – 'Practise everything as if nothing were more difficult.' We'll see.

I must say that one aspect of these letters – their dominant aspect, in my reading – took me by surprise. I've always seen the studio, the concert hall and the study as the natural habitats of Thomas Lang. He has appeared to me as a sort of urbane hermit, as a man who carries his own landscapes with him. Now I have these romantic, bucolic, almost rhapsodic scenes with which to contend. Would you be able to show me any other letters comparable to the Paray sequence? This is a very exciting stage for me, like venturing into a forest myself. And do you know where he was when he wrote the third letter?

## *Christopher Lang to Michael Dessauer*

Not the remotest idea about the geographical origin of letter three. Should you be hell-bent on pinpointing Thomas's bolt-hole in August 1976 (and were I obliged to assess the intensity of your intention, hell-bent would be my estimate), I suggest that you get hold of the annual guide to the *Logis et Auberges de France*, dispensed for a nominal charge by the French national tourist board office on Piccadilly (open normal office hours). Then all you have to do is compare the maps within this estimable publication with a chart displaying patterns of vegetation in France: one is to be found, I am sure, in any self-respecting French college of agriculture, or in any French university's geography department come to that. You can limit your investigations to the area defined by a two-hundred-mile radius from Paray I'd have thought. Sounds like rudimentary detective work to me. Do let me know how you get on.

Regarding your penultimate request, I hope the enclosed suffices. Owing to the vagaries of the Italian postal service, this letter didn't reach me until June 1977, some four or five weeks after it was written. I assume the national airmail pigeon was in quarantine. At the beginning of the previous month Thomas gave a concert during the Maggio Musicale, having stepped in at short notice for a famously temperamental pianist of Latinate extraction. There's no date on the letter, but I'm sure it would have been written before the recital, as it wasn't his custom to hang about in a city once his duty was done. I hope this fits your revised master plan.

*Caro Cristoforo,*
I dropped in on John Wycherly's sister, the remote Leonora, now married to a shinily handsome and faintly saurian young man, the scion of a house of upwardly mobile bandits from the deep south. He tells me his father could ride from Bari to the west coast of the Italian peninsula in the knowledge that at every village the mere mention of his name would elicit twenty offers of hospitality. Having seen a photo of papa Franco, I can believe it. He looks like he'd make a casserole of your donkey as soon as shake your hand.

Franco junior has become one of Tuscany's leading authorities on agricultural subsidies and their attendant frauds, and now is waxing fat on the handouts he receives for producing inedible olives. I found it difficult to follow his explication of the finer points of his venal enterprise, but it is almost impossible to listen attentively to a person whose eyes are perpetually obscured by sunglasses, however low the circumambient light. The three of us went up into the Mugello to eat at a restaurant owned by a member of the cadet branch of Franco's clan, and passed a very pleasant evening, but every time my host turned to me I was confronted by the reflection of a candle flame in each of his inky lenses. Rather like staring at keyholes, but without the sense of imminent discovery.

Leonora, possibly the only person alive who can attest to the present existence of young Franco's eyeballs, took me for an educational turn round the Accademia, her magical influence circumventing the queue in a trice. Doggedly we cleft a path through the throng within, and dutifully I gazed upon the David of Michelangelo, a lascivious and witless lump I have always thought, and think so still. The gigantic adolescent is installed in a ridiculous little alcove that makes him look like he's preening himself in a changing room: 'now, which way suits me better – sling over this shoulder, or sling over that?' The paintings brought no joy either, an infinity of dogged variations: Madonna and baby with two chins, baby with three chins, baby with four chins, baby turned forty-five degrees from viewer, baby turned ninety degrees from viewer, baby in blue, baby in red, baby in the buff, baby smiling, baby not. As I think I overheard one exasperated matriarch declare – Jesus Christ, what's with all the babies? And who's this guy Fiorentino Ignoto? So prolific, and yet so pungently, poignantly, polystylistically uninteresting, don't you agree Sir Kenneth?

And such bad faith too. Half these pictures aren't saying what they say they are saying. This Crucifixion isn't about the Crucifixion, it's about the view from the workshop window, or the creepy face of the local baker, or the luscious colour the artist discovered by mixing the contents of the first three pots that came to hand. And this Madonna is nothing of the sort – it's a tribute to a local girl's beautiful eyes, or her birch-twig fingers, or the high style of the wife of the man who'd paid the painter a year's wine allowance for a glossy two-foot by three-foot. A forced march through the Uffizi was suggested, but this I declined as too high a price even for Leonora's effervescent and scholarly companionship.

By two o'clock I was heading southwards cross-country, along lanes half-blocked by mounds of solidifying brick-coloured slurry washed down from the hills in last week's rains. It had poured for forty-eight hours without a break, and it looked like the sky was preparing itself for a repeat performance. Clouds as big as the Andes, with anvil heads and bases the colour of graphite, were sliding closer to the horizon minute by minute. About ninety minutes out of Florence, the sky sealed over completely – gradations of grey from pole to pole. Everything took on the tone that tells you a storm is about to break, that dim greenish light that seems to emanate out of the ground. And then, without any sort of preamble, it was straight into the tempest, the first thunderclap smacking the air so hard that the car rocked in the shock wave. There were no crescendoes, no rumbling off into the distance, just these thumps of thunder that felt as if they were exploding right overhead, twenty feet above ground zero. I had a couple of minutes of this, getting buffeted every twenty seconds, before the rain started, and like the thunder it came in at full blast, like I'd driven right into a car wash.

I switch the wipers to super-fast setting. They are swiping the windscreen in demented prestissimo, but visibility is still two feet, if that. It's as if the car has been draped with grey silk curtains. Off with the engine, on with the hazard warning lights – I could be parked in the middle of runway three at Pisa airport for all I can see – and I sit there, slammed by the thunder over and over again, thrillingly anxious, like someone who's run out of fuel in the middle of a safari park.

The rain gets heavier. The spatter looks the same, but the drumming on the roof has become so loud that I can only feel the thunder rather than hear it. Thinking I might be able to see slightly farther if I were not squinting through glass, I wind the window down infinitesimally, and it's as if someone standing out in the road has chucked a glass of water at me. And then, just as I get the window shut again, everything around turns bright white-blue and I hear this terrifying sound, a shrieking hiss that hurtles off over the hill and is gone within half a second. I'm trying to think what it sounds like – it's like a blade wiped fast down a steel cable – when again everything goes bright and the sound comes again, at the same moment as I realise that what I'd just heard was lightning. I lean over to open one of the back windows, because I want to hear it again, as clearly as I can, but that's the end. Suddenly the thunder is retreating: it's miles off, stuffing pillows of fat noise into the valleys as it goes, all amiable and blustery. I've got a foreground again, and weaving over the road are these snakes of bouncing water, the sort of implausible rain-pattern you get in movie cloudbursts. The waterfront meanders away, waving across the fields, and I listen to its diminishing hush for a minute or two.

Time to get under way again – but there's one last flourish to come. A stamp of sunlight hits my hand, and I crouch forward slightly to see where the sun has broken through. It's lodged at the top of a long crack in a mass of clouds the colour of a two-day bruise. My eyes trace the crevice right to the earth, and just a degree or two north of that point of contact stands a small tree, its branches touching the ground to the left and the ground to the right, and between them a wedge of air in which steam or smoke is drifting slowly upwards. The bark is hanging off in strips, as if a grizzly had just stropped its claws on it.

From Wagner to Debussy. Within an hour a thick wet mist had come down, a mist so bad that I decided to stop for a while in a hilltop village which I noticed above the murk. The village itself was engulfed almost as soon as I'd installed myself in a bar opposite a broken-backed church, *caffè corretto* and map in hand, ready to come to a decision about the day's final destination. I was driven from my lair by the occupants of the adjacent table. The lead character was a young American male, florid cravat blossoming from the neck of his tightly buttoned blazer with what I imagine he imagined to be Baudelairian panache; he was piping preciously about the non-completion of some restoration project in the village. His companion, attired as if he had just wandered into town from the eighteenth green, was grunting affirmation of the unreliability of all things and persons Italian.

'The tourist people, the people in Siena, they promised me, they *promised* me, that it was all OK. *Finito, si, si, si*. But come *on*, nothing's changed. *Nothing*. What's their problem? I was here last fall and I recognise it *all*.'

'Tell me about it. Get service—'

'No but I know this *dust*.'

I fled into the fog, following a wall until I happened upon a brick loggia, a huge open hall where six or seven orange plastic chairs had been arrayed, presumably so that the citizens might comfortably enjoy the civic prospect, which at that moment was so thoroughly obscured that I determined to await its reappearance. I was joined by a local gentleman whose approach was soundless and invisible – he was just suddenly there, stepping out of the fog as if he'd been precipitated by it. He took a seat at the far end of the loggia and for a good fifteen minutes we waited, each of us absorbed by the featureless view. Then gradually the village square came on like a photo clarifying in a developing tray, the darker lines slowly firming, the walls coalescing, the eaves merging, the arches in the campanile rising now distinct above the clock, no colours at first, just tones of glistening grey, every mottled roof tile and stone glazed by the mist. My companion and I exchanged nods of respectful approval. Bloody good show we thought.

And yet the best was still to come. I set off again, in light rain, no direction in mind, in fact backtracking for a while. I drove along a crest that ran parallel to a stream I'd crossed straight after the deluge, when it had looked like a narrow mustard-coloured carpet rolled out in the base of the valley. It was now wide as a motorway, its margins dragged by waterlogged branches, vast mashes of grass and leaves rolling in the yellow swill. A couple of miles farther I passed a sign for Cortona – never been there, so decided to head that way, and turned right to ascend the flank of the valley. It was then, reaching the ridge, that I saw the most magnificent scene, the day's last Sublime. I slewed off the road, got out of the car and gaped.

Try to see this Chris. Wet tarmac in the foreground, rinsed by little waves of rainwater flowing across the camber; overhead, gunmetal clouds extending almost unbroken right across the sky, with rags of cloud coloured dove-grey and charcoal hanging from their underside, in places touching the line of the road's verge. Through the gaps in these rags I can see, in the middle distance, portions of the fields in the valley floor, obsidian under the lid of the clouds. Beyond them, an ungaugeable distance beyond, there's this panorama lit by the hidden sun with a neon glare, tiny fields that are white not green, a glimpse of some other world without shadows. I tell you, it was like a view of unpeopled heaven.

Next morning, I walk to the piazza where the buses come into the centre of old Cortona. It's like a balcony overlooking the Valdichiana, but this morning the Valdichiana isn't there. Only Montepulciano and Monte Amiata (I think) are jutting above a mist so milky that I can't even see the cars climbing the road up into Cortona. The mist is flat as a pavement, but there are globules of cloud sitting on it, showing where the villages are located below. I can hear the traffic in the lower town, and the trains pulling into Camucia station, and they are like noisy phantoms, so close but invisible. Haven't yet decided whether to work out where that loggia was.

Wherever he went he took with him his mania for ambiguity.


### Michael Dessauer to Christopher Lang

The letter from Italy suggests another armature for the biography: the notion of Thomas Lang and what we might term the Germanic soul, his predilection for tragic landscapes, annihilating forces, intimations of the infinite, the heroic loneliness of Beethoven and Schubert, the archaic worlds of the 'triptych'. But Thomas's comments on art do not ring true to me – I find them too strenuously philistinic. The laboured irony of his account of the gallery I take to be a sort of transferred epithet: Thomas is redirecting his irritation with this man Franco, whose wife I take to be Thomas's former lover. However, her name is in fact Sylvie rather than Leonora – as I'm sure you know. I'm unable to extract much more information about her from her brother, as an unbridgeable rift has opened between Sylvie and the rest of her family, a consequence of Franco's committing some deed that remains too heinous to be discussed. Do you know anything more about Sylvie and Thomas? It would be indelicate and fruitless to press this line of enquiry with John Wycherly.

## Christopher Lang to Michael Dessauer

Thomas's indifference to the visual arts was genuine, to my regret and, sporadically, to his own. And don't get overheated by the vision of Tom amid wolves, ravines, canyons and torrents. If you had to earn your living sharing big rooms with hundreds of weirdos – and audiences for Tom's kind of fare are the oddest of the odd – you'd develop a passion for vast empty landscapes. Until I unearthed this letter I had forgotten that Wycherly had a sister, so am unable to help you on the subject of his involvement or non-involvement with her.

## Michael Dessauer to Christopher Lang

I'm playing with the idea of punctuating the chronology of the life with a sequence of thematic sections. Thus material might be extracted from the Paray and Tuscany letters for an exploration of the subject of 'Retreat', interwoven with some of your recollections of Thomas as a child. A chapter titled 'Romance' might gather together the various quasi-Arthurian/Wagnerian threads. For 'Memory' there's an embarrassment of riches. Anyway, here are my notes for a prototype – 'Chopin'.

1. From the *Guardian* review of Thomas Lang's Wigmore Hall recital, March 1968.

Lang's Chopin is marked by fierce control and economy of means . . . Lang might be cool in comparison to some other exponents of this music, but his coolness packs an emotional punch. In the context of the meticulous brilliance that had preceded it, the molto fortissimo closure of the D-minor prelude sounded indeed like the clangour of overthrown reason . . . Chopin's antipathy to Beethoven is common knowledge. It is typical of Lang that he should set about demonstrating that these antagonists are brothers beneath the skin . . . Lang's account of the last studies of the opus 10 and opus 25 sets were saturated with the spirit of Beethoven's late sonatas, and when Lang played the thunderous bass ostinato of the A-flat polonaise, one heard echoes of the *Hammerklavier* . . . Some protest that Lang's Chopin speaks in too stern a voice; I respond that genius speaks in many voices.

2. From *Music Now* review of Lang's third recording, June 1973.

Other virtuosos have made more seductive recordings; none has ever matched Lang's sense of driving purpose . . . Technique is always at the service of feeling, and feeling never divorced from thought . . . When Lang plays an étude you know that, for all its passion, this composition is a study: not unmediated emotion, but rather – to use the word with no pejorative undertones – rhetoric . . . This is not the darling of the Paris socialites, but a man with iron in his soul.

3. Reading Lang's reviews, one is struck by the extent to which the criticism of musical performance is condemned to the discourse of analogy: the sign of a sign which itself functions in the most ambiguous way. One writer characterises Lang's style as 'noble and limpid'; a second,

discussing another musician's performance of the same Chopin piece, praises his 'lucidity and nobility'; yet the two performances are completely dissimilar. Recurrent phrases such as 'clean technique' and 'purity of tone' raise affinities where none are to be heard.

4. On the day after the Antwerp competition, Lang was asked by a local journalist if he could explain his 'affinity with the spirit of Chopin'. Lang's reply was: 'I know the notes; I know nothing about the spirit.'

A review by a Polish musicologist, published in *Le Monde*, condemned Lang's reading of the opus 40 polonaises. 'His principal shortcoming is a failure to understand the soul of the Polish people.'

5. Lang was known to express admiration of the playing of Alfred Cortot, a musician whose disregard of textual niceties is scarcely compatible with Lang's attitude to precision. There is a parallel here with Chopin's praise for Adolf Gutman – of all his pupils, the one whose style was most unlike his own. It was said of Gutman that he could knock a hole through a table with a chord.

6. In the year before the Antwerp competition, Lang ceased to play Chopin's music on his piano at home. Like an artist who sketches at home but paints in a studio apart from his residence, he worked on Chopin only at college.

7. As played by Thomas Lang, the central section of the C-sharp minor scherzo – the chorale theme adorned with rivulets of notes – becomes the confrontation of opposing facets of the composer's spirit: that which would succumb to the pleasures of experience, and that which is driven to

transmute all pleasures into art. We might bear in mind that Chopin composed many of the preludes with a copy of Bach's *The Well-Tempered Clavier* beside him. During the last days of his life he was reading Voltaire's *Philosophical Dictionary*.

8. The beauty of Chopin's manuscripts has often occasioned comment, but as remarkable as the staves of delicate notation are the erasures they contain. First drafts of individual notes, or even whole bars, are cancelled by so many strokes that the individual lines often merge into a single block. Perhaps these deletions were intended to ensure that the text could afford no opportunity for the investigation of the process by which it came to be written. Yet the deleting marks are far denser than is necessary simply to obscure the original conception. It is as though the intention were to obliterate these first ideas: as if, buried below these slabs of ink as below the lid of a tomb, these discarded fragments might decay to nothing. Thus purged of these traces of contingency, the score appears as the transcription of an unimprovable improvisation. A parallel with the perfectionism of Thomas Lang is suggested.

I am now sketching the Schubert section, perhaps to be titled 'In search of liberated time'.

## Christopher Lang to Michael Dessauer

Remarks on Cortot wide of the mark – if Tom did say he admired old Alf, he was definitely pulling some-one's leg; otherwise fragments passable, pleasing, platitudinous by turns. I'd take the 'signs' down if I were you. They'll date you as badly as flares. When you get round to 'Beethoven' make sure you include this: 'In whatever company he might chance to be, he knew how to produce such an effect upon every hearer that frequently not an eye remained dry, while many would break out into loud sobs . . . After ending an improvisation of this kind he would burst into loud laughter . . . "Who can live among such spoiled children!" he would cry.'


## Michael Dessauer to Christopher Lang

I can't remember now – did I tell you that I announced the biography in the music press a few weeks ago? Forgive me if I didn't. Anyway, its entrance into the public domain is beginning to pay dividends. The first half-dozen replies were inconsequential, the second-hand reminiscences of souvenir-collecting types. Then on the Wednesday of the week before last the postman delivered an envelope containing a pamphlet entitled *The Concerts and Recordings of Thomas Lang*, compiled by one Ralph T. Kahnweiler and printed in New Haven, Connecticut, in 1989. It's a two-part catalogue, that's all, but put together with exemplary attention to detail, listing in chronological order all Thomas's platform appearances and all his recordings, with full details of releases worldwide, right down to a bootleg of Thomas's 1972 Hamburg performance of Mozart's K.466 concerto. (This recording was briefly available in Germany and Italy. I must hunt down a copy, if for no better reason than to relish its aura of destiny – the Hamburg concert took place in the course of the tour during which, a matter of a month or so later, I first saw Thomas play.)

Enclosed with the pamphlet was a brief letter from Mr Kahnweiler, giving me permission to make use of his work. He asks for no fee, simply an acknowledgement. Last night I rang him to thank him for his generosity, and we ended up talking for more than an hour. He actually met Thomas once, in the summer of 1978 in Vienna, where Thomas was recording the *Two- and Three-Part Inventions*. Kahnweiler was a research student at the time, completing a thesis on Mahler and the Secession. He was sitting in a café, reading a newspaper, when Thomas came in and took a seat at the only unoccupied table, which was in an exposed spot between two large mirrors directly opposite the door. From his alcove in a corner of the room, Kahnweiler watched Thomas extract from his coat pocket what appeared to be a batch of letters, but he'd no sooner begun to read them than he was accosted by a waiter who requested an autograph. Next, one of a nearby trio of Viennese matrons rose and approached Thomas in respectful silence; she extended a hand, had it shaken, and wordlessly withdrew to resume her place alongside her friends.

Kahnweiler offered to exchange places with Thomas, an offer gratefully accepted. Sitting deep in the well-screened armchair that had been vacated for him, Thomas completed the scrutiny of his correspondence undisturbed. When he left, he stopped at Kahnweiler's table and asked if he was the addressee of the postcard that Thomas had found underneath his table. He was. Thomas passed him the card, thanked him again for his consideration, and departed. The following year

Kahnweiler received a parcel forwarded from the address he had vacated a couple of months earlier; inside was a copy of the *Two- and Three-Part Inventions*, its sleeve signed by Thomas Lang. Kahnweiler sent a letter in reply, care of DRGG, but there was no further contact between them. It was shortly after this that Kahnweiler began his tabulation of Thomas's career, simply as a chronicle rather than as the basis for some more searching project.

Between the arrival of Kahnweiler's pamphlet and my conversation with him, I heard from an equally useful respondent, by the name of John Henry Leysham. In addition to possessing almost all the recordings listed in Kahnweiler's index, Leysham has also amassed what he believes to be Britain's most comprehensive collection of Lang-related printed memorabilia. Having spent an afternoon trawling through his archive, I think he's probably right. He lives just outside Northwich in a tiny two-bedroomed cottage – the smaller contains his bed and a few bits of furniture, the larger has a hi-fi system, one chair and a wall of box files, one for each year of Thomas's career. Each of these box files is packed with reviews, stories and photographs culled from newspapers and magazines published in all the countries in which he has contacts. As he was formerly a press officer with ICI, half the known world has been drawn into his network. It seems that every person with whom Leysham ever did business was soon made aware of his passion, and thereafter supplied him with whatever material they could find. He has folders full of stuff he cannot understand: record reviews in Portuguese; concert notices in Hebrew; career retrospectives in Polish; letters in Turkish; even an editorial in Basque, printed for some reason below a photograph of the young Horowitz, whose name would appear not to be mentioned in the article. Some of this material might prove valuable, if I can enlist a cohort of linguists to assist me.

For the time being, I have distilled from this great vat of information the essence of what could be an interesting diversion in the biography of Thomas Lang. Altogether, Leysham has some eighty-three different pictures of Thomas – publicity releases, album covers, magazine shots, programme photos. Of these, seven recur with greater frequency than the rest. I'm sure you'll recognise them.

1. Taken while practising in the Salle Pleyel, 1970. Thomas's left hand is extended to its fullest extent, each finger depressing a key in the middle range of the keyboard; his right hand is stretched over the upper reach, thumb downturned to within an inch of the keys, fingers splayed and parallel to the plane of the keys. His eyes are lightly closed.

2. Just Thomas's hands. A picture first published as an illustration on the leaflet enclosed with the *Hammerklavier* recording. The left, cupped to play a chord, has something of the smooth and lifeless tone of an old film studio portrait; it resembles a hand carved in wood. The right is a spatulate blur, in which only the nail of the index finger is defined.

3. From September 1974, the rehearsal for Beethoven's fourth concerto in Stockholm. By positioning himself below the lip of the stage, the photographer has framed

Thomas's face between the arcs of his arms. His hands are hidden. One assumes he is playing, but from the angle of his face he appears to be looking not at the piano but at the floor. A coil of hair has swung over his eyes, and only his mouth can be seen, the teeth clenched as if in pain.

4. From the same rehearsal. Thomas's composed, alert expression suggests that he is awaiting his entry; the conductor leans forward, baton extended like an épée, but the three violinists caught in half-focus are looking at Thomas, not at the conductor.

5. Another rehearsal shot, New York, October 1980. Tie and collar awry, Thomas grips one side of the piano with his arms outstretched, peering into the frame. He seems to be scrutinising an object resting on the bottom of a pool.

6. Taken during a break in the recording of the Chopin preludes, March 1971. In the foreground three technicians are working at a microphone stand; through the thicket of legs one sees Thomas slumped in a steel and leather Bauhaus chair, a paper cup between his feet and a towel draped around his shoulders. The flank of the piano obtrudes on the right of the picture. Lang stares in that direction, his look that of a matador assessing a bull of uncertain temperament.

7. Thomas leaving the stage after playing the Brahms B-flat concerto in Berlin, June 1973. In the background the audience is on its feet, applauding with hands raised. One woman appears to be weeping. Approaching the steps leading down from the stage, Thomas is

frowning at his hands, which he holds out from his body, flat, as if testing a phantom keyboard.

This last photograph, like the third, is in a sense inaccurate, since Thomas Lang's dispassionate bearing on the concert platform is more faithfully represented by the studio photographs on the covers of his records. (I think it most likely that the seventh photo in fact shows Thomas reaching for banisters that are just out of shot.) The popularity of both is perhaps due to the fact that they seem to reveal the creator behind the creation, the turmoil from which the perfected image is supposed to have been wrought. Though misrepresenting the accidental as the essential, they have some merit as metaphor.

In addition, this seventh image has another significance. Judged simply by technical criteria, the other six are all superior to the Berlin picture, which has the poor contrast and blurred outlines of an amateur's snapshot. Yet, paradoxically, it is in this very deficiency as a photograph that the potency of the image resides. It resembles not the crisply defined and stilted studio shots posted in the foyers of theatres, but rather the sort of image that might be brought back by an expedition in search of a near-extinct species. Snatched in half-light, the photograph warrants the rarity of the creature, the preciousness of the moment of its sighting. In just this way, the Berlin picture is the emblem of Thomas Lang's elusiveness. It does not show the 'real' Thomas Lang, but it augments the mystique of the virtuoso.

Something else struck me as I skimmed through the visual record of Thomas's career, as indeed it would have struck anyone else. Among the various publicity photos from the last five years of his life – and with the exception of a shot of Thomas leaving Steinway's in New York, and one of him with Daniel Barenboim in the Place des Vosges, that's the only kind there is – there's not one picture in which he isn't clad entirely in black. Before 1982, a fair number of the photos plausibly suggest that they show Thomas Lang's day-to-day appearance; after, there's no hint of such spontaneity. It's certainly a look that suited him, but I can't help finding its uniformity counterfeit. It's a little too demonstratively self-denying, as though calculated to signify that the high seriousness of Thomas's musical style expresses itself in every aspect of his life. I find it, in short, banal, a word I would never have imagined myself using in relation to Thomas Lang. But then again, perhaps the Black Angel look was Thomas's concession to the marketing people. After all, if his records didn't sell he wouldn't get to make them. I still harbour a sentimental distaste for the hard business of art, for the image-mongering side of the profession – in short, for the professional side of the profession. Part of Thomas's attraction was always his integrity, and I am slightly discomfited by this appearance of compromise. A poor reflection on myself, I know.

Finally, allow me to introduce a third accomplice. This very morning I received a letter from a woman whose anonymity I think I should preserve, though she has not asked me to do so. Born two years before Thomas, she saw his performance in the final of the Antwerp competition, to which she was taken by the doctors for whom she worked as an au pair. Thereafter she attended more than sixty Lang concerts, taking three or four short holidays each year to see Thomas play in Europe. In October 1970 she even flew to New York to see his Carnegie Hall debut. I travel to Edinburgh next week to meet her.


## *Christopher Lang to Michael Dessauer*

Your squeamishness leads you astray. I agree that Tom's sales figures were not harmed by the 'sensitive raptor' image, to quote a phrase I have instantly coined, to my immodest pleasure. But to accuse Tom of collusion in the manufacturing of this image is – once again – to go galloping off in pursuit of a chimerical quarry.

Tom loathed portraits of any description, and especially detested the species of photo sham demanded by his record company. All those nonchalant violinists, those conductors gesticulating at non-existent orchestras, pianists languidly displaying the length of their fingers on the keyboards of gleaming Steinways. What you see in these publicity shots is not a collusion between Tom and his sellers. It is genuinely what Tom happened to look like on the day he was blackmailed into showing his face in the snapper's den.

In the long years before his mutation into monochrome Tom was known to his intimates as a singularly inept dresser, a deficiency hidden from the public by the ingenious framing of his mugshots. Though hawk-eyed in many respects, in this crucial field Tom possessed the visual sense of an axolotl. Even in the context of the general sartorial delinquency of the

1970s, a period during which the only people who dressed well were the members of the armed forces, it was apparent that my brother possessed a special gift for the ghastly.

As you might expect, Tom's vulgarities were not those of the common man. He deplored the excesses he saw all around him – the hypertrophied lapels and flares, the absurd contrasts of billowing sleeves and tight tank tops, the high-voltage patterns, the stacked shoes. His taste was subtle. He preferred plain colours, discreet tailoring, understatement. Yet, left to his own devices, he always managed to get his wardrobe wrong. Exquisitely, excruciatingly wrong. For a start, he had not the faintest idea as to which colours looked good on him, however often it was explained to him that certain hues flattered only Vikings, and others only equatorial Africans. He persisted in applying all conceivable colours to his frame as if he were a blank canvas. Worse than this failing, though, was his inability to judge the compatibility of colours. A characteristic touch would be to wear a blue shirt with a jacket of a hue so close to that blue on the spectrum that it set up a savage discord. He was also unable to discriminate between the high-class and the low-class in high-class guise, like those people who fork out hundreds on oil-painted reproductions of photographs. A seersucker pinstripe jacket in an acetic blue-grey comes painfully to mind.

For a while Jen used to escort him on shopping forays. She was able slightly to dampen Tom's enthusiasm for the hideous, but could do nothing to prevent his returning from foreign appointments bearing suitcases crammed with outfits that should have been covered by the Geneva Convention. Slowly he learned that he would never learn, and the evolution into black was achieved. At least in this colourless attire he ran few risks of violating the esoteric codes of good grooming.

Your woman sounds like she might be the dingbat who used to send white roses backstage. It happened once or twice on every tour. Tom would return to his dressing room to find it had been converted into an alpine floral tribute in his absence. Somewhere amidst this morass of petals there'd be a card, and on it always the same message – 'Thank you'. Emetically pathetic isn't it? Once in a while Tom might be half tempted to dispatch a flunkey to track down his admirer, but always his curiosity would be countermanded by his distaste for such obsessiveness – cringing, abasing obsessiveness of this kind, I mean, not obsessiveness per se, of course. I can just imagine her: the dressing table like a tabernacle consecrated to Thomas, the vigils outside his hotel, the unobserved observer at the stage door, the joyless contentment of devotion, so much richer than mere happiness. Spare me.

## Michael Dessauer to Christopher Lang

Your lady of the white roses is a different person. We made the same mistake, you and I, which makes a change. I had extrapolated from the letter a character not unlike the one you sketched, but as someone less desperate – one of those high-society types who latch onto stars as if in the belief that propinquity is akin to patronage. However, there is nothing deluded about this woman.

She is a solicitor in a practice specialising in employment law. She's handsome, tall and constantly mindful of her bearing, with frank grey eyes and a voice that's light and pleasantly sibilant. Her way of speaking is remarkable, very rapid but with each stress so precise that one can almost hear the punctuation. She talks about herself openly and disinterestedly: when she says 'I did such-and-such' or 'I felt such-and-such', she seems to be recounting the narrative of some distant historical entity named 'I'. There's nothing provisional about her recollections or her comments on them – it's impossible to imagine her saying 'as far as I recall', or 'I suppose I did this because . . .'. To my thinking, there was no element of obsession in her attachment to Thomas.

She is, I believe, a self-sufficient, measured, clear-headed person who saw in Thomas the perfection of self-sufficiency and clarity of thought. Furthermore, there is something about her manner, the fleeting expressions around her eyes and mouth, the cadences of her voice, that suggests – and here I realise that I am perhaps venturing farther than I am entitled to go – someone for whom the intimacy with which most people are contented is something too flimsy to be satisfactory. A person not so much disillusioned as unillusioned. I would propose that the experience of listening to your brother play the piano was as intense for her as the experience of love, equally intimate and enriching, but untainted by the egoism and dishonesty that love often entails. For her, perhaps, the greatest fulfilment is to be found in this – in the communion, however brief, of two minds raised to a pitch of extreme concentration.

I learned a lot in the course of the afternoon, though more about her than about Thomas, I admit. Most pertinent to the biography were her remarks concerning the changes in the way Thomas used to begin his concerts. The insouciance of the early years, the customary graceful hauteur, was succeeded in the years of the Bach recitals by what sounds like an almost hieratic severity. In the mid-70s he would intimidate the audience into a silence that was protracted ever further with each appearance, as if he were gauging the limits of his audience's attention. Then, when he came back to the concert hall after the sabbatical of 1978 (and I now know the reason for this break), he had changed completely. Now he crossed to the piano at a quick march and gave the most perfunctory of bows, staring down at the stage, as if the sight of another person might make him forget the reason for his presence.

His demeanour while he played never changed, however. His face was cast in an expression at once distanced and attentive, seeming to listen to sounds his audience could not hear, as if moment by moment he was hearing and judging all the developments the music might take. His hands, meanwhile, never rose more than a few inches above the keyboard, the fingers seeming to coax the notes from the piano with simple flexings and strokes, such was the smooth economy of his action. She saw him play the *Goldberg Variations* with such rapt delicacy that a 1,000-seat concert hall felt as small as a cell; she saw him play the *Appassionata* with such violence that from near the back of the hall she could see the piano shake; and on both occasions no expression of emotion passed over his body, no movement betrayed a reaction to the music he was playing.

As for the manner in which Thomas conducted himself at the concert's end, I am told that in the early years he tended to regard the auditorium with what my witness terms 'a frigid graciousness', a character-isation that matches my own memory closely. Later, from the mid-70s to the early 80s, he appeared more relaxed but preoccupied, unsmiling, as if he had come through an event that required immediate recollection and consideration. In the last years he was subtly different again. When confronted by the inevitable ovation he looked – and here I quote the exact words – 'like a philosopher-prince emerging from his study to find a grand ball unaccountably in progress in his own house'.

This image brought our interview to a close, and it's the last image I'll gain from this source. Courteously but firmly she informed me at the outset that our meeting would be our only one, and I shall not press the point.

A footnote. From the testimony of a couple of my minor respondents it would appear that Thomas often had an uneasy relationship with his public, in however modest a grouping they came. One Katia Phillips sent me an account of her brief encounter with Thomas on the afternoon following a recital in Avignon. (July 1975 she thought; Kahnweiler says September.) She found herself face to face with him outside a shop, where he was waiting for two people to extricate themselves from a jammed revolving door. She complimented him on his performance, at which Thómas looked utterly bemused, as if Ms Phillips had told him something deeply embarrassing about her private life. After a pause, he remarked that he liked her brooch, smiled apologetically, then strolled off down the street.

The experience of Gavin Crowley, formerly a BBC journalist, makes Katia Phillips's exchange look like a meeting of minds. Having been introduced to Thomas at an after-concert reception in London (1980; Kahnweiler confirms), he remarked, 'perhaps injudiciously', on the exceptionally slow tempo that Thomas had chosen for the main work on that evening's programme – Schubert's B-flat major sonata. Thomas appeared stunned by the comment. He opened his mouth as if to speak, sighed, closed his mouth, inhaled slowly, opened his mouth again, set down his glass, shrugged his shoulders and walked away without saying a word.

No Thomas Lang letters for a long time. Any likelihood of receiving more in the near future?


## Michael Dessauer to Christopher Lang

Back to the photographic theme, by an unexpected route. I received this morning a letter from a Mr Colin Allason, proprietor of South Street Cameras, Dorchester. He tells me that on the first Monday of October 1974 a young man came into his shop to place a huge order for equipment and materials: 'a top of the range Durst enlarger, gallons of chemicals, a drier, a guillotine, boxes of papers, bulbs, tanks, trays, filters, and so on. He wouldn't leave a name or address. He paid for everything up front in cash, and said he'd call back in a couple of weeks. He was in my shop for about ten minutes, and in that time he spent a good four-figure sum. Two weeks later he returned, and spent another few hundred pounds on a Leica. He paid for that in cash too. He wasn't flashy; he seemed a shy character, but he knew what he was talking about. We only found out who he was a few months later, when we saw one of his records in the library.' Any light to shed on this?


## *Christopher Lang to Michael Dessauer*

Be careful what you do with Crowley's brush-off. Its only significance lies in Tom's dislike of jumped-up BBC types, whom he tended to regard as the self-satisfied vanguard of the new illiteracy. The substance of Mr Crowley's comment is beside the point. Tom was impervious to criticism, just as he was impervious to praise. He didn't enjoy being exposed to either, just as he didn't enjoy being exposed to sleet, I'd imagine. But neither praise nor criticism nor sleet could penetrate his hide.

He abominated launch parties, after-concert parties and all other events at which he might expect to be subjected to torrential approval. For really big productions – like the shindig after his Carnegie debut, where the entire White House staff, half the UN and a dozen pretenders to obscure European thrones seemed to be present – Joshua Thorpe had to organise a stake-out of Tom's dressing room to prevent the guest of honour from sloping off. Even then, I recall a scuffle in the car park of some top-notch venue, when Thorpe apprehended Tom in the act of attempting to dodge surveillance disguised as a chauffeur. For lesser occasions Thorpe would usually run through a speech about the pleasure Tom's presence would bring to the other party-goers; and Tom in the fewest possible words would assure Joshua of his best intentions; and Joshua would praise the manifold qualities of the aspirant hosts, who even now were ranging the champagne glasses in readiness for Tom's arrival; and Tom would nod; and Joshua might essay a few parting remarks about social obligations and reciprocal respect; and Tom would bugger off home. Which I think was best for all concerned, having once witnessed Tom laying waste to a gaggle of dignitaries from the Belgian arts ministry. Warm, well-rounded, intelligent people all of them, and utterly sincere in their enthusiasm for my brother's art. But Tom blasted them with one of his adamantine silences, his eyes drilling the carpet, his mouth set in a sort of post-mortem rictus. The poor stooges looked like courtiers in the presence of a capricious despot, suspecting they have committed a mortal gaffe but unable to fathom what it might have been.

In the early years Thorpe used to detail a minion to garner Tom's reviews and package them off to him. Ninety per cent of them were strongly positive, but nonetheless Tom soon requested a cessation of the service. Concert reviews were an absurdity to his way of thinking, their primary function being to affirm or modify the memories of the impressionable. Record reviewers at best belonged in the company of philatelists and numismatists, at worst in the ranks of petty demagogues, peddling prejudice as doctrine. I think his records received in total about twenty international awards, but there's no trace of any of them among his effects, unless you count the badges that DRGG insisted on printing on his CD covers.

Yes, every chance of further letters. A bonanza sooner or later – but patience, please. 'Untainted by the egoism and dishonesty that love often entails'? *De profundis*, eh?

## *Michael Dessauer to Christopher Lang*

I must disagree with you. I think Thomas could not tolerate criticism. Gwen Hanna, who must be accounted one of his most loyal friends, tells me that for three years Thomas refused to talk to or even acknowledge the existence of one of his fellow students. The offence? He had once joked that Thomas was already famous in his own mind – not, in view of the evidence of Thomas's admirers, an unjust observation. John Wycherly, another staunch member of the Thomas Lang camp, says that if anyone dared to challenge Thomas's way of playing a piece, he reacted with barely stifled anger, as if the offender had carelessly broken an irreplaceable object. And of course Clement-Johnson has tales by the caseload.

Now, I appreciate that we are talking about Thomas as he was in his formative years. He was ambitious, and in the sphere of activity for which Thomas was marked, success does not simply fall onto the shoulders of the talented. It was not enough just to be himself. It was necessary to create the figure he was going to be, and then grow into that figure. This process would have been precarious, and we can forgive a young man if, in such circumstances, he is overly protective of himself. But later in life, when Thomas had, as it were, securely become the character of Thomas Lang, he could still display an exaggerated sensitivity to criticism or anything he perceived as criticism.

Matthäus relates an incident during one of the Munich sessions. Someone left lying around in the reception area a magazine that contained uncomplimentary remarks about Thomas's Chopin recordings, comparing them detrimentally to Rubinstein's. Thomas glanced at the article then put it aside without comment. Next day, before the recording began, he warmed up by playing a few Chopin preludes. He played in a manner that was sprightly, debonair and immensely attractive, but it was not the manner of Thomas Lang. Just in case the point was missed, his face bore the expression of a man who is waiting with growing impatience for his boring boss to finish talking. Thomas was playing at being Rubinstein, and was not impressed by the experience.

Furthermore, what the Germans tell me is that Thomas could quote verbatim from any of his reviews, and took great pleasure in reciting his less favourable notices in a querulously punctilious voice, a voice they took to be that of nay-saying academia. It may well be that Thomas did not want his home cluttered with cuttings, but the notion that he simply disregarded the press is not borne out by the evidence.

But back to the photographs. Anything to say? And while I'm at it, anything you want to tell me about Marcus Taylor? I ask because I was recently talking to Mr Allason, who informed me that once in a while Thomas would phone through an order for materials and ask for them to be set aside pending collection. More than once the collector was a certain Mr Taylor, who from Mr Allason's description would seem to have been quite the most dapper odd-job man on the face of God's earth.

## Christopher Lang to Michael Dessauer

'What the Germans tell me' – sounds like one of those daft lines Mahler used to scribble on his symphonies: 'What the trees tell me'; 'What the birds tell me'; 'What the children tell me'; 'What the Germans tell me'. Case not proven, however.

For one thing, your witnesses are not participating in a laboratory memory test. It's not as if you're asking them to remember the colour of the curtains in their parents' dining room. They are contributing to a narrative that's been taking shape since Tom became famous. When they recall how Tom appeared to them, they are reading back into Tom's life what they are being prompted to recall. For another, I come back to my analogy. Remarks of the uninformed are like rain: nobody likes to stand in the rain; the rain is a bloody nuisance; but the rain is not capable of inflicting grievous injury.

In answer to your question: Tom liked to take photos and as a rule he trusted people only for as long as he kept them in sight. Therefore he wasn't likely to entrust the local chemist with his irreplaceable pictures. No mystery here.

I can't let you get away with your aside about Tom's 'year off'. Yes, our parents died in 1977, father on September 1st, mother on November 26th. You'll find such patterns of mortality common among long-married couples. There is some truth to the implication that bereavement was a factor in the hiatus in Tom's concert schedule, but you should not assume that Tom required a rest to recover his equilibrium. Avaricious and geographically diverse relatives made the disposition of our meagre inheritance a more protracted business than it need have been. Tom and I found it necessary to devote a considerable amount of time to needless correspondence and dull legalities.

Speculation on my brother's state of mind in the aftermath of our parents' deaths is pointless, as is most speculation about my brother's (or anyone else's) state of mind at any time. He attended both funerals, but never visited either grave thereafter, a sin of omission for which Aunt Margaret, our family's standard-bearer for all the uglier aspects of suburban culture, could never forgive him. She made valiant efforts to extenuate his offence by apportioning some of the blame to the sort of people Tom mixed with in his line of work, but in the end fell back exhausted from the endeavour, and cast my brother, regretfully, into the outer darkness. I should imagine that Thomas for his part regarded graveside observance as a self-dramatising ritual, albeit one that rarely attained the heights of Aunt Margaret's bravura demonstration of inconsolable bereavement. I cannot say for certain, as I never discussed the issue with him. Offhand, I cannot recall Thomas initiating a single conversation about our parents after their decease. From this I would deduce nothing. I would say merely that it is probably valid to depict Tom's year-long absence from public show as an administrative rather than a recuperative necessity.

Regarding the irksomely persistent Mr Taylor – perhaps you simply underestimate how lucrative freelance blue-collar labour can be in certain zones of the leisured world.


## *Michael Dessauer to Christopher Lang*

Writing this book is sometimes like scrolling through the wavelengths to find a station on the radio. I get a letter from you, and it might be like a blast of white noise, or a voice momentarily coming through clearly against the interference. An imprecise image, but I confess to being disheartened. The biography of Thomas Lang is slipping away from me. Letters, recordings, memories seem on some days so insubstantial, just the trace of an hour. I read through my notebooks and it's like watching a plane's trail fade in the sky.

I need to see Thomas's house, because it's there that I'll find the firmest imprint of his identity. A man's house cannot be out of character – his choice of friends may be, even his own words may be, but not the environment in which he chooses to place himself when he is alone. It's imperative that I see what Thomas saw when he was at home.

*Re* Taylor – I know skilled craftsmen are at a premium nowadays, but I doubt if any earn enough to dress in the manner in which Mr Taylor customarily dressed, nor to drive a brand-new Jaguar.

## Christopher Lang to Michael Dessauer

Calm down, relief is at hand. You want to snoop around the Dorset fastness? I shall assist, although I harbour doubts about your line of reasoning.

OK, we are at my brother's house, a humble, four-square chalk-coloured Georgian lodge, a satellite structure to a mansion long ago demolished. To our left, three superb ash trees mark the limit of his land. To the right stands the squat tower of the church of Saints James and John, allegedly the masterpiece of an anonymous assistant of the Bastard brothers (I do not jest). We have the front door open. (Trust me, it wasn't worth lingering on the outside. Standard issue, circa 1810.) The hallway runs straight ahead, bisecting the ground floor, forming a right angle with the staircase at the end farthest from the door.

On your left as you enter is the bathroom, an idiosyncratic arrangement, and not the last. On the right, a room containing Tom's piano, a piano stool, a standard lamp and nothing else. An arched opening links this room with the study, where bookshelves bracket a desk that's placed against the wall farthest from the arch. Light enters the room from a large window to your right as you sit at the desk, close to which there is an armchair, leather, Chesterfield-ish, provenance uncertain. Shelving occupies almost all available wall space; contents much as you'd imagine, books indicative of a wide-ranging intelligence with a musical bias. A few prints hang on the walls – Beaux Arts drawings of Ionic capitals, reconstructions of the Forum, the Colosseum, the Golden House. This is the only room decorated with pictures. I must say I'm getting bored with this already. I'll try to remember to take a few Polaroids when I'm next down that way. You'd like that, I'm sure.

Onward. The staircase rises steeply to a landing lit by a narrow window of blue glass, the only apparent customisation of the external fabric.

(Sorry, I forgot – back downstairs. Door opens onto hall from study, opposite door to kitchen. Contents of latter exclusively culinary, underused by the look of them.)

So now we're at the top of the stairs, staring at the blue glass. Turn ninety degrees to face the door of what was once a minuscule bathroom, converted by Tom into a darkroom. We'll go in here, I think, as the rest of this floor is pretty dull. No, let's get that out of the way first, as there are only two other rooms.

No. 1: music room, extending the full depth of the house, over the study and piano room, containing one preternaturally acute hi-fi rig (amps with heat sinks the size of sharks' fins; speakers like small wardrobes; record deck machined from titanium and granite), one sofa, x-hundred LPs, ranged alphabetically by composer (notable gaps in the 'T' section, ditto 'M', 'S' and 'R').

No. 2: bedroom, housing bed, couple of ladder-back chairs, wardrobe – for which I cannot bring myself to compile an inventory.

We return to the darkroom, where we shall not linger on the apparatus and fittings, which I am sure are indistinguishable from those of any well-heeled hobbyist or long-term subscriber to *Amateur Photographer*. Let us instead concentrate on the filing system. No, believe me, this will interest you. It even interests me, slightly.

We have shelves flanking the door. To the left, a rank of film canisters occupies most of the shelf at eye height. Each canister contains an exposed monochrome film, and each bears a label on which is written the name of a city and a month. Thus on one we read 'Köln / October 1987'; on another 'Brussels / November 1987'; on another 'London / January 1988'. But Tom wasn't in Cologne in October 1987; he wasn't in Brussels that November, either; and of course he was not in London in January 1988, being dead by then. A clue as to what is going on is offered by the last canister in the line, labelled 'Mantova / May 1988'. Got it?

The shelves to the right of the door are packed with photograph albums, also arranged chronologically and each labelled with a city and a date. Beginning at the top left with 'Luxembourg: December 1974', these albums contain black-and-white contact sheets and a few enlargements. On the bottom shelf is a batch of empty albums, concluding with one marked 'Mantova: May 1987'. Plain now isn't it?

Take September 1982 as an example. Tom would have returned home from his recital in Madrid, unloaded the film he had used on the preceding days, and placed the film in a canister labelled 'Madrid / September 1983'. He would then have removed the canister at the far left of the line, shunted the rest along to fill the gap, and placed the newest one at the end of the line. In the same operation he must have labelled an empty album 'Madrid: September 1982', then added it to the albums on the bottom row, presumably after removing the earliest empty folder, 'London: September 1981'. Into this album he would place the prints soon to emerge from the canister marked 'London / September 1982', the one he had previously extracted. So much work, and for what purpose? The terms of Tom's will of course forbid release of these pictures, but the world shall not in any way be impoverished by this ban from the grave, for here I proffer a survey of those London shots.

1.  A delivery van, its back doors open; stacked messily inside, two tables, a mattress, three tea chests, a standard lamp and two armchairs, in one of which sits a shop mannequin, its right arm chipped, revealing white plaster.

2.  A massive granite fist; a child standing under it, one arm raised to touch the stone knuckles.

3.  A Roman marble head of Perseus in one-third profile; in the foreground, out of focus, the back of the head of a dark-haired woman, and her right hand, raised, holding a pencil.

4.  A funerary stele; standing around it, forming an arc, a group of young adults, each consulting a Bible; a child holding the right leg of one of the adults, weeping.

5.  A puddle, the base of a broken bottle upright in its centre; on the wall above, a paint-spray graffito – 'Do It' – with annotation in same script – 'Too Id'.

6.  In the left foreground a digital clock, showing noon

or midnight; behind it a clock with a cast-iron case, showing five o'clock; on the right, a woman hailing a taxi in what appears to be an empty street.

7.  A shop-window display of three record sleeves featuring the faces of Kiri Te Kanawa, Georg Solti, Thomas Lang.

8.  A long loop of hawser in a shop window, beside a small steel capstan and a pile of anodised karabiners; on the glass – 'LAST DAYS OF SAIL, 30% OFF'.

9.  The end of a building-site fence; top left, a hard-hat symbol; below, the ragged edges of torn superimposed fly-posters, now reading: 'THE GREAT /THE /ONLY / THE /WHAT'.

10.  Three pedestrians turned to observe an incident or object outside the frame: one puzzled, two smiling. In the background, a dog in the road, paws evenly straddling the white line.

11.  A shop interior; a young woman standing within a buttress of light that rises from bare-boarded floor to high window.

12.  A man seated on a splintering crate, a pat of squashed fruit between his feet, close to a toppled cider bottle, a flattened cigarette butt, a sports page.

13.  A ripped bag of cement, from which rises a thick fume of dust, blowing across the face of a young man holding a cigarette.

14. A dark-haired young woman facing the camera full on, pulling back a cotton jacket to reveal a T-shirt printed with the slogan *'Perchè no?'*

15. A scene of shadows projected onto a blank plaster wall: a small tree, a huge dog, part of a bicycle wheel, a bollard, a shopping bag.

16. A polished brass nameplate, its embossed lettering eroded to: MASTERSON, JONES & ONE, SO ICI OR.

17. A street hawker crouched over an upturned box on which are ranged twenty-four perfume bottles; propped against the box a sign – 'Eve St Laurent'.

18. A young man and young woman: his hands are clamped to the side of her face; he looks into her eyes, smiling; she looks down, not smiling.

19. Two taxis head-on, headlights six inches apart; each driver leaning out of his cab, one arm extended; a passenger disembarking from cab on right.

20. T. Lang's left hand holding a cigarette between index finger and middle finger, a flysheet between index finger and thumb; only the top line is in focus – 'LESS PROTEIN LESS PASSION'.

21. A queue outside a theatre; the third person from the front seems to be asleep, with mouth ajar and back jammed against a drainpipe; the sixth is kissing the seventh; the tenth is holding a child upside down by the ankles; the thirteenth lies supine on the pavement.

22. Five women in a line on a kerb, all grimacing: three looking to the left, one looking at her sodden skirt hem, one straight at the camera. The first four share a golf umbrella; the last holds her linked hands above her head.

23. A flat asphalt roof, sleeked by rainwater; two empty crisp packets, two beer cans; at the roof's edge, the back of a London Underground sign.

24. Two men in evening jacket and bow tie leaning over a parapet; behind them the Royal Festival Hall; below, a strip of glossy silt.

In all humility, I admit that I find my pen-pics a damned sight more engaging than the originals. But, having come so far, we cannot let the matter rest here, can we? What can they mean, these images, so provocative in their ordinariness? A diary of sorts, notebook jottings in silver nitrate? But to what end? Surely Thomas Lang the memory man had no need of souvenirs? A meaning lies here to be discovered, for nothing done by Thomas Lang was without meaning. The lives of the great can boast an unflagging significance to which the humble can aspire only in their dreams, yes? Everything has its rightful place somewhere on the path to the heart of the labyrinth. Let us posit, then, an exegetical soliloquy by Thomas Lang.

'Each scene is but the catalyst for a sequence of visual recollections. Each image, as soon as seen, releases the consequences of the moment it shows. It is as if the picture thaws into life – the figures move, the shadows slither, the colours seep back into the bleached frame.

The picture I'm looking at now becomes animated by the smoke's quick dispersal, by the pastel harmonies of near-white powder and near-blue smoke; this one by the way the sun catches the umbrella's fabric, and by the cobalt of the scarf worn by the woman who passes a semi-second after the shutter clicks; this one by the strangely aged hands of the nearest reader, his skin as scored and hard as a root. And sometimes a scene will become something that I have never experienced, as a new atmosphere rises from the print. It's like sitting beside the sea when the view suddenly ceases to be interesting, and the relentless sound of the waves, previously almost sealed out of hearing, builds to a pitch that obscures every other thing. It happens with a picture here. This woman is in love. As her pencil traces the lines of the statue's face, her hand is in fact stroking in air the skin of her lover's cheek. She maps the contours of that marble head, poised in the knowledge that she is loved. She breathes slowly, as in the depth of night, her hand moving slowly on the paper.'

I don't know about you, but I've half a mind to be convinced. I could get a taste for this guff. It's a lot of fun, the mode empathetic. What a relief to tread such lush and carefree pastures after the desiccated plains of historiography. What blissful irresponsibility.


## Michael Dessauer to Christopher Lang

I was going to keep the testimony of one of my respondents out of our correspondence, but now, for reasons I suspect do me little credit, I feel disinclined to edit myself. The enclosed letter, dispatched from Oxford on 12 April 1976, was returned one week later by your brother, opened, in an envelope that contained nothing else. I've spent the last week away from Thomas Lang, reading a couple of other biographies, some memoirs, a few essays. This letter is what drove me away from him. In the interim my feelings about it have moderated, though I still wish I had never seen it.

Something you wrote at the start of all this now makes more sense to me, after my week's study: I am beginning to comprehend how benumbing Thomas's life might at times have been for him. I can see it as a life of repetition, but a life lacking the security that repetition often imparts: a succession of arrivals and departures, of towns he knew chiefly as a road from an airport, a hotel room, a dressing room, and yet another audience demanding wonders. I can feel something of the discontent of touring alone – the profusion of acquaintances and dearth of friends, the house that's come to seem little more than a wardrobe, a bed and an accumulation of mail. I understand how Thomas might have perceived his talent as an entity quite separate from himself, how he might have felt tyrannised by that gift. I can even imagine that he might have been relieved had something happened that would have made it impossible for him to play again, releasing him from the imperative to practise, to maintain for others the identity to which his skill condemned him.

I suppose I've lingered on these ideas as an alibi for what emerges in this letter, both directly and indirectly. (It's obvious there's a lot more to be unearthed.)

I'm troubled by the evident cruelty of his actions, a cruelty so difficult to reconcile with the sensitivity revealed by his playing. It's unnerving to face the possibility that Thomas Lang, a man uncannily competent in the evocation of emotion through music, was considerably less adept with the emotions of brute reality.


Dear Thomas,

I was going to begin 'do you remember?', but of course you remember, Thomas. I don't mean 'do you remember?' do I? I mean 'Please hear me out, for once. Try not to get bored.' It won't cost you much, just another fifteen minutes of your time and I'll be gone, back among the muttering shades of your love-struck girls and other unfortunates.

So anyway, Thomas, there was that evening when we needed an alibi – sorry, when I needed an alibi. And I rang Jane, to tell her that I was supposed to be with her. She made light of it: 'Of course it's OK. I've no self-respect at all.' It doesn't seem funny, now I come to write it, but still. So she said that, and I looked over to you, as if I was expecting you to react to her comment, which of course you could not possibly have heard.

You were standing with your back to me, gazing out at the garden. It was a beautiful afternoon. (Sorry, I know how much you hate that word. 'Beautiful', that is.) Two fat magpies were swaggering across the grass – they looked like a couple of mafiosi, one of us said. You, I suppose. My coat was slung over the back of the chair, and as Jane carried on talking I saw your hand fall onto the collar, as if of its own accord, and then I saw your head turn to see what your hand was up to. You looked at your hand, then you looked at the coat, and it was as if you were looking at something that had absolutely nothing whatever to do with the present, with us as we were then. As I thought we were then.

I don't know, Thomas. I can't find the words for it, the way you looked at that damned coat. Perhaps a sort of sorrowing pity. It was as if it were something you'd been given by a friend who had completely misjudged your style. Or as if you'd found it lying there after a party and were recalling the star-struck little bastard who'd left it behind, having stuck to you like a leech all evening.

We went on for weeks after that, didn't we? But from that moment onward I felt that I was living in the past tense. We even seemed to make love in the past tense. ('Making love' always used to strike me as a stupid phrase. Not any more.) And just from the way you looked at that coat, I knew exactly what it was that had killed me off. It wasn't that you were troubled by the morality of what we were doing. I think my husband's existence, my torment (no other word for it, I'm afraid), were just the incidentals of my being, like my unpunctuality or my clumsiness, which once you found so charming. No, what you couldn't stomach was the vulgarity of our situation, all the paraphernalia of deception. I thought we were in love; you thought we were in bad taste.

I suppose I should take some comfort from this. My self-esteem should be able to survive a failure that was not mine but ours. I was not inadequate in your eyes, my company was not banal – we just conformed to a type of banality, and that was intolerable to you.

But fuck it all Thomas, I was not the mere shabby embodiment of an endlessly recurrent type. I was a married woman who was prepared to ditch everything for you – her husband, her career, her family, her friends, everything damned thing. You knew that, and you abused me. You wrapped me around yourself like a blanket against whatever inclement climate you had contrived to create for yourself, and when your private season took a sunnier turn you suddenly saw what a tatty old thing our 'relationship' was, and you cast it away.

I can recall whole paragraphs of your speech. Not as perfectly as you might recall every last one of my inconsequentialities, I'm sure, but clearly enough to cause me pain. There's one word I can never hear you say, though, and that word is 'feeling'. I try to hear your voice forming those syllables, and it always comes out like a contemptuous diminutive – 'princeling', 'underling', 'feeling'.

To be fair, you never said you loved me, even when – as you told me – it would have been easiest to do so. I think I wish you had taken the easy way, and placed my happiness before your own integrity. 'Isn't what I do enough?' you asked me once. Really, you did. What you did, what you performed, that was what was true. Why did I need a paraphrase of it? Well, what I needed wasn't a paraphrase, it was more a guarantee. I wanted a certificate of authenticity. And besides, what exactly was it that you did? Ignore my letters, never be at home when I phoned, act as though we had never been friends, let alone lovers.

I was going to ask to see you again, even though I know I'd have gone weeks without an answer. The thought may be nine-tenths of the act, but I feel some sense of virtue, some consolation, in having resisted desire as much as it can be resisted. I did follow you one day. I may as well now confess. I found out you were at Abbey Road in February. (Don't fret, your agent didn't let you down. Everyone in his office is well drilled in stonewalling the ardent fan.) I don't know why I trailed you that day. Perhaps in the hope that you might somehow seem diminished without an audience, like the actor I once saw in a shop, who looked just like himself but wasn't himself, if you see what I mean. I might have hoped that when I saw you from a distance you might just blur into the crowd and I could leave you there.

It was pitiful. I actually sat on a wall across the road from the studio for a good three hours, waiting for you to come out. Finally there you were, with a couple of men behind you, walking half a dozen deferential paces adrift. But the whole thing would have been a disaster even if they hadn't been there. You had your head slightly at an angle, with that sceptical, attentive look on your face, as if strange ideas were being whispered in your ear, and then that little nod, as if conceding a point, for the time being. I saw you rub the skin to the side of your left eye, closing the other eye as your finger rubbed away. And that silly way you stand with your toes precisely on the front edge of the kerbstone, waiting for the traffic to clear. Those little mannerisms of yours seemed even more beguiling than usual, I suppose because I had you at a disadvantage, watching you without being seen. And they gave me such a feeling of tenderness, Tom, that I couldn't have risked ruining it by speaking to you.

But I think I'd have followed you until you saw me if I hadn't been crying.

Did you love me Tom? Perhaps you did, more truly than I loved you, in not wanting me intemperately, perhaps in not really wanting me at all. You could be so kind, so concerned for my well-being. You were the only man whose advice I could trust. That should have warned me.

Still, after all these months, I see you every day. In the street I sometimes see a man move as you might move – raise a hand to touch his hair as you do, shrug his jacket on his shoulders. And in that moment, though I know it is someone else, it's you I see. It is as if your reflection had flashed on a window, blanking out the figure on the other side. The pain of these moments is so sharp, and yet the pleasure of them sometimes seems as substantial as anything you have left in my memory. Hopeless bloody ecstasy, Tom, that's what life with you became.

Don't worry Thomas, you shan't be hearing from me again. I wish you continued success in everything you do, superfluous though that sentiment may be.


### Christopher Lang to Michael Dessauer

You never cease to disappoint me, in a rather bracing sort of way – so excitable, so suggestible, so wrong. On the basis of a single letter you swiftly settle into the opinion that Tom was another Don Juan – this, I more reasonably assume, is what the prim remark about things still to be 'unearthed' is intended to convey. It seems not to have occurred to you that this letter

195

could have been written by a besotted lunatic. She has a plaintive turn of phrase, I grant you, but since when has style been a reliable gauge of character? For all you know, this letter might have been preceded by such a barrage of verbiage that Tom could take no more. Do you know what had happened before the heart-rending incident of the waddling magpies, if we allow for a moment that such a scene occurred in the way described?

Furthermore, your extenuation of my brother's 'guilt', besides attesting to a weakness for the banal dichotomy of private vices and public virtues, is based on a fallacy. You should be wary of drawing conclusions from the shape of events, in this case, the dates in a diary of engagements. History on any scale is only secondarily about events – a point with which I have frequently belaboured my young charges, though still they cussedly prefer tales of medieval battles and vendettas to the microeconomics of pre-industrial European society. (You're also misunderstanding, incidentally, the point of mine to which you're alluding.)

In my opinion, Tom did not find his life dull, ever, and loneliness he regarded (with Jacobin inflexibility) as an ailment of the inadequate – so you can dispense with the 'idea' of sex as a palliative. From the start of his career, Tom played music almost every day of his life, and Tom was never bored by music. (Bear in mind that you're talking about somebody who cheerfully submitted himself to *Parsifal* on three nights of the same week.) As a child he was always listening to his own music, even if he wasn't playing. He'd sometimes lie in the front room, with the curtains drawn and the lights off, running a piece through his head in preference to trying it out on the piano. At least that was what he said he was doing, and whatever Tom's faults, he was not pretentious, even (singular distinction) as an adolescent. Tom said he could practise some things better without the distraction of the noise of the music, and as the results seemed to bear out this claim I was not going to get embroiled in the metaphysics of it.

Sometimes the family would go on a drive, and Tom would stare blankly out of the window while he played something to himself, leaving me to sit next to a lump of silence. For a short trip, he'd pick, say, a Mozart concerto and be gone for twenty minutes; for a drive to the coast, he might select *Figaro* – half on the way down, an interval while the earthlings sported on the beach, then the rest on the way back.

Incidentally, I was amused by the disclosure that the *soi-disant* biographer of Thomas Lang regards music as something distinct from that quaint but brawny abstraction, 'brute reality'. This would seem to be another disqualification, or am I missing something? And one last thing. If we take your heartbroken lover at face value, it would appear that Tom was capable of strong emotions actuated by another person, and of cruelty and dishonesty towards that person. Sounds like love, as defined in your earlier ruminations upon the subject.

## Michael Dessauer to Christopher Lang

The letter must be taken at face value (I've spoken to its author), and the contradiction between Thomas's artistic sensitivity and his callous personal behaviour seems to me a paradox that must be pursued, as does the contradiction between his superstitiousness and his analytical lucidity, between his passion for Wagner's elephantine operas and his love of Chopin's exquisite miniatures, and so on. The resolution of these problems is vital if I am to be confident of the biography's tone. The detection of these paradoxes might not be new, but novelty is not a prerequisite of the truth.


### *Christopher Lang to Michael Dessauer*

I beg you, no more of your old fond paradoxes. I've never had much patience with the paradox myself, regarding it as a vice of the lazy mind, on a par with a penchant for card tricks. Nature knows no paradoxes, as I wish someone had once said. Let us give a twist to your Chopin problem, for example. Let's suppose that the primary attraction of Frédéric C., to my brother's ears, was the tension between open and closed structures – a timid enough idea. Then let's say that Richard W.'s work displays such tension on a massive scale – look at *Tristan*, a classically closed love story floated on a raft of ambiguous, open harmonies, or at the *Ring*, a perfectly cyclical tale, emerging from the void and returning to the void, but one riddled with self-contradictions and partial resolutions. And there goes your paradox. Anyway, Franz Liszt had no problem holding Chopin and his own son-in-law in tandem, so why should you? But in view of your insatiable craving for tales of my brother's odd behaviour, herewith a toccata on the theme of a character idiosyncratic, contradictory, enigmatic, unique . . .

With minimal provocation – the sight of a cinema billboard might suffice – Tom would give loud voice to his disdain for the civilisation of the United States. He would refuse to look at any publication that contained any mention of Frank Sinatra, Judy Garland or James Dean. Billy Graham was known to him by the alias Belial Graham; Richard Nixon could be explained only as a Maoist agent provocateur. To summarise the failings of that sterling country, Tom would on occasion impersonate a certain journalist from a prominent West Coast magazine, a man grotesquely deformed by ambition, envy and fleeting intimations of the extent of the areas of human knowledge that lay beyond the confines of his miserably constricted mind. This hack collared Tom at a reception in Los Angeles, and tried to goad him out of his sullen silence by endlessly reiterating the notion that Mozart, were he alive today, would be living in LA and writing for the movies. Tom thought that LA was the city that all other American cities aspired to be; Tom thought that LA was a sump.

And yet Tom was also given to comparing the slack-phrased and under-researched journalism of the English press with the well-turned and expansive prose to be read in US publications such as *The New Yorker* and *Nature*. He admired no one more than he admired Noam Chomsky, whom he was apt to portray as the latter-day repository of the spirit of the American Revolution. Whereas many Europeans, when told to 'Have a nice day', affect to take it as an insult, Tom took it as an echo of the eighteenth century, an acknowledgement that in daily life civility was often more important than sincerity. He enjoyed the habitual courtesy of middle-class, middle-aged Americans, almost as much as he enjoyed the more elaborate and perhaps more suspect courtesy of the French. France was, I think, the place where he was happiest, though the contempt in which he held the French style of piano-playing was of a Johnsonian trenchancy, surpassed only by his contempt for ninety per cent of French music, an antipathy as intense as his reverence of Blaise Pascal.

Tom saw the modern western world as a culture cursed by the gramophone, an invention he decried as an agent of ignorance, in that it allowed people to carry the enthusiasms of adolescence into adulthood. Yet he preferred the recording studio to the concert hall.

He enjoyed driving, and was an excellent driver, but refused to learn anything about the machines he drove, even though he readily grasped the complex technicalities of sound recording, keeping himself informed of every engineering innovation. As soon as one of his cars went wrong he sold it, however inconsequential the problem. A self-willed mechanical idiot, he professed himself in awe of Arturo Benedetti Michelangeli not because the Italian maestro played the piano superbly but because he could strip down any engine and rebuild it without recourse to a manual.

Tom told me that the reason he liked Munich so much was that it was within easy reach of the Zugspitze; once he even flew down to Munich from Hamburg, where he was playing, just so that he could take the cable car to the summit. He loved the view from the narrow parapet on top of the unfinished nave of Siena cathedral, for my money the most frightening spot in Italy. To my knowledge he went to Ireland five times, and on each occasion drove across the country from Dublin so that he could peer over the lip of the Slieve League cliffs. So he was thrilled by heights – but he hated flying, even though he ran a greater risk of premature extinction every time he tiptoed round the crumbling tower of some mountain-top ruin. On every flight he would have the blinds pulled down on take-off and landing. There were certain makes of plane on which he would not travel. He once missed a rehearsal rather than get on board a plane that turned out to be powered by a type of engine different from the one the reservations clerk had informed him it was fitted with. After each air disaster he would scan every newspaper report to learn if there were some new factor he should take into consideration when choosing his airline.

In most cities he loved travelling by taxi. An exception was of course New York, where the taxi drivers were taken to be exemplars of the democratic spirit gone mad; in the States one could become a taxi driver simply through designating oneself as such, as demonstrated by the prevalence of drivers unfamiliar with the topography of the city in which they plied their trade, and underendowed with orientation skills. In London, however, he might hail a cab and ask to be driven to a place he had no reason to go other than the pleasure of the arcane route the driver might take. He also thought London cabbies were all crypto-Nazis, and if one persisted in talking to him he'd stop the car and get out.

He loved fine food, but was a useless cook, as intimated earlier.

He would stuff fifty quid into a church collection box for African famine victims, while professing a hatred of all religions except the wackiest self-eradicating, pebble-contemplating Oriental regimens, regardless of the fact that Zen monasteries are not renowned for their charitable works.

His home was in England . . . No, sorry, I've had enough. Truce.

## *Michael Dessauer to Christopher Lang*

I may be on the brink of a gold strike, and I think you are the person on whom my success depends.

Merely to tie up a loose thread, I went back to Joshua Thorpe to ask him for details about the secretary/PA referred to as 'Jen' in the Paray letters. Her name turns out to be Jennifer Ma, and she ceased to work for Thorpe at the end of 1989. Her resignation was unexpected, greatly regretted and not adequately explained. However, Thorpe reports that she seemed increasingly distracted after your brother's death, and had become somewhat uncommunicative in the weeks immediately before her departure.

It took me half a dozen phone calls to trace her – she is now a director of a public relations firm in Clerkenwell. My last call was at twelve-thirty from a phone box just a hundred yards from her office, to give myself maximum leverage. I was right outside, I told her. I'd take only a few minutes of her lunchbreak, would she mind giving me a few words? And then, on the dot of one, I was face to face with her. It was rather like walking into a glass door.

She is the most astonishing woman to look at, black-haired, slender, with an orientalised Hibernian face – very pale complexion, open features, shallow-set pewter/green eyes, narrow plumb-line nose. Her way of moving is amazingly fluid and refined, almost courtly. She doesn't so much sit down as set herself in place – everything about her manner seems to imply a millennium's breeding. She's someone you feel could walk through a warehouse in a blackout and not bump into anything. I'd have thought her no older than thirty, but I suppose, as she was working for Joshua Thorpe back in 1976, she must be a little past that.

She was unflaggingly courteous to me, but it would have been impossible to talk trivialities: the intensity with which she looked at me compelled me to justify her attention. I proceeded straight to the matter in hand, but in answer to my questions she told me nothing I didn't already know, indeed nothing that anyone would not have known after an afternoon in the library. When she asked me for an assurance of confidentiality, I thought this might be leading to something significant, but it rapidly became apparent that we were going nowhere. And then I produced a photocopy of that 'Last Months of Thomas Lang' piece. She read it very quickly, as if uninterested, but when she gave it back to me I saw her eyes flinch momentarily. 'That's terrible,' she said, and then she asked me if you knew about it. I told her you did.

I asked her if I might talk to her again at a later point. She said she would have to talk to you first.

I didn't press my luck, and left soon after. Outside, I was trembling with exhilaration at the realisation that I had discovered a new protagonist in my story. I am sure that Jennifer Ma was your brother's lover, and that you alone could persuade her to talk to me properly.

### Christopher Lang to Michael Dessauer

Not quite on target with Ms Ma. There's something to be said for your summary of the exterior of her head, and – within certain limits – for your genetic analysis. You were right about the confluence of nationalities, but your excitement over her perceived thoroughbred bloodlines is misplaced: her father was a compositor on Fleet Street, and was born in Hong Kong; her mother was a waitress somewhere round Holborn and hailed, I believe, from Roscommon. Her age is a smidgeon more advanced than you estimated it to be. She was twenty-two or twenty-three years old when Thorpe Associates took her on as a graduate from the University of East Anglia, where she was one of the first students on whom I was permitted to exercise my half-evolved tutorial techniques. I have been in contact with her ever since.

The possessor of the most baroque name of any student then enrolled at UEA, Jennifer Jacinta Ma was also the most *soignée* member of her year, a supra-fashionable self-created young woman who drifted around campus in home-made black trouser suits modelled from photos of pre-war Chanel creations. She was also extraordinarily guileless, while radiating a sense of invulnerability. As she looked then pretty well the same as she does now, you may gather that she was irresistible to many of her male contemporaries – her name had an unrivalled rate of incidence in the graffiti of the men's toilets, and her entry into the common rooms never went unremarked. These gauche and scruffy boys, however, were too obvious for young Jennifer, who tended to address them with the frank, asexual affection with which a twenty-year-old might address a randily adolescent half-brother. As far as I was able to determine, the only people she ever regarded as mating material were on the faculty side – and you would be astonished at the ethical depths an expert on canon law or trade routes in the sixteenth-century Levant can plumb.

Academically she was in the top flight, but was not suited to the desiccated life of the research student, as she came to realise shortly after embarking on her Ph.D. thesis (Thirteenth-Century Monastic Reform, as I recall). I could picture her as a luminary of the French aristocracy, presiding over a dazzling salon. Madame de Staël would have been more of a soulmate than ninety-five per cent of the inky creatures to be found nesting in the darker recesses of the university library. In their eyes, anyone who washed her hair three times a week was manifestly frivolous. She in turn would sooner have swigged a bottle of No. 5 than fraternise with anyone who wore an anorak indoors.

After leaving university she seemed incapable of finding a real job, chiefly I think because she was incapable of feigning ambition in order to flatter a possible employer. She didn't care what she did, as long as it left her with time to read and enough money to hit the sales twice a year. I was instrumental in getting her a position in Thorpe's office, and within six months she was effectively his second in command. He could have been hit by a bus and none of his clients would have noticed.

Which brings me, at last, to the present situation, which is more delicate than you suppose. At the time Tom wrote the letter from Paray, he and Jennifer were not lovers – Joshua Thorpe and Jennifer were. Their relationship had quickly developed beyond its professional limits, and I believe my brother played a small part in this. Joshua benefited from his proximity to Tom, but not, as you might think, because he in some measure partook of the virtuoso's glamour. Quite the reverse. Jennifer was never in thrall to the idea or the person of Thomas Lang, an almost unique distinction among persons of her gender and education.

There is no possibility whatsoever that Jennifer Ma was ever involved with my brother in any manner not covered by the terms of her contract. She admired him, and she went to all his London concerts, but at the same time she was repelled by him. I think that is not too strong a word. She felt there was something monstrous about him. The tales of his precocity and stupefying memory appalled her, but far worse was the sight of Tom in performance. She never missed a concert, but she couldn't bear to watch him play – she'd put her chair right at the back of the box, so she couldn't see the stage.

Tom's apparent aloofness disturbed her, certainly. Yet the essential problem lay, I think, not with my brother as an individual but rather with virtuosity in itself, with a technique that achieved its result with what appeared to be an unnatural lack of effort. Jennifer couldn't stand it, the sight of his wrists swaying like the waist of a heavy-hipped woman walking slowly, while his fingers bounced and darted from note to note as if independent of each other. I was there when she was introduced to him for the first time, backstage at the Festival Hall, and I saw her shudder when they shook hands. She was shocked, she said, that his hands were no larger than her own.

Joshua's worth was proved by his unexceptionalness. It was as though he daily glimpsed the abyss and had elected for ordinary decency. This common-or-garden niceness got him by for a good couple of years, and then I think Jennifer began to tire of having to look to her books for a challenge. They parted amicably, as you'll have deduced from the continuation of her employment with him.

And now a confession. The reason I allowed myself to become embroiled in this correspondence – the primary reason I should say – is guilt. A few months after my brother's death, I talked to Jennifer about the last letters I had received from him. This was not, I must emphasise, by way of an attempt to 'comprehend' what had happened. The conversation was idle, directionless, comforting reminiscence, nothing more. We talked about the letter Tom sent me from Norway, the penultimate one, and I must have mentioned a remark on its last page. 'I am trying to get the music out of my head,' he wrote, after joking that Beethoven had become his 'sitting tenant'. This comment, grotesquely misrepresented, magnified out of all resemblance to its true proportions, evidently became the basis of the Ackerman farrago.

As for Jonas Ackerman himself, this oleaginous reptile appeared in Thorpe's office some time around the middle of 1989, and announced that he was on a commission from some trendy US monthly to write a celebratory piece on Tom. Thorpe deflected him towards me, and I deflected him straight out the door. For one thing, he had a way of smiling that made me feel as if my place had been taken by a six-foot mirror. For another it soon became clear that my function was merely to corroborate whatever colour-supplement ideas he had brought with him from the airport. He kept telling me that Tom 'was so much of his time', which appeared to mean little more than that his face might not have looked out of place in a Warhol movie, and he peppered his chatter with sideswipes at Vladimir Horowitz, which is one thing coming from Thomas Lang but quite another coming from a man who thinks that a sforzando is a Renaissance despot.

However, by some mysterious process Ackerman managed to infiltrate himself into Jennifer's confidence and affections. (I am reluctant to believe that his Rolex, pheromones and weak resemblance to Victor Mature did the trick, but stranger things have happened, I suppose.) After a month he promptly took himself back home, and was never heard of again until the day you broke the news that his meretricious little project had not imploded through its own inanity, as I had thought it would. Now you see why Jennifer was upset by that piece – she was its immediate source, though I must take much of the blame for its appearance.

I am appealing to your goodwill, Mr Dessauer. Please don't bother Jennifer again. Anything she knows that might be relevant to your book I know too.

## Michael Dessauer to Christopher Lang

Would it be possible to let me have a transcript of the Norway letter? You have my word that I won't approach Jennifer Ma again. However, I would appreciate more candour on the subject of Marcus Taylor. I have made further enquiries, and I now know that whatever it was he did for a living, it did not come under the category of toil.

## Michael Dessauer to Christopher Lang

In the absence of a reply, another draft. This section is to be titled 'JUNE 1984: DRGG 413 449-2'.

The front of the sleeve of Thomas Lang's most controversial recording carries a photograph of Thomas Lang below a cartouche in which appears the text: Thomas Lang / Beethoven / Der letzte Klaviersonate / The last piano sonata. The back bears the minimum of information. At the base of the sleeve it is stated that the recording was made in the Salle Pleyel, Paris, on 10 March 1983. Above this single line, side by side, are photographs of Beethoven's death mask and his 'last piano, gift of the Viennese piano-maker Konrad Graf'. Over these pictures are printed the contents of the record:

Side A – Klaviersonate nr. 32 in c-moll op. 111 (sonata no. 32 in C Minor, op. 111);

Side B – Klaviersonate nr. 32 in c-moll op. 111 (sonata no. 32 in C Minor, op. 111).

The performance of the sonata on Side A, taken in

isolation from its coupling, received widespread praise. In Britain both the *Guardian* and the *Telegraph* selected it as one of the ten best recordings of the year, and *The Times* rated it as 'perhaps the finest achievement of Lang's career to date'. The reviewer for *Music* magazine believed that 'no musician has ventured so far into the arctic heart of late Beethoven's sound-world', and – like several others – cited the lecture given by Wendell Kretschmar in Thomas Mann's *Doktor Faustus*, on the theme 'Why did Beethoven write no third movement to the piano sonata opus 111?' This literary reference was deployed at greatest length in a celebratory piece published in *Schallplatten*, a quarterly journal produced in Hamburg at that time.

'The pages on which Beethoven drafted this valedictory sonata are scarred by the composer's hand. Discarded notes are so violently erased from the stave that in places the furious pen has scraped right through the fabric of the paper . . . This opening movement is the trace of a mind on the verge of derangement, enraged by the failings of its own means of expression, dashing onwards to the brink in its impulsion to eliminate these failings . . . a great calm descends in the silence that lies between the wings of this extraordinary diptych, and out of this calm, as if an extrusion of the silence, emerges the *Arietta* theme. The development of this theme is the most painful progress in western music; it is destined, as Thomas Mann wrote, "to vicissitudes for which, in its idyllic innocence, it would seem not to be born". Yet, under the hands of Thomas Lang, the "black nights and dizzying flashes" of these variations come out of the theme with the inevitability of Greek tragedy. We are listening to a man who discovers within his own words a terrible meaning, a truth that implacably demands elaboration until the point is reached at which the soul can bear no more. And at the edge of this abyss – the terminal brink, for everything now has been said and nothing has brought peace – Beethoven achieves grace through the assumption of convention, a rediscovery, as Mann wrote, "conditioned by death". As played by Thomas Lang, the colossal trills towards the sonata's close are like spring water rising from the cracked earth. Lang's classicism contains and transcends the romantic – it is a classicism predicated upon the romantic, that contains its own critique and is of irreducible value because of this awareness of its own fragility.'

On Side A of DRGG 413 449-2 the second movement – the *Arietta con variazioni* – lasts almost eighteen minutes; on Side B Lang dispenses with the music in little more than fifteen. This is a statistic upon which as many reviewers founded their condemnation of this version as had founded their praise of the other reading their quotations from Thomas Mann. 'Where the one performance has urgency,' wrote a reviewer in *Gramophone*, 'this merely has speed. Beethoven the tortured poet is replaced by Beethoven the show-off, an unattractive and implausible character.'

'To be charitable,' concluded *Music Today*, 'one could say that this rebarbative effort has some sort of spontaneity, as it clatters through the music unimpeded by any sense of what the human ear can abide. Perhaps Thomas Lang imagined that he was showing us something new in making this sonata out to be some species of demonic improvisation. I confess bafflement at this recording, but am disinclined to pursue the matter further.' There followed the verdict: '9 out of 10 for Side A; 3 out of 10 for Side B'.

From *Keyboard* magazine came the most hostile assessment. 'Everything about it is shallow: its ideas are shallow, the sound is shallow and wearying, as if the microphone has been taped under the lid. This wilfully ugly performance proceeds with no logic, and ends without arriving anywhere. A dolt once asked Beethoven why he hadn't added a third movement to this sonata; the composer replied that he just hadn't had the time. Lang plays the opus 111 as though he believes this explanation. This is not playing Beethoven. It's playing around with Beethoven.'

Six months after the record was issued, however, a more favourable review did appear, in *Neue Kunst*, a short-lived Munich arts magazine which primarily concerned itself with the visual arts. This article, written by one Tadeusz Landesmann, obliquely commended both of Lang's performances of opus 111 by addressing 'the problem that is the key to the critics' responses to this work'. It was Landesmann's contention that the writers were all troubled by Lang's record 'because it assaults the issue of sincerity. The frivolity of the second version is a scandal . . . it is not even true light-heartedness, but rather it is facetiousness. This frivolity casts its shadow back over that which had defined its insincerity, and so if B is insincere, how can we now believe the sincerity of A? None admits to the fear this dialectic raises, but it is the real subject of the critics' accusations and gives them their venom.'

Landesmann ends by posing a question. 'If Lang had played these sonatas on successive nights in different cities, instead of presenting them simultaneously on a disc, would the controversy have been as intense? Had an employee of the record company altered the dates on the sleeve, to make it appear that one version preceded the other by a year, would the note of desperation have been quite so loud in the critical chorus?'

This rhetorical question elicited a reply, published in the subsequent, and final, issue of *Neue Kunst*. An anonymous employee of DRG Grammophon wrote: 'Would the note of desperation not have been louder if the full session of 10 March 1983 had been released? The performance on Side B was recorded in a single take from 9.30 a.m. The one on Side A was recorded at 3.30 p.m., also in a single take, and was the fifth single-take recording of that day. It was followed by one more, as distinct from the Side A version as it had been from its predecessors and as they had been from each other. That day's music-making is, I believe, the most astonishing recital ever caught on tape, and it is to be hoped that one day the public will be allowed to hear what a privileged few heard on that day in March.'

These recordings have never been released.


### *Christopher Lang to Michael Dessauer*

I'm sorry, but I no longer have the letter Tom sent from the north – call it a victim of bereaved irrationality. As compensation I can offer an item I'm positive will make you happy: the last correspondence I ever received from my brother. Can't find it at the moment, but I'll look again, I promise.


### *Michael Dessauer to Christopher Lang*

I await eagerly. In the interim, more of the biography – the nucleus of the section on memory.

When one talks about Thomas Lang with anyone who knew him personally, it is inevitable that the subject of his memory will arise. It is also inevitable that one will be told that the full depth of Lang's capabilities, or rather the full extent of his range, was unknown to those who knew only the public figure.

Istvan Markov, who in 1973 twice conducted Lang in the Chopin E-minor concerto, says that within a few hours of their first meeting it had become apparent that his soloist knew by heart the full orchestral scores not just of every concerto then in his repertoire, but of several others too, including concertos he was adamant he would never play, such as Tchaikovsky's – which of course he never did play. After the second rehearsal, Markov made some comment about a certain recording of *Die Meistersinger*, a remark of which he can recall nothing except the response it elicited from Lang, who returned to the piano to play a perfect transcription of the prelude to that opera. This he then elided into a sequence of phrases from the symphonies of Mahler and Bruckner, a seamless extemporisation maintained in parallel with an equally fluid spoken counterpoint, here explaining a point in the music he was playing, there introducing a fragment he was about to play. This two-part argument was sustained with such ease and such a superabundance of invention that it seemed Lang would have gone on for hours, had one of the orchestra members not come back into the hall, an interruption that abruptly finished the amazing display.

Christophe Radiguet, chief engineer on the recording of the Chopin sonatas, recalls that the sessions lasted for two weeks and that on each day Lang would come into the studio an hour before work was scheduled to commence. In the presence of perhaps one or two technicians, he would begin the day by running through a few Domenico Scarlatti sonatas – and he was never heard to play the same sonata twice. Before his appearance in Stockholm in September 1974 he stayed in the villa of the music publisher Erik Sorman. There he spent much of the day playing mazurkas, preludes and studies by Scriabin, another composer whose works featured on none of his concert programmes but of whose output he seemed to possess complete mastery.

Lang's memory is often described by his acquaintances as though it were a perfectly passive faculty, a simple process of adhesion. Incidents, images, texts and sounds, it seemed, became lodged in Lang's mind purely by virtue of their coexistence with him. In conversation with Thomas Lang, any subject might release deluges of information, much of it recondite yet none of it committed to memory by conscious effort, or so it would appear.

One example will suffice. A week or so after returning from a brief holiday in Florence, Joshua Thorpe held a dinner party for a Swiss industrialist, sponsor of a series of chamber concerts which Thorpe was organising. The other guests were the industrialist's wife, a visiting American conductor, and Thomas Lang. Towards the close of the evening, Joshua Thorpe happened to mention his visit to the Casa Guidi, the Florentine house in which Elizabeth Barrett Browning died, and to the nearby Specola museum, with its lurid array of anatomical waxworks. On this dissonant combination of little-known sights – a shrine to a minor poet and a museum of wax corpses – Lang constructed an extraordinary monologue, a performance of tangential shifts and provocative ideas. From an impromptu parody of Elizabeth Barrett Browning ('A sparrow on my sill expired . . .') he launched into an excerpt from Robert Browning's 'Paracelsus', a poem little read even by those with a great affection for its author. At this point he embarked on a disquisition on the birth of iatrochemistry and the career of the historical Paracelsus, a figure of 'inspirational charlatanry', as Lang characterised him. Thence he moved into a veritable fugue of subjects – the Medici family and their patronage of the sciences; the publication of Copernicus's heliocentric system in the same year as Vesalius's pioneering anatomy; Paracelsus's burning of Galen's books of anatomy; the depravity of the Roman games in the time of Galen – and as he spoke he seemed to lose all awareness of his audience. Connection sparked connection at ever greater speed until finally, looking at Joshua Thorpe as though awaking from a dream to see that the person of whom he had dreamed was actually present, he stalled in the midst of a digression on Boccaccio and the plague in Florence.

Let us briefly consider one other aspect of Lang's memory. His recollection of the distant past rarely had anything of the free-floating quality with which our memories are normally endowed. Fragments of utterances or isolated visual images usually seem to drift against a vaguely defined backdrop within a chronological scheme of no great stability. Thus we might recall two distinct remarks made to us by a friend, but be uncertain which was made before the other, or what we had done on the day each remark was made. Thomas Lang, by contrast, could remember how he played a certain phrase on a particular evening, and mimic it, ten years later. He could remember which ushers had been on duty at the concert hall that evening, the comment made by the stage manager just before he went on stage, that day's weather.

One last example. The first time Elisabeth Charniot met Thomas again after leaving the RCM was in the mid-1970s, backstage at a Paris production of *Fidelio* for which she had helped rehearse the chorus. They went out for a meal

216

together, and on their way to the restaurant she joked that she knew she'd one day work on *Fidelio*, as she'd always had such an affinity with Leonora. Ignoring the self-mockery, Thomas corrected her – she had not always liked *Fidelio*. In fact, she had once thought it 'sententious'. Elisabeth protested mildly that this was surely not the case. Thomas was provoked into reconstructing the setting of that disowned judgement. She and he had talked about *Fidelio* on the steps at the back of the Albert Hall; it was a day on which he had loaned her Schnabel's recording of the *Hammerklavier* sonata; she had been wearing a white PVC coat, one of her sister's cast-offs. They had talked about the cycling holiday in the Vaucluse that she was planning with her flatmate, but then had gone home to find that her friend's bicycle had been stolen from the hallway of their block. The burglar had forced the door of their flat but hadn't taken anything except a pair of patent-leather shoes. And so on, citing a dozen trivial circumstantial details, enough of which were sufficiently familiar to convince Elisabeth that all had happened exactly as he recounted, and even to stir what might have been the faintest echoes of recollection. And so, like many of Lang's acquaintances on many occasions, she was placed in the incongruous position of having to revise her own life in the light of Lang's vicarious experience of it.

(As an aside, it's interesting that Elisabeth Charniot describes this brief reunion in Paris as an uncomfortable episode, attributing their awkwardness in part to their acquired discrepancy of status but chiefly to Lang's lack of attachment to their shared past. This indifference did not surprise her, nor did she take it as any slight to herself – Lang had always had a strict antipathy to nostalgia, a vice he detected even in the most innocent social reminiscence.

He might use an anecdote to correct a matter of fact, but never for the pleasure of revisiting the past.)

We might be tempted to envy Lang's preternatural memory, but perhaps we should not. In a recently published book by Professor Magnus Thompson, we read of a man with severe amnesia, the result of a viral infection. His long-term memory was impaired, and his medium- and short-term memory all but destroyed. This man had been married for five years before his illness; now, each time he entered a room in which his wife was present, he experienced their meeting as though it were a reunion after months of separation, even if he had only left her side a couple of minutes before. Whenever he and his wife went out together (and his disability made it impossible for him to go out except in her company), she was obliged to maintain a conversation about the purpose of their trip throughout the journey, otherwise he would arrive at their destination with no idea as to why he was there. At the start of each day she had to tell him what they had done the day before, and what he was going to do that day. In effect, she had become the retainer of his identity.

Perhaps the life of Thomas Lang, in a sense the converse of this tragic case history, contained something of its loneliness. On the one hand we have the individual whose atrophied memory places him, as it were, under society; and on the other we have a man whose overdeveloped memory places him beyond society, thereby compounding the isolation of virtuosity. Again and again Lang would have been placed in the position of being the guarantor of the validity of what he remembered. His memory of an event could carry such conviction that it could persuade the forgetful protagonist of that event to adopt his recollection as something akin to a replacement memory. But who is to say that the lack of definite external confirmation did not to some degree lessen the weight, if not the clarity, of that memory in Lang's mind, reducing its gravity from that of the real to that of the imaginary? Could it not be that he found some refuge in the concert hall, in the creation of a society of common knowledge, albeit a transient society? A flippant remark he once made to Elisabeth Charniot – 'I'm a memory bank with manual extensions' – acquires a touch of pathos when heard in this context.

To take a slightly different path, let us look at the bare plot of Lang's public life.

From 1967 to 1969 the music of Chopin accounted for some eighty per cent of the items on his programmes, and one hundred per cent of the solo music he played, excepting the programmes for the Antwerp and Trieste competitions. The only other pieces he played were the two Brahms concertos and Beethoven's third, fourth and fifth concertos. During this period he recorded Brahm's second and Beethoven's fifth. In 1970 a huge percentage of his performances were given over to a very limited selection of the works of Schumann – during this period he did not play a single concert which did not feature either the *Études symphoniques*, the *Davidsbündlertänze*, or the first sonata.

The years 1971 to 1974 represent the most wide-ranging phase of his career: Mozart, Beethoven, Boulez, Schoenberg, Debussy and Prokofiev supplement the composers previously listed on his concert programmes. During this period he recorded Chopin's second and third sonatas, the *Études* opus 10 and opus 25, and the opus 28 *Préludes*.

At this point Lang's focus narrowed rapidly. From 1975 to 1977 he played nothing but the solo keyboard works of J. S. Bach – the *French Suites*, the *Goldberg Variations*, the *Three-Part Inventions* and the *Partitas* being the most frequently chosen. In 1977 he began recording *The Well-Tempered Clavier*, a project completed in 1978, when the recording of the *Two- and Three-Part Inventions* was also released. He gave just one concert in the latter year. From 1979 to 1981 the great majority of his concert pieces were by Schubert (Liszt and Beethoven are the only others); he recorded Schubert's *Impromptus* and the last three sonatas. From 1982 until his death he played nothing but Beethoven in concert, and released recordings of the last four sonatas, the opus 126 *Bagatelles* and the *Diabelli Variations*.

There was a joke in certain circles, one that gained currency as Lang's career unfolded. 'I saw Thomas Lang play in Paris last week,' the jibe went; 'Oh really? What was he playing – programme A or programme B?' It has to be admitted that Lang's repertoire comprises a remarkably sparse list, and it excludes numerous staples of the concert pianist's curriculum vitae. Most of the barnstorming concertos are missing. Lang never played the Grieg concerto, nor any by Rachmaninov or Tchaikovsky. Of the solo literature, he spurned Liszt's bravura pieces in favour of the terse, angular final works. Most of Schumann he ignored, and most of Debussy – he played the *Études* a few times, plus a couple of the *Préludes*, and that's all. Haydn doesn't feature on any of his programmes, neither did Ravel after the first round at Trieste, when he was obliged, like all the other contestants, to tackle *Gaspard de la Nuit*. He played none of the Mozart sonatas, none by Scarlatti, nothing by Scriabin.

What can explain this extreme selectivity? Certainly not unfamiliarity or any technical considerations. We know that Lang's knowledge of the repertoire was prodigious, and that the transition from knowledge to performance was an unhindered, almost instantaneous process. Furthermore, the chart of Lang's career shows a proscriptiveness more absolute than could be explained by personal taste: it surely cannot be the case that Lang regarded all Russian music except Prokofiev's as unworthy of attention, or that Lang in his thirties had outgrown his enthusiasm for Chopin, or that in the mid-1970s he never felt any desire to play music other than Bach's. Rather, it is as though Lang imposed the structure of necessity on his life, creating the appearance that his career was shaped by the will of the music rather than by the personality of the performer.

It's striking that the variation form was crucial to each phase of this career. Lang played Schumann's *Études symphoniques* at least eight times in 1970; the *Goldberg* he played eleven times between 1975 and 1977; the *Diabelli* featured on no fewer than twenty of his programmes after 1982 (never having appeared previously). In addition, of course, Beethoven's opus 111 sonata was the best-known of all his recordings, and in earlier years his performances of the *Appassionata*, another sonata containing a variation movement, were universally acclaimed.

Viewed one way, these performances can be taken to exemplify Lang's consistency of vision. Other musicians might present a set of variations as the image of the volatile, episodic nature of human experience; when Thomas Lang played a set of variations, one felt that the root theme had been present throughout the music, that the vicissitudes of experience had been subsumed, after whatever struggles, by a shaping mind. This was as true of his Schumann as of his Beethoven.

Viewed another way, Lang's performances appear as points along a trajectory that was destined to end with the recording of the *Diabelli*. It's a deliberately significant progress, from the romanticism of Schumann, through the corrective asperity of Bach, to the recasting of convention at the close of the *Diabelli*. Lang's career appears as a journey of intense self-scrutiny, a journey recapitulated in Beethoven's valedictory variations. What more is there to achieve after the achievement of the repose at the conclusion of the *Diabelli*?

When Lang told Konrad Seibert that he would never record again, he was perhaps merely stating something that could have been deduced as surely as plotting a graph line from a sheaf of statistics.

## *Christopher Lang to Michael Dessauer*

The artist's life as a work of art – a mushy notion that should have become extinct with absinthe, along with the loneliness of the creative mind. Besides, you're forgetting your own 'revelation' that my brother had plans to make other recordings, including recordings of pieces he hadn't played in public (cf. letter to Joshua Thorpe, 25 October 1987). There is a more prosaic explanation for Tom's comment to Konrad Seibert, and it lies in the way the *Diabelli* sessions ended.

Even by Tom's exigent standards the *Diabelli* was an arduous business. The recording dragged on over four weeks or so. On what should have been the penultimate day, Tom and the crew were listening to a playback when they noticed a creak or a tick or something in the middle of the eighth variation. As there were a dozen takes of this passage on tape – none of them to Tom's liking in its entirety, but all presentable – one of the engineers suggested that

222

they sample these alternative versions and splice in the best replacement for the ruined segment. Not as weird an idea as you might suppose – most records are mosaics of various takes, and the backroom boys at DRGG are so adroit that no one would have spotted the deception. No one except Tom, that is, who vetoed the idea straight away, on philosophical rather than sonic grounds. Integrity was paramount, and integrity was not contingent upon the audience's perception of it. With Tom, any continuous piece of music had to be caught on a single take, which is why – bearing in mind we're talking about a man who could find irregularities in the shape of a raindrop – a piano sonata played by Thomas Lang could take as long to get finished as a whole opera.

Rather than bow to the inevitable and resign himself to an unscheduled extra half-day at the console, the advocate of splicing decided to make an issue of it. Next morning, he asked Tom to listen to something he had knocked together overnight. It was a recording of the third variation, created by blending three different takes: all Tom was asked to do was listen, and if he couldn't spot the joins, then perhaps he might reconsider. This impertinent suggestion – rather like asking Van Gogh to try painting plastic flowers – was received in a rage too profound for utterance. His silence was mistaken for receptivity, and within seconds the collaged masterpiece was booming around the studio. Tom duly identified the splices. He then set to the task of re-recording the eighth variation. He played all day in sulphurous silence, finally pronounced 'That one will do', and left without saying another word to anyone.

Tom bore grudges with the vehemence of a deposed dictator, and I think what Konrad Seibert got was just an efflorescence from the simmering lake of choler. In time he would have cooled down and gone back to the studio, on condition that capital punishment be exacted for any future act of insubordination.

## Michael Dessauer to Christopher Lang

I won't dwell on this point, but Thomas didn't go back into the studio, and that being the case, my theory that the *Diabelli* was the necessary terminus of his career is at least as valid as your conviction that it would have proved otherwise. Nothing yet set in stone, however. Can I quote you on 'the vehemence of a deposed dictator'?

## Christopher Lang to Michael Dessauer

Your grand design is a product of that false perspective against which I warned you at the outset of our correspondence. I believe that the significant aspects of Tom's death, like most, encompass a few seconds only. It came about perhaps by a mechanical fault in the car or in himself, an avalanche of chemicals in his brain – or perhaps just a flash of light on a mirror, or an animal in the road. I don't know, shall never know, do not wish to know, and cannot conceive the value of knowing what happened in the moment his car left the road.

## Michael Dessauer to Christopher Lang

We had best change tack I think.

I've almost reached the limit of my capacity for biographies of musicians – other people's biographies, that is. Some read like accounts of a Caesar's triumphal progress, some like gossip from the court of Louis XIV, some like an extended press release, some like an annotated airline timetable. Yet for all their various modes of mediocrity, they have at least one thing in common: all have been written as if with a view to obtaining the subject's posthumous imprimatur. There's not a bad review or poor performance in sight. A few tantrums are admitted, but chiefly as a way of guaranteeing the genius of the artist. I'm going to devote an entire section to the adverse comments that Thomas Lang attracted (though much of it is simply mirror-image praise).

I've already quoted the Polish critic who deplored Thomas's playing on what we might term ethnic grounds. In addition to that, I have tracked down a brace of unenthusiastic reviews of the Chopin releases, one from the States and one from France, both of them unhappy with Thomas's temperament. The French reviewer is excessively fond of thermodynamic metaphors and tends to weaken his attack by spending too much time polishing his metaphorical sabre instead of using it, but the basic point is simple – Thomas Lang's Chopin is too dispassionate and uninvolving. The New York journalist takes a similar line – 'Chopin is sometimes crazy,' he writes, 'but Lang is never anything if not rational.'

This is an approach taken up at length by one

Charles Mizrahi, in an article published in 1982 in *High Fidelity* magazine, under the headline 'Doubting Thomas'. The writer begins by expressing his admiration for Thomas Lang, concurring with the 'received opinion' that 'Lang's technique is astounding'. He goes on to say: 'I am willing to accept that Thomas Lang is able to play any piano music that the human ear is equipped to hear.' He goes into a panegyric of Horowitz, citing his legendary performances of Scarlatti, Clementi, Schumann, Chopin, Tchaikovsky and Prokofiev as evidence of his 'empathetic range'. He then recapitulates his admiration of Thomas Lang's talent ('as a piano player he is second to no musician of his generation'), but continues – 'I have almost given up hope that one day I will join the legions of Thomas Lang's fans (and "fans" is the word), for never have I heard a Lang performance, live or recorded, that has approached the emotional commitment achieved by Horowitz, and a host of now unfashionable masters, as a matter of routine. I'm least unhappy when he plays Bach. No one could fail to be exhilarated by Lang's sheer éclat. But so often with Lang there's more than a hint of the pedagogue. He is so incontrovertible . . . You won't find the flux of emotion in Lang's Beethoven – his Beethoven is all about music, not about passion . . . and sweet, pastoral, lyrical Schubert is mutilated by Lang's severity. Vienna in the time of Beethoven and Schubert was a rural town; listening to Lang, you'd think they never opened their study windows, let alone walked in the woods.'

This piece, characterised as 'an heretical tract', is quoted approvingly in the *Daily Telegraph* in March 1982, in a review of Thomas Lang's *Hammerklavier*.

The review concludes 'he has presence, but it's a powerfully impersonal presence: there's more to a musical personality than perfect tone control and perfect articulation. A hint of fallibility would work wonders.'

(Interesting to note that the author of this last piece is listed as one of the three chief contributors to the *Essential CD Guide* [Hillendale Press, 1992], in which the Lang *Hammerklavier* is given a three-star recommendation, along with the recordings by Emil Gilels and Maurizio Pollini. Also recommended in this book is Lang's version of Schubert's posthumous sonatas, 'a set of classic status . . . perhaps the finest modern recording of Schubert's piano music'. The A-major sonata is singled out for special praise: 'The sleeve note tells us "this is music of irreducible unhappiness . . . the embellishments of the *Andantino*'s theme are like the smile on the mourner's face, the moment's helpless recollection of a moment's bliss". This might sound precious until you hear Lang's performance, of which I can only say that if there exists any music more desolate than this, I have never come across it.')

I'm still at work on this section, but I think I've found the quotation with which to end it. It's from a Toronto newspaper. 'On this showing Thomas Lang does not have much time for the *Moonlight* sonata. Eleven minutes and four seconds is the time he has for it, by my watch: a record, I'll be bound. It does not seem to have occurred to Mr Lang that this music acquired its nickname for a good reason. No moonlight here, no romance. In their place the glare of searchlights and the headlong flight of an escaped prisoner.'

### Christopher Lang to Michael Dessauer

Perhaps, by way of retaliation, I'll send you a draft of the essay on which I am currently engaged. It's a reappraisal of the career of Maurice de Talleyrand, Prince de Bénévent, Bishop of Autun, republican ideologue and virtuoso of pragmatism. 'Shit in silk breeches', Napoleon once called him; needless to say, mine is a revisionist analysis of truculent trenchancy. I have prefaced it thus: 'Let us then not ridicule those who are honoured on account of rank and office, for we love no one but for borrowed qualities.'

Enough of my teasing. I invite you to superimpose your blueprint of my brother's life on the enclosed documents, twenty-odd letters extracted randomly from my inheritance. Some I find interesting, others not, but I am handing them over exactly in the order of their extraction, and I have changed nothing except to append the likely date wherever Tom has omitted to supply one, as he frequently did. You are welcome to quote from them freely.

No. 9 loosely translates as: 'Medieval crudity gives way to the rise of the fine arts: the piano is the chief instrument of modern education. Trains are also of benefit to family life, since they make it easier for us to keep a distance from our family.' Apologies if the translation is superfluous.

1. *October 1980, New York*
Remember Robbie Allenby – works at Steinway, mock-morose, strong as a forklift truck, never without his Crèvecoeur, plays pool left-handed for money, yes? He's in love again, just in time for my arrival, as

always. The woman in the case is a young and thrusting academic from Buffalo, weightily proficient in her field, art history. Having met her, I have no doubt that sooner rather than later she'll publish her way into the professorial post she plainly regards as her entitlement. But Jesus, she takes herself seriously. She talks as if her every utterance were being transcribed, as if every person she meets might one day be called upon as a character witness.

Yet Robbie has a strong sense of irony – or at least he did, before he started knocking the corners off his mind to lay it more closely against hers. *Où sont les nuances d'antan?* I fear the worst. He's a strange young man, unbending as a totem pole when dealing with men, pliant as a poppy with women. What good does it do him in the long run?

It did him no good with Maria Paoli, a three-foot semi-Corsican junkie who fancied herself as a mordant observer of the wackier side of New York life. Always carrying copies of Balzac and Dorothy Parker, just in case her bit-players didn't get the point, which they didn't, as she combined the psychological acuity of Neville Chamberlain with the linguistic panache of Dwight Eisenhower. In moments of especial bleakness that stridulant little voice comes back to me, declaiming her catchphrase – 'crazy place, crazy girl'. Which of course she wasn't. She must have spent three hours every morning making sure her clothes didn't match. And there was Robbie going home in the evenings to try to work up a few offbeat idiosyncrasies, to make himself a 'character'. Then came the evening when she regaled us with the outline of *Rebuilding my Soul*, Work in Progress no. 309 in an infinite series – 'accessing the core of my being', 'life, it's an intensely personal thing'. Godalmighty. Poor Robbie – I've never seen anyone so unsmitten. He looked like a kid who'd just caught a glimpse of Santa Claus having a cigarette round the back of the Xmas Grotto. Ms Paoli is nowadays tyrannising some video cooperative in New Jersey. Robbie penitentially showed me their latest publicity handout – word is that she's discovered a means of 'subverting the phallocentric gaze'. A Pulitzer awaits, I'm sure.

To be fair, the latest inamorata is similar only insofar as she rates herself very highly, and in this instance there's good ground for her self-evaluation. She boasts an impressive tally of appointments and papers for a sub-thirty-year-old. And to spend a moment on those crucial superficialities, she does look very good indeed. Paoli was straight out of some medieval homily, the hideous externals making manifest the turpitude within. Annelise Morgenstern is indubitably attractive, in a cute commandant kind of way: almost hipless, wide-shouldered, about five-eight, cheekbones covered with the bare minimum legal requirement of soft tissue, blonde hair that has an uncanny permanent-wet sheen, irises so blue the pupils seem to stand a millimetre out from the eyeball, and quite remarkably long hands. She appears to have been fitted with extra metacarpals.

I spent a lot of time looking at these hands yesterday evening, when it was incumbent upon me to bear witness to Ms Morgenstern's qualities at an open lecture in the only unheated building in Manhattan. I rather enjoyed the talk, which I hadn't expected to do, despite Robbie's big build-up. 'Some Aspects of Religious Iconography in Dugento Italy' – doesn't quicken the pulse, does it?

I can't say that the attendant slide-parade did much for me, but I did admire the structure of the show – thirty minutes building up a few hypotheses, then thirty knocking their foundations away. The remarkable hands conducted our attention to a gallery of thirteenth-century Christs and saints, some from chapels in the fastnesses of northern Italy, others from the vaults of robber barons somewhere in Zurich or New York. We were invited to be buttonholed by these pictures, by their boldness, by their immediacy. (I've just remembered another Paoli afflatus – remember her prose poem, *Crucifiction*? Aaaaagh.) And then teacher turned nasty. Who, she demanded, could tell her more than three facts about the career of Frederick von Hohenstaufen, the *stupor mundi* (1194–1250)? A smart-arse in the front row wavered a hand, but the rest looked sufficiently sheepish. Being able to spell Frederick von Hohenstaufen was enough, muttered Robbie. Collectively we knew next to nothing, she posited sternly, about Ezzelino da Romano, reviled by the people of thirteenth-century northern Italy as the Son of Satan, condemned by Dante to spend eternity mouth-deep in boiling blood. (Must look him up.) We knew damn-all about the obscurantist heterodoxies maintained by people of outwardly respectable bearing in thirteenth-century northern Italy. Yet these things, nowadays the preserve of specialists, are fundamental to any understanding; and how many other things, she grimly wondered, are just as essential yet remain unknown even to the art-school boffins? What do we know of the people who commissioned these particular paintings? Is it not the case, Ms Morgenstern demanded, that all we know about these pictures is how we felt when we saw them? And so, Madame, we are where we began, more or less, peering through a smeary telescope.

We went for a meal after the talk, Robbie, Annelise and I. She was congenial enough, but too much of a monorail for my tastes, and with no apparent liking for what's left of Robbie's humour. Somehow (by which I mean that the full story isn't worth the telling), a somewhat fractious discussion arose, prefaced by her pious apology for the fact that she didn't really understand classical music – 'understand' in this context having a significantly different hue from its appearance earlier in the evening. She 'admitted' that she 'loved' soul music, which I think I was meant to take as evidence of her complexity. By this confession she gave herself the opportunity for some ponderous acrobatics in the semantic penumbra of the word 'soul', and you can just imagine the nonsense that ensued. Promise me Chris that you'll have the words ALL ARTS ARE PERFORMING ARTS carved on my gravestone. We parted with handshakes, having met with cheek contact.

Perhaps Robbie's trying to prove to himself that he doesn't have a type. A laudable project, but there are less strenuous ways of achieving that end. I know that next time I'm in town I'll be hearing the post mortem report; I've never managed to win him to the view that a trouble shared is a trouble doubled. Not to worry; he's never so happy as when he is melancholic.

## 2. *Munich, 1 September 1979*

Disharmony in the house of wax, where Rainer, one of the backroom boys, has decided on a new career move. He's decided to become a psychotic. The day before yesterday I'd returned from a visit to one of nutty Ludwig's houses, and was sitting in a warm and odoriferous *Kaffeehaus* in the environs of the Asamkirche, my thoughts on Strauss (R.) and his smug little parables, when in lurched our man. The proprietor riveted Rainer with a practised eye, gauging in one glare the alcohol to red blood cell ratio to the tenth decimal place. Rainer ordered a coffee, and slotted himself beside me before I had a chance to flee.

Rainer, hitherto a man so orderly I could imagine him using a set square to position the stamps on his envelopes, confides to me, in a whisper which is audible halfway across the Alps, that drink has been taken. Beverages of every conceivable deleterious type have been imbibed in huge quantities over an extended period. He's been gargling with beer, brushing his teeth with schnapps, cooking with cognac. This man is in a state, and he's telling me in some detail what a state he's in, staring at me as if he's reading his script from an autocue on my eyelids.

He tells me he's started being rude to shop girls and parking his car where it might inconvenience his fellow citizens. He has let people know what he thinks of them, without consideration of the consequences. He has left the phone off the hook in friends' houses and scrawled abusive messages on political posters. He has sent an anonymous letter to his boss, making allegations so gross he cannot divulge them even to me. He doesn't like the way he's behaving, but it's an experiment. 'I say to myself, am I the kind of person who could do such a thing? Well, I am doing it, so I must be that kind of person.' Yesterday he told his girlfriend to go to hell – but he loves her. What did I think of that? The German ministry of culture should restrict the circulation of Nietzsche's writings, that's what I think, but now he's telling me that 'the chemical reactions to produce the smile, they happen before we feel happy.' What did I think about that? – or 'Fotyu zzzinkdat?' to be precisely onomatopoeic. I respond, quite truthfully, that I find this an interesting notion and should appreciate a more detailed explication of it at a later date. Rainer, finding the maintenance of narrative cohesion quite beyond him, informs me that he admires my 'working', by which he seems to mean the quantity of my labours rather than their quality. I tell him that I'm a lazy person who simply keeps busy to hide his laziness. He ponders whether I am joking (as do I), then whether the joke is on him. Mid-ponder he slithers to the floor. I left a waiter grappling with Rainer's floppy form – a moving tableau, reminiscent of a Michelangelo *pietà*.

Hours later, Rainer has run amok in the studio, bouncing ball bearings off the console and tying knots in the wiring. It's possible he swallowed the odd capacitor he found lying around. This has knocked my *Impromptus* a bit out of kilter, but nothing decent had come out of the previous session anyway. In retrospect I can put the failure down to an impalpable atmosphere of impending dementia.

I spent part of the washed-out day in the archive, listening to my '71–'73 recordings, something I haven't done for many a year. Préludes and études stand up OK I think, but the Chopin B-minor sonata had my attention wandering before the scherzo. I found myself bored with myself, or at least bored with this creation that bears my name. A rare and pleasant experience, being wafted by gusts of boredom. Time has a terrible constancy when I am playing; every second demands the same attention, has the same weight. But as a listener I can enjoy the experience of time as something elastic, become disengaged for a while, feel the texture of time thin out. It's a luscious, self-annihilating feeling. There's a thesis here, Chris – on the congruence of boredom and extreme excitement. Ecstatic Boredom, a New Way to Personal Growth.

## 3. *April or May 1970, Paris*

Yesterday was a day in a major key. I pulled back the curtains seconds after waking and it was like a fanfare as the sunlight crashed into me. Within five minutes I was out on the streets, eager for a day of indolence. The avenues of buildings seemed like a special form of nature, as soothing as avenues of trees, the light coming off them as softly as sunlight filtered through leaves. Everything seemed slower, more measured than usual, everyone seemed more mannerly, the traffic processional. For an hour I sat in a café looking through a pane in which a single fat cloud was framed like the sky of a landscape painting. I took a book to Père Lachaise and spent all afternoon there, not thinking of a note. Everything was delicious: I took the metro just to relish its smell – dusty and sweet, with a tang of hot rubber and hot metal. Even the evening rain was special, lit by the streetlamps at the top of the metro steps like a scatter of aluminium pins. Nothing was going to perturb me yesterday, not even the proximity of two of the less pleasant technicians, a loutish pair who seem to be kept keen by the anticipation of disaster. Came back to the hotel, took a cool shower, ate alone, fell into a sleep I knew would be dreamless.

Then today I woke up with nerves clenched at the prospect of another three-legged race with history. Fled the hotel at 6 a.m. to walk the foreboding out of my system. Peripatetic ennui instead. Trudged past innumerable deeply significant locales, unable to detect the ghosts of Napoleon, Berlioz, Molière, Proust, Rameau, Balzac, Robespierre. Feeling enervated and stupid. But around nine o'clock I was standing in the Place de la Madeleine, when I realised that I was standing where Roth's Franz Tunda stood at 4 p.m. on 27 August 1926, bereft, with no idea what he should do. And in that instant I had a sudden sensation of intense sadness, as if the hopelessness of that character had been carried to me like a taste carried on the breeze. Why should I feel so strongly the presence of someone who had never existed, when the presence of the eminent dead had eluded me? Perhaps because Tunda and his sorrow had been intended for that location, and that location alone. I don't know, but whatever the reason, Tunda's momentary appearance immediately propelled me into action. Rehearsal brilliant, success assured.


4. *7 March 1978, Vienna*
Recording of *Well-Tempered Clavier II* completed. Very pleased with it. In euphoric, *carpe diem* mood I've decided to go for the Alfa Spider we looked at last

week in Battersea. Could you give the dealer a call for me, tell him I'll take it if it's still unclaimed? Remember not to expunge your glottal stops – he might make exorbitant profits, but he likes to pretend he's a man of the people. He promised a one-year warranty – see if he'll make it eighteen months for cash.

5. *October 1980, Louisville, Kentucky*

A slow drive, all day on the move but for one stop to gaze over the fence of a stud farm the size of an English county. Strange thing, the love of horse racing in these parts: sport as the expression of a badly disguised affection for the old world's hierarchies. Soporific roads, with gradients like gentle sea-swells and long, long curves. Put the radio on – country and western to aggravate myself into concentration. I've dreamed up the archetypal C&W album.

Side one

1. Come on in (and stay).
2. True Sue.
3. Not round here we don't.
4. I've seen some suns go down.
5. Sure seemed real to me.
6. If it ain't bust, don't fix it.

Side two

1. Tell me (I won't mind).
2. Win some, lonesome.
3. Two miles to your door, ten miles back.
4. Guess it must have been love.

5. High as the sky, then twice as blue.
6. Just have to break my heart in.

## 6. *10 April 1981, Modena*

Arrived last night to find that my recital has been turned into a metaphysical exercise. On the discreet grey poster my name is interwoven with the words *Musica/Silenzio*, in a diaphanous italic script. The programme has been printed like a menu, each dish annotated with a caption: first half, the *Hammerklavier* – 'the struggle against silence'; after the interval, op. 111 – 'the pathway into silence'; to conclude, late Liszt (*Unstern!-Sinistre, Nuages gris, RW-Venezia*) – 'the triumph of silence'. Beautiful font, I'll say that much for it.

A copy of this document was waiting for me at the hotel reception, along with an invitation to the Puccini festival at Torre del Lago, a consequence of an unguarded moment in which I revealed that I'd be on the Italian peninsula in July. So I find myself in a bit of a quandary. My potential hosts are the most civilised people imaginable, with a *palazzo* in the core of Lucca, the most civilised town imaginable. But could I bear to sit through one of Giacomo's debauched spectacles; can I fake an interest in hunting, fishing and screaming? Probably.

## 7. *August 1985, Hamburg*

Unnerving incident when I came back from the hall last night. The hotel lobby was packed with corpulent, crop-haired, gimlet-eyed characters who fell strangely silent when anyone passed within earshot. A convention of paranoiacs. I slalomed through them and into the lift, which then broke down between the first and second floors, trapping me for five minutes with a ghastly character who seemed to have modelled his appearance on that of Erich von Stroheim, right down to the monocle. His choleric fat face looked as though an invisible hand had clamped him round the carotid, and his hands were squeezed into leather gloves as taut as sausage skins. As the lift juddered to a halt he glanced at me for a moment, wrinkled his snubby nose, and uttered what at first I thought was a sort of dry spit of disgust, but I then realised was the word 'Turks'. His wife, a triumph of the embalmer's and upholsterer's arts, nodded primly. She had a primped little Pekinese under her arm, clamped to her side as if she were taking it upstairs for vivisection. 'Bulgars' I rejoined; the monocle nearly vanished into the grimace of uncomprehending contempt.

I saw him again this morning, communing in a dark corner with a gang of weasel-faced young bloods, who looked away in unison as I passed. Plainly a gathering of Nazi revisionists. They turned out to be an extended family of dispossessed aristos who used to own half of East Germany. Charming people, says the manager. Very cultured. Isn't that what they said about Hans Frank, with his delicate white hands?

8. *New York, March 1986*
Took the Staten Island ferry this afternoon for no other reason than to escape the mayhem of the streets. Stood on the prow, Garbo-like, trying to find the magic in the view, but thinking I'll never come back here again unless it turns out I'm contractually bound to do so. Then out of nowhere the close of the *Diabelli* came

to me – not a memory of it, but an irruption, as if headphones had been clamped onto my ears. And so, for reasons that had nothing to do with what I was seeing or what I had been thinking, the scene became elegiac, a valediction. I looked across the water and dredged up some adjectives to describe the city, trying to clamber back to visible reality on a ladder of words, but it didn't work. I had to close my eyes as the words bobbed about on the outside of the music. The perils of being a humble vessel. For three minutes I was staring at skyscrapers and hearing Beethoven hearing the eighteenth century.

## 9. *Munich, August 1979*

Mittelalterliche Roheit
Weicht dem Aufschwung schöner Künste:
Instrument moderner Bildung
Ist vorzüglich das Klavier.

Auch die Eisenbahn wirken
Heilsam aufs Familienleben,
Sintemal sie uns erleichtern
Die Entfernung von der Sippschaft.

## 10. *July 1975, Lisbon*

Surrounded by charming, slightly mournful people, all seemingly mindful of their country's former glory and its decline in the eyes of the world. This city is not the place for me – an inchoate mess, solidified into decrepit grandeur in one or two spots. Out of gratitude for her Ariadnic services I've agreed to take Maria Coutiño, the Gulbenkian's publicity chief, to a London theatre next month. Do you mind scanning the Sundays for something suitable? My guest insists that she has an aversion only to musicals, and for my sake stay clear of radical reappraisals of the dynamics of the theatre space, and no comfy-chair plays either. Shakespeare must be a safe bet – I can close my eyes and think of England, as long as it's not one of those plays full of regional dukes and two-minute battles. Restoration stuff would do nicely as an alternative. She's arriving on August 6. If the best candidate looks like it could be a sell-out, could you go ahead and book a couple of seats – three if you feel like coming along.

Maria presented me with a selection of cakes from the shop which, she assured me, makes the best pastries in Lisbon. I must bring you back a carton of these things. Buff-coloured and irregularly shaped, they come nestled in shredded paper, so they look like a litter of stillborn marsupials. Their exteriors have the consistency and flavour of lightly baked cardboard, while the interior tends to be stuffed with a viscid substance that has the colour of custard and the taste of nothing at all. Either the Portuguese mouth has evolved into an organ unlike any other in Europe, or it has something to do with Catholic self-abnegation. And let me tell you, as one who has recently watched a cohort of woebegone young men advancing on bare knees across the plaza in front of the church at Fátima, that Portuguese Catholicism is no slouch when it comes to self-abnegation.

11. *May 1971, Paris*
In need of decompression after a morning with Chopin, so I went for an afternoon film show near St Germain. A Jacques Tati double bill, warmly recommended

by chief engineer Lavardin. Having counted three laborious jests in an hour that felt like a day, I had to leave. The rest of the audience, a gaggle of young *philosophes* by the look of them, were chortling suavely at an attenuated gag they had already seen six times before.

Dejected by this mirthless pantomime, I took myself off to a record shop I'd noticed in a neighbouring street. Big Johnny Halliday promotion in progress, with six-foot posters and piped pap to all floors. Ever heard of Johnny Halliday? He's France's state-sanctioned pop star, dresses like a bank clerk in rock 'n' roll fancy dress, all black leathers and studded mittens, sings songs that sound like margarine adverts. He's inordinately popular over here, even among those young enough to know better. The shop was packed with people miming to the soundtrack as they browsed, mouthing the words with a dim intensity that proclaimed the words' unique specialness to the mouther. If M. Halliday were dumped on the USA or Britain with no explanation of his provenance, he might briefly be taken for an inept parodist. The French just cannot see what tepid, derivative posturing this is, and we in turn cannot hear what the French are hearing. Do they hear J.H. as something vital, rebellious, sincere, dangerous? If that is indeed the case, it's a reasonable deduction that they don't hear anything the way we do, and that makes me wonder what I'm doing here.

Depressed deeper, I took refuge in the riverside bookstalls. Present coming for you under separate cover – the illustrations from Diderot & D'Alembert's encyclopaedia, sans text.

12. *Bayreuth – perhaps August 1970*
At last the omphalos. Orchestra superb, perfect acoustics, no distractions except for the punitive seats. A wallow in the eternal present. But now has come the interval, and the talk is all comparative analysis, or comparative boasting: 'The cast of '66 – Windgassen, Nilsson, Talvela, Ludwig. Nothing will match it.' '*Ach*, I saw Flagstad. Flagstad was the one.' '*Nein, nein, nein . . .*', and so on until some old bat whose *grandmutti* was on first-name terms with Bismarck trumps the lot with some yarn that demonstrates beyond all dispute that Wagnerian singing has been in an inexorable decline since the heady days of Ludwig and Malwina Schnorr von Carolsfeld. Air thick with mephitic mixture of extreme self-satisfaction and extreme self-abasement before R. W. *Übermensch*. Some might find this very German. I hear bells. We are being summoned for the resumption. Oh to be a Ludwig, with a little Wagner grotto in the bowels of my burg.

13. *Venice – perhaps March 1977*
I can't trick myself into liking this place. It should be pleasurable, the counterpoint of water and a city that's completely artificial. But Venice is now just the world's biggest reliquary for a cult that has no substance but homesickness. History as commodity – wasn't that one of your lectures last year?

However, I have made the acquaintance of an Armenian cartographer, a man of chastening linguistic facility, fluent in six languages (one of them Farsi), proficient in another six (one of them Mandarin), and with a working knowledge, it appears, of every tongue recorded by UNESCO. He was formerly a monk in

243

an Armenian community out on one of the remoter islands of the lagoon, and he took me over there yesterday, in the company of a Swedish lexicographer, an Italian journalist, a Colombian coffee merchant and a Vietnamese gentleman who does something with recycled undergarments.

A fascinating tour, with our guide nimbly interpreting questions and answers in all necessary languages. The monastery would seem to be almost the only spot where people still do any meaningful work in Venice – they have a very impressive computerised printing press, with full-colour technology and polyglot fonts. Tigran, our host, gave me a gift on parting – a print of a map of an Indian island, drawn in the eighteenth century by a monk who, it turned out, was going off his head at the time. Every last indentation of the island's coast is absolutely true, and all the features of the surrounding sea-channels and islands are marked precisely, but every feature of the island's interior – every hill, river, valley and village – is imaginary. It's not known whether this was an anti-colonialist gesture, nor whether anyone perished while using the map.

Had an unusual encounter early this morning over on San Giorgio Maggiore. I was waiting at the vaporetto stop, looking over at the Doge's Palace, when I became aware that I was being scrutinised by a young Japanese couple standing ten yards off to my right. I turned a quarter-circle in their direction, which seemed to impel them to make a decision. The man hurried over to me, halted at just over arm's length, and asked 'Excuse me sir, you are Thomas Lang?' with the sort of inflection that suggested the bafflement of someone who felt he could no longer rely on the evidence of his senses. It was as if he'd asked 'Excuse me sir, this is Venice?' I was so disarmed by his tone that I had to confess I was indeed he. Whereupon my man frowned, bowed, scuttled back to his diminutive spouse, bowed with her, and escorted her to the church door, where they paused briefly, surveyed the pavement and myself with a sombre and undifferentiating gaze, then went inside. It made me feel as if I were my own tombstone.

Enclosed dusky Polaroid shows the statue of local hero Paolo Sarpi, anatomist, priest, friend of Galileo and defender of the Serene Republic against the autocrats of the Vatican. He is much admired for the fine phrase: 'non dico mai bugie, ma la verità non a tutti' (I never lie, but I don't tell the truth to everyone). Ten words to encapsulate the slithery ethics of Venice, inventor of the diplomatic service. I happened upon Paolo on my way back from the train station, returning from the edge of the Dolomites, a spontaneous excursion inspired by the view of the peaks from the bell tower of San Giorgio shortly after the traumatic Japanese encounter. Took the train up to Belluno, where the town square cringes under the peaks. The Dolomites don't bother much with the rigmarole of foothills – they just start point blank, with thousand-foot precipices and blades of naked rock receding to infinity. Spent an hour hypnotised by a constant procession of small clouds moving slowly out of the ravines, as if exhaled by the mountains. When the rain eventually fell it came as a silky drizzle that put a delicate gloss on everything. The shiny rail lines, glazed with water, reminded me for some reason of the little block of sodium that used to be kept under oil in the chemistry lab. Remember the way it gleamed when sliced freshly? I always wanted to bite it. Such a sensual and perverse substance: a bright metal as soft as clay. Enough.

No impact made on me by Belluno's contribution to the artistic heritage of Italy, viz. the work of one Andrea Brustolon, a dextrous woodcarver who could cram an entire Calvary onto a cherry-stone, or some such futility.

I've bought you a pair of padded yellow leather gloves, as worn by water-bus conductors when lassoing the capstan as the boat sidles up to its stop. You'll like them.

14. *Dorset, June 1982*
[Letter enclosed with copy of *Classic Sound* magazine, issue no. 1.]
Have you seen this rag? It just flopped through my letter box, accompanied by a semi-literate note from its editor, Darius P. Nelson, who hopes that I will enjoy his 'insightful' and 'user-friendly' publication, which aims to 'chart the leading edge of the contemporary music scene'. Emphasis is on 'scene', I suppose. How else can one reconcile this bold mission with the cover story, a slavering profile of a cute little automaton whose fiddle has never been required to sound a single note written after the advent of the internal combustion engine? Perhaps you recall its author? He's the swivel-eyed buffoon who called my Bach 'bathtime for the soul'.

The meat of the *Classic Sound* carcass is to be found between pages 10 and 64. Here, as you can see, Mr Nelson has devised a clever system for grading the

246

records that pass under the gaze of his 'hand-picked team' (one must infer that other magazines assemble their hacks by means of a random cull of the phone directory). Each disc is awarded up to five stars in each of four categories: 'interpretation', 'performance' (inexplicable this division, I know), 'sound quality' and 'value for money' (I wonder what the rate of exchange is at the moment – 1 Beethoven symphony = 3 Sibelius = 5 Shostakovich?).

Your attention is directed (as was mine) to page 17, where you will find 'The Core Collection', a regular slot intended to help the chronically insecure to garner a small but choice record library that is guaranteed humiliation-proof should a classics buff swan into the neophyte's living room unannounced. First through the turnstile is Ludwig van Beethoven and his 'nicknamed' *Emperor Concerto*, as interpreted by Arrau, Kempff, Serkin, Horowitz, Schnabel, Brendel and myself. Arrau is 'expansive' and 'thrilling'; Kempff demonstrates 'firmness'; Serkin has 'fire and brilliance'; Horowitz is 'powerful and poetic'; Schnabel is 'searching . . . profound'; Brendel is 'eloquent'; and I – to my inexpressible relief – am 'magisterial'. The conclusion? Older records sound a bit – how shall we put it? – 'older' than newer ones, and Beethoven's immortal music will bear the attentions of a legion of pianists. Each of us has his strengths – and, respectfully implied, his weaknesses too. Hold the front page.

This boy should be writing for car magazines, but I shall refrain from dispensing this insightful advice, lest he find it user-hostile. He hopes we can discuss a 'future profile'. I give it six months at the outside.

### 15. *Lyon – perhaps July 1972*

Postcard shows the pick of this museum's dull land-scape paintings – a tautology, if you ask me. Icons and pin-ups I can allow, even portraits, but landscapes? What's the point? I did like one picture here, but they don't have a card of it, presumably owing to embar-rassment. Its yellow pigment has faded away over the last couple of hundred years, leaving lush foliage the colour of the sky. A podgy shepherdess and her swain are now swooning in the shrubbery oblivious of the Martian growths all around them. Only other item of interest was cracked display case of unexplained significance, holding a skull, several unlabelled lit-tle phials half-filled with congealed, amber-coloured muck, and a slew of anatomy books. *Et in Arcadia ego.*

### 16. *Madrid, late summer 1973*

Suffered another of Joshua's hallucinatory phone calls this morning – he woke me up at 8 a.m. to pro-pose a recording of Mozart sonatas on a fortepiano. He heard his first fortepiano last week, and later that same day had met its maker – charming man, I'd love him. Complete irrelevance, of course, if one doesn't love the Mozart sonatas and cannot abide the crepitating racket of the fortepiano. I told Thorpe that my enthusiasm for this project defies conventional mensuration. He seems to think this is a negotiating position.

I could have done without this irritation. The heat's murderous and nothing looks straight – the roof tiles are shimmering, and the air wobbles so much that looking down the street is like peering through a waterfall. Air-conditioning in this room is ferocious

– it just creates a pod of chilled air in the midst of the oven, with no comfortable median zone in which to rest. Can't sleep either, as the entire field of the Spanish Grand Prix seems to be conducting its practice sessions outside my window from 3 a.m. to dawn. Room service comes courtesy of a young woman who would appear to be a lineal descendant of Torquemada. When she came in this morning she was quite blatantly disappointed to find that I haven't been taken off by a nocturnal stroke, and she has a way of depositing the tray that suggests she might have laced the coffee with strychnine, and am I man enough to risk it? You should see her turn a doorknob – in her mind she's wringing the neck of every guest in the hotel. I risked a 'buenos días', and was granted a dazzling glimpse of teeth such as one sees only on those who eat nothing but raw meat. The piano in the hall isn't the one that was here last time. I'm going to cancel.

## 17. *Toledo, 11 April 1980*

Spent an hour trying to get the point of El Greco, but he triggers my immune system into overdrive. This lachrymose Hispanic sanctity makes my stomach churn even more violently than do his acrid colours. I don't understand these pictures, let alone like them. Isn't Christian tragedy a contradiction in terms, or am I being literal-minded? I shuffled round with a tough-looking Franciscan, who gave every portrait a quick fierce glance, like a splenetic general inspecting a poor parade-ground turnout. As one who has stood on the crag of La Verna, scouring my soul on Francesco's landscape, I was with him all the way.

## 18. *Entrecasteaux, August 1983*

Picked up an open-top Porsche in Paris and blasted south over the skirt of the Alps through Gap. Beautiful day, crystalline air, fat sun, no clouds – Edenic. And then I drove into the aftermath of a crash on one of those ridiculous three-lane roads they have over here, where lunatics dare each other to stay out in the middle of the tarmac. I didn't know what was happening as I slowed behind a line of six or seven cars, then suddenly I was creeping past this van with its engine hanging out and its wheels wrenched round in a pool of broken glass. There was a young man standing by the driver's door, with his hand on the roof. The driver was still in his seat, looking out at the traffic with an exasperated stare. Because there was no blood, I didn't realise, until the young man moved to the front of the car without looking in at the driver, that the driver was dead. The traffic slid by. Two minutes ago someone's husband; now just a bit of a smashed-up car.

I booked into the first hotel I came across, and switched on the TV to take my mind off the smash. French TV would take your mind off the Day of Judgement – watch enough of it and it'll erode your brain to the size of a walnut. Now, I'm as tolerant of popular culture as the next overpaid globe-trotting concert pianist, but I draw the line at some things. I spent twenty minutes looking at this quiz show, in which some seedy old man with a shiny blue suit and ivory teeth challenged sluggish members of the public to identify the mistakes in the pictures projected behind them. Photographs of three Eskimos walking down Fifth Avenue, Leaning Tower of Pisa with hippo in foreground, Leonardo's Last Supper with a supernumerary bearded extra fingering the tablecloth. One smart alec got six right in a row (after much prompting), and progressed to phase two. Blue Suit then conducted him through a blizzard of sequins to a perspex booth, where he was required to don head-phones and listen to snippets of doctored soundtrack – commentary on French victory at Parc des Princes, with spliced-in reference to eminent tennis player, commentary on liberation of Paris with wrong date, etc. etc. . . . I think he was on course to win a young woman in a bikini, but I may have lost the thread.

In the evening I collided with a doggedly stupid programme about Chopin. Mention Poland and we get the Chopin statue in Warsaw being adored by locals in baggy hemp trousers, the whey-faced victims of a society in which free speech has no part. Mention Bach and we get a mugshot of bewigged old gent and a few bars from the '48'. Mention Majorca and we get a shot of hairy-shinned indigenes stomping through the thorny undergrowth. Couldn't bear it, so briefly switched channels for a cheery travelogue about some Caribbean idyll with pellucid lagoons, vibrant festivals and spiders the size of wheel hubs. I presume they broadcast this sort of thing to save people the trouble of going there themselves. Rather like my line of work, when you come to think of it. I'll stay here a week.


19. *Dorset, March 1984*
Something peculiar is happening. I'm awash with a feeling of regret, but I can't for the life of me think what it is I wish I had or hadn't done. It might be workaday melancholy, depression, ennui, lassitude . . . But it does seem rather to be regret, a feeling with a root

cause. I'm ransacking the years, but nothing's come up. Perhaps it was brought on by listening to too much Palestrina. Must get out into the garden for some horticultural therapy, but I'm still torn between two courses of action – should I go for the low-maintenance alpine array or the lush English rose bower? Hope you're well.

20. *Dorset, September 1978*
It is possible that I am about to cause you some embarrassment. As you can see, one of your former places of employment intends to plant an honorary doctorate on me. Refusal of this bauble is the only possible course, partly because my acceptance would be irksome to real scholars, partly because they expect me to deliver some kind of oration in return for my gown and mortarboard, but primarily because they also intend (as you can see from the enclosed) to salute a character who to my certain knowledge is chairman of a firm that peddles its chemical wares in parts of the world where the expression of any aberrant political sentiment is likely to get you a slap on the backside with a 5,000-volt cable. I do not yet know by what form of words I shall decline the gift, but I shall decline it, I hope without making a parade of my ethical foibles. Thought I should warn you.

21. *Ferrara, October 1984*
These shows are becoming ridiculous. Last night I still had my hands on the keyboard when a wave of profoundly moved students tried to vault onto the stage, only to hit a breakwater of security guards. Utter bedlam, like a re-enactment of the Sabines. One girl threw her sunglasses at me as she was borne away.

I just can't go on doing this, playing to pre-frenzied audiences. Mass atavism is such a depressing sight. I keep remembering that trip to Siena when I saw the Palio, and that horrible moment when I realised that all the hysteria was absolutely genuine. I seem to be committed to three more Italian dates in the next three years, then no more.

22. *New York, November 1981*
Robbie A. has shown me an interesting item in a Los Angeles newspaper – a profile of me written by one Paul Marnham DiSantis, a person whom I have never met – or at least I have never met anyone operating under that ludicrous name. It's a very aggressive piece, very personal, and I must say that I object to it. Look at this – 'He's intense, scarily intense. When he looks at you it's like he's looking straight through you . . . His friends will tell you he doesn't suffer fools; others say this is a man you just can't work with unless you're a genius . . . Lang is slow to praise, quick to fault . . .' and so on. DiSantis does concede that I'm 'great' – it's a word for which he has a particular fondness. At one point he even ventures that 'Lang might be the greatest living pianist under 60' – who's the 61-year-old he has in mind? But then again 'Lang's flare-ups are legendary, as is his unreliability . . . you buy a ticket knowing it's even money on a no-show . . . snubbed by Lang at an age when the pianist should have been showing more respect to his elders, one eminent American conductor talks of his "superiority complex" . . .' and so on.

This creep doesn't actually state that his nonsense is based on a face-to-face talk, so I suppose it's not actionable, even if it perpetuates the folk memory of events that never happened. Could you ask Matthew Kirkham what he thinks? I'm sure he'll say it's tendentious rather than mendacious, but it would be nice to frighten Mr DiSantis with a litigious missile.

23. *London – perhaps May 1965*
[first page missing]
. . . found myself on the fractured staircase of a condemned tenement somewhere near the Arsenal, joining the back end of a queue of gatecrashers, none of whom had any better idea of where we were than I had. Turned out to be a fancy-dress party, and the boozed-up Valkyrie on the door was refusing admission to all plain-clothes dullards. Fine by me – I was on my way back down through the plaster fragments and fag ends straight away. E.C. protested that we could just swap clothes. Valkyrie confirmed that transvestism would comply with the dress code of her establishment; I confirmed that I was heading back to my sanctuary. Altercation ensued. Did my companion feel no compunction about subjecting me to such factitious jollity? She did not. Was I content to be branded a prig in the eyes of my peers? Yes I was. Have we spoken a word to each other since my withdrawal from the fray? We have not.

24. *Paris – perhaps March 1980*
*Nel mezzo del cammin* . . . The end of the recital was hellish. Charged into the Schubert B-flat and instantly knew I'd rehearsed it once too often. Right from the start I felt it slipping away from me – imagine hearing what you're about to say and knowing you don't

think that any more, but being unable to stop because you haven't thought through the alternatives. Terrible experience, playing the whole thing out of sync with myself, but I think I managed to present a unified front. Gentlemen of the press didn't spot anything amiss, but I'm rethinking the Frankfurt programme for next month.

Having fled the hall, I allowed myself to be inveigled into a cinema for a much-praised film by a much-lauded British team. It was like watching an animated waxworks through sepia-tinted goggles, and my concentration was ebbing after twenty minutes. I really was trying hard, because every time my eyes glazed over I'd hear the Schubert swilling around my head, sounding more wretched with each repetition. Assailed by the Furies, I swivelled my unresponsive retinas back to the screen, where men in white suits and girls in crinolines were suffering terribly in photogenic, dirt-free, sun-blessed foreign streets. 'I love you, Daphne. I love you. You do know that, don't you?' Pause. Roger brushes leaf from his linen sleeve. Gazes with pent-up fervour into eyes of the beloved. 'Could you love me, do you think?' Pause. Daphne averts face, watches a bird's slow traverse of the azure sky. Roger gazes with adoration at shell-like ear of the beloved. 'Could you?' Daphne raises a white-gloved hand to her cheek, daintily dislodging a bead of moisture. 'It's so hot, Roger,' she replies. Long pause. Glossy horse trots into view, pulling a landau occupied by a behatted gentleman and his copiously veiled consort. Terracotta-coloured dust rises from the whirring wheels; it billows and falls. Wistful Roger watches the vehicle recede. 'Yes. It is.' Pause. 'Shall we walk?' he asks. Daphne regards the tattered plaster Virgin in a nearby niche; a faded garland lies at the figurine's feet; a candle burns behind the grille below, its flame wavering through red glass. Daphne smiles an inward smile, looks into Roger's eyes, and takes his arm. It would try the patience of Job. Why does everyone assume that the human species was propagated by binary fission in the Victorian age?

When it was over I endeavoured, against my own conviction, to persuade my companion that this stuff traduced the English national character, but she unanswerably reminded me that box-office proceeds tell a different story. So depressing, to think that I bear the mark of Europe's laziest nation. Turned out she'd liked the film, and as I couldn't trust myself to maintain civility in my troubled state, we parted, she to Montparnasse, I to pace the streets awhile (three hours), walking disastrous Schubert out of my head.

To skip the mechanics of the plot, by eleven the next morning we were speeding west on our way to her native village, a tiny place six or seven kilometres from Anet. Forgoing the opportunity to visit the Manet garden en route (no chance of my feigning tolerance there), I urged her on to her homeland, imagining that I was about to be immersed into one of those familial communities out of Balzac or Fontane, which is indeed exactly what was in store. We processed round the village church, stopping on the steps to greet M. Boulin, retired farmer and long-time friend of her father (now deceased – I saw the grave). M. Boulin, whose rubicund face seemed to be kept under pressure by strong, barely suppressed emotion (not sure whether it was hilarity or wrath), misled us into the bar for a glass of the wine produced in the vineyard of the Mme Grosjardin, whose widowhood – I was allowed to infer – he may or may not have once lightened with an autumnal dalliance. I know, I know. In the bar we encountered the buxom and wall-eyed Louise, now the maths teacher at the school where my escort and she were once classmates. Louise conducted us to her house for coffee; there we were introduced to her daughter, Sophie, aged eight and already showing something of her mother's caustic wit. Ever seen your mannerisms mimicked by a waist-high child?

Thence we took a stroll to the bridge over the river on the outskirts, and there met the man who used to fix her father's tractors. He'd caught a fish (species unknown), which we admired (even though it was puny and looked as if it might have decided to commit suicide) before ambling back through the streets to greet the baker, the florist and the rest of the plausible cast, each of whom assumed I was her latest beau. This misapprehension began to have a very interesting refractive effect on my vision of her, an effect amplified by the affection with which she was evidently regarded – the barman, Léon, patted the back of her hand as she reached for our tumblers; neighbour Adèle (82 this year) gave her the sort of long appraising look a woman might give her grandchild; Aunt Marguerite (in fact unrelated) couldn't keep herself from stroking her hair. Quite easily – but invisibly, I hope – I placed myself in the part I was being assigned, and found that I enjoyed it hugely. The qualities of my companion (immanent and reflected) were of course the preponderant causes of this enjoyment, but there was another factor at work.

I was falling for the allure of a second-hand *Heimat*. God help me.

Ever wondered what would have happened to us had our parents not expunged the more vulgar locutions from our speech, thereby casting us adrift from our authentic milieu? Mired in warm, loving, supportive tedium no doubt. The conundrum of Cleopatra's nose.

This all feels as if it might turn out to have been a rehearsal, but for what I don't know.

25. *Budapest, March 1985*

Went to a festival performance of *Bluebeard's Castle* last night – the first time I've ever seen the thing, not being a great fan of Heart of Darkness allegories. A fine hour it turned out to be, though I did wonder how the non-Magyar newcomer would have got on with it, as the programme's English synopsis was strangely selective and uncertainly translated ('art thou frighted?'; 'he shows his flowers with bloods'), and the stage action was no model of clarity. It seemed to be set in a drab furniture showroom, where a dyspeptic sales assistant was reluctantly presenting his wares to a rather overwrought lady – 'We don't like this suite Madam? Perhaps this one is more what Madam had in mind?'. Instead of the flood of sunlight at the opening of the fifth door ('his expensive domains are spread'), we received the anaemic glimmer of a couple of 60-watt bulbs, as if they'd gone to the broom cupboard by mistake. At the grand finale the three incarcerated wives trooped out to meet the new arrival like a trio of factory girls taking their tea break after a five-day shift on the conveyor belts.

Good singing from Bluebeard himself, a young man with a voice that seemed to emanate from somewhere in the region of his lumbar vertebrae – astonishingly rich, steady tone, if a little stentorian. Judith was raspy but one hell of a sight, trundling round like a geodesic dome on castors.

My Budapest contact seems to think that he's getting me into the Gellért baths tomorrow, for a float amid the massed pallid adipose tissue. He don't know me too well, do he?

### Michael Dessauer to Christopher Lang

Passing quickly over the proof that Thomas was not, after all, immune to boredom, could I ask if you know the identity of the woman in letter 24? And if this fund of invaluable material is to be followed by more?

### Michael Dessauer to Christopher Lang

Dare I hope that the delay in receiving a reply means that you are compiling more letters? My thoughts on the twenty-five will be with you soon.

### Christopher Lang to Michael Dessauer

Now I've almost had enough. Of course Tom experienced boredom; my earlier point was a tactical rebuttal. I have no idea whatsoever as to the identity of Tom's evanescent paramour – I think we've already covered this subject anyway, haven't we? You have enough here for whatever anecdotal glitter you might need. Please spare me your thoughts on the twenty-five, amusing though those thoughts may be.

## Michael Dessauer to Christopher Lang

No more questions then, except these – are there many more letters, and am I to see them?

## Christopher Lang to Michael Dessauer

I have many more letters, for the time being. I have hundreds upon hundreds of documents. I have so much material that a phalanx of archivists could make no more than the feeblest furrow on its surface were they to devote an entire week of their joyless lives to its indexing.

There is something I have lied about, is there not? It is time for me to come clean about Marcus Taylor. Mr Taylor owns land in the vicinity of Tom's house, and on a plot of this land stands a facility for the use of which my brother paid Mr Taylor a sizeable fee each year. This facility is a disused storage building on the periphery of a field which Mr Taylor leases to another party. Let us go there.

Shielded from the road by a tall hedgerow, the shed is about the size of your average lock-up city garage, but with the difference that its entrance measures no more than three feet by five, and the walls are built of stone blocks so large they could probably withstand a direct nuclear strike. Inside, the only light is what the doorway lets in – there are windows, but both were blocked by my brother with stacks of identical dun-coloured cardboard boxes. Stout crate-like things, like butter is packed in, were piled by him on all sides, almost to the ceiling in places. They are all the same size, all arranged lengthways, laid as closely as the blocks in an Inca wall. The first time I saw them, the week after Tom's death, I sat for a while in the midst of these boxes, regarding them, I admit, with some trepidation. Eventually I hauled one off the top and carried it out onto the grass.

The lid squealed off, revealing a file of upright papers, not bound but held tightly in place by pressure. Letters, most of them, and all received within a span of a couple of months, but they were not arranged in any apparent order, and were randomly interleaved with concert programmes, flysheets and postcards from the same period. I went back for another box, the one underneath the one I'd opened. The same story: letters and ephemera from one particular season, jammed into their container in no order that I could make out. The first box dated from 1975, the second from 1981, the third – top of the pile next to the one the others had been in – was from 1978, the one under that from 1967. I found another 1981 against the wall opposite the door, another 1978 to the right of the door. It appeared that Tom had thrown no paper away since the day he left home.

That afternoon I skimmed through two complete boxes and sampled I don't know how many others – perhaps twenty. I have returned several times, but shall return again just once.

Allow me to give you a glimpse of the contents of a box from 1981: a roll-call of characters now doomed to remain absent from the biography of Thomas Lang. Some names have been altered.

## Peter J. Ensheimer
Living in Pasadena, born some time in the 1950s I would judge from circumstantial evidence. A radio engineer. He seems to have written more than fifty letters to Tom, c/o DRGG, over a period of ten years (1971–81); I infer that most of these concerned the piano tone on Tom's recordings. It is apparent that he received at least one reply.

## David Prendergast
A trader in antique furniture, his letterhead informs us (Prendergast & Nauman, founded 1960). It would appear that Mr Prendergast had recently spent two hours in Tom's company in the departure lounge of Frankfurt airport; his six-page letter commences *in medias res*, and is plainly a continuation of a conversation that ranged over the following subjects.

1. The relative merits of Seattle Slew and Secretariat.

2. The prevalence and ethics of drug abuse in Olympic competition, with particular reference to gymnastics.

3. The economics of olive production.

4. The techniques of Japanese lacquering.

5. The origins and power structures of the Mafia.

6. The various philosophies of architectural restoration represented by the bomb-damaged cities of Berlin, Munich, Treviso and London.

7. The Irish-owned vineyards of Bordeaux.

### Jane Morgan
Staff writer on a national Sunday newspaper. She reports that she has been approached by a young Belgian model named Isabelle Lavardin, offering her the story of Ms Lavardin's 'night of passion with Thomas Lang on the Greek island of Kos'. Ms Morgan repulsed her informant with the observation that there is a distinction to be made between a famous person and a celebrity, and that her tale 'might just about have been a story if it had been a night of passion in the Albert Hall'. The tone suggests that this was not Jane Morgan's first letter to my brother.

### Kristin Em
Student at Uppsala. She thanks Tom for an unspecified present which he sent to her in return for a good deed: it is probable that she prevented Tom from stepping off the pavement into the path of a car, and possible that she then acted as his advocate when a passing policeman attempted to fine him for unruly conduct.

### Maddalena Gaffori-Mannozzi
Letter bears the rubric of the Trattoria al Teatro, Áscoli Piceno. Signora Gaffori-Mannozzi informs Thomas that her nephew Pierangelo has just returned from a trip to Montalcino, where he bought 'a special Brunello for you'.

### Sir Gavin Deayton
Advises Tom, 'in all confidence', against 'the investment in question'. He suggests that they discuss certain 'less precarious' ventures over dinner at White's.

### Michael Fiennes
This young man would seem to have crashed his car into Tom's, somewhere in the vicinity of Maiden Castle, sometime early in the year. He is anxious to avoid the involvement of his insurance company. He declares himself a fan.

### Gabrielle Mitchison
An Arbroath clairvoyant. Her name appears on a poorly printed business card, above a poorly drawn image of Saturn and its rings.

In just three anecdotes it is possible to convey the complete image of a man, or so the mustachioed sage believed. Are Thomas Lang's three definitive anecdotes hidden in the correspondence of this box from 1981? Are they in another stratum of this mountain of paper, or are they not there at all? Perhaps you have already discovered them? Let us hope so, for all this memorabilia is to perish in my own Bonfire of the Vanities, as soon as I can organise the transport.

## *Michael Dessauer to Christopher Lang*

Dumbfounded by your letter. I beg you to delay until we have had an opportunity to discuss.

### Christopher Lang to Michael Dessauer

Discussion futile. Immolation to proceed – cue finale of *Götterdämmerung*.


### Michael Dessauer to Christopher Lang

I can only proceed on the assumption that I still have time to prevent the disaster. I implore you to preserve Thomas's archive, if not for my use, then for future writers. You are our richest source. Please phone me.


### Christopher Lang to Michael Dessauer

In partial atonement, and with apologies for my tardiness, I present you with the text of Thomas Lang's last written communication with his brother. Dated 16 October 1987, and postmarked Dorchester, the message is on the reverse of a postcard of Franz Liszt, in his youthful, jaw-jutting, smug incarnation. Text is as follows:

'After reading Marcus Aurelius am now pondering an idea for garden improvement: a circle of yews around a horizontal granite slab, bearing inscription in deeply incised Roman lettering: name, dates, and the words AN END TO NOVELTY – in Latin, your department.'

Here I think I shall take my leave. I'm sure you'll be able to continue your dialogue alone. Please don't think that I've done whatever I've done because Thomas

Lang was my brother. I'd have done the same for anyone.

## Michael Dessauer to Christopher Lang

Perhaps you have not heard that Helen Gilray's illness has a very poor prognosis. I had hoped to present her with the manuscript of my biography. Please allow me to complete my work before she dies. You and I must at least meet once before I can consider concluding my research.

## Michael Dessauer to Christopher Lang

I'm chasing a lead given to me by a commissioning editor at Faber, who tells me that Thomas once submitted a proposal for a book to be entitled *The Cult of Expertise*. Does this sound at all familiar to you?

## Michael Dessauer to Christopher Lang

I have on my desk a photo of the hollow ash-figures from Pompeii, husks of people set where they died, curled against the suffocating clouds. Perhaps that's what I'll have on the cover of my book, but instead of hardened ash my figure will be clad in photographs, sheets of music, letters, postcards and reels of tape. Please, let us meet. These unanswered letters are like a second death. I'm marrying Hildegard Schuster, and we'd be honoured if you could attend our wedding. It will be in Munich, three months from now.

All Fourth Estate books are available at your local bookshop or newsagent, or can be ordered direct from the publisher.

Indicate the number of copies required and quote the author and title.

Send cheque/eurocheque/postal order (Sterling only), made payable to Book Service by Post, to:

Fourth Estate Books
Book Service By Post
PO Box 29, Douglas
I-O-M, IM99 1BQ.

Or phone: 01624 675137

Or fax: 01624 670923

Or e-mail: bookshop@enterprise.net

Alternatively pay by Access, Visa or Mastercard

Card number: ☐☐☐☐☐☐☐☐☐☐☐☐☐☐☐☐

Expiry date ...............................................................

Signature ...............................................................

Post and packing is free in the UK. Overseas customers please allow £1.00 per book for post and packing.

Name ...............................................................

Address ...............................................................

...............................................................

...............................................................

Please allow 28 days for delivery. Please tick the box if you do not wish to receive any additional information. ☐

Prices and availability subject to change without notice.